Katherine felt a quiver of alarm

She had known
of men might
Perhaps not fo
such a find coul

'I have not to
reminded him. 'It may be that my father was
mistaken…'

Alain's eyes were steady on her face, but held
warmth, a concern that made her heart race.
For a moment she thought that his feelings
towards her were more than mere courtesy. 'If
I gave you my solemn word that I will return
them to you when we reach England, would
you trust me?'

Katherine hesitated, and then nodded. Instinct
told her that if she could not trust this man
then she could trust no one. Hesitating but a
moment, she picked up the pouch and handed
it to Alain.

'I believe there is enough here to give
credence to my father's discovery, but you
may study these and give me your opinion.'

'I thank you for your trust in me, Katherine,'
Alain said, and hesitated, then reached out to
touch her cheek. It was the merest graze of his
fingers but it sent tremors running through
her…

Dear Reader

To become a true knight a youth must strive to attain perfection in all things. He must be able to read the scriptures in Latin, must know all the rules of chivalry, and be as skilled in matters of physical excellence as in those of the mind. It is a hard, rigorous training.

Alain de Banewulf was luckier than most boys for his mother begged that he should receive training at his father's hands, rather than be sent away. But Alain has always felt that he cannot be a true knight, as his magnificent half-brother Stefan is, because his life has been easy. Adding to this feeling of inadequacy, he believes his prowess is due to a sword with magical powers that was given to him by his brother when he went to the Crusades. Now he is returning home, covered in glory, but still not satisfied that he deserves his reputation as a fearless knight. It is only when he rescues the thin child Katherine and swears to protect her, gradually coming to understand that she is actually a warm and loving woman, that he is given the chance to prove himself in every way.

I hope that you enjoy this last book in the series, which gives a hint of the spiritual nature of the age as well as the exciting physical action of kidnap, fierce fighting and love.

As always, I love to hear what you think. Visit me at www.lindasole.co.uk

Love to you all

Anne

HER KNIGHT PROTECTOR

Anne Herries

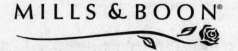

MILLS & BOON®

First published in Great Britain 2005
Harlequin Mills & Boon Limited,
Eton House, 18-24 Paradise Road, Richmond, Surrey TW9 1SR

© Anne Herries 2005

ISBN 0 263 84380 7

Set in Times Roman 10½ on 13 pt.
04-0805-89266

Printed and bound in Spain
by Litografia Rosés S.A., Barcelona

Anne Herries, winner of the Romantic Novelists' Association ROMANCE PRIZE 2004, lives in Cambridgeshire. After many happy years with a holiday home in Spain, she and her husband now have their second home in Norfolk. They are only just across the road from the sea, and have a view of it from their windows. At home and at the sea they enjoy watching the wildlife and have many visitors to their gardens, particularly squirrels. Anne loves watching their antics, and spoils both them and her birds shamelessly. She also loves to see the flocks of geese and other birds flying in over the sea during the autumn, to winter in the milder climes of this country. Anne loves to write about the beauty of nature, and sometimes puts a little into her books, though they are mostly about love and romance. She writes for her own enjoyment, and to give pleasure to her readers.

Recent titles by the same author:

THE ABDUCTED BRIDE
CAPTIVE OF THE HAREM
THE SHEIKH
A DAMNABLE ROGUE*
A WICKED LADY

Winner of the Romantic Novelists' Association
ROMANCE PRIZE

and in the Regency series
The Steepwood Scandal:

LORD RAVENSDEN'S MARRIAGE
COUNTERFEIT EARL

and in
The Elizabethan Season:

LADY IN WAITING
THE ADVENTURER'S WIFE

and in
The Banewulf Dynasty:

A PERFECT KNIGHT
A KNIGHT OF HONOUR

Chapter One

'What will the bards sing of us?' Sir Alain de Banewulf asked of his friend as they drew rein to contemplate the vista before them, which was one of sun-baked hills and lush valleys. It was some months now since they had left the arid heat of the Holy Land, joining forces to make their journey back to England. 'Will men say of us that we are sad failures or praise us for the taking of Acre?'

Sir Bryne of Wickham looked at him, narrowing his gaze against the sun, wondering at the strange, bleak expression in the younger man's eyes. Alain had been quiet for some days, and now perhaps he was ready to speak of what ailed him.

'You are still angry that we failed to take Jerusalem from the infidel?'

Alain was silent for a moment, his thoughts mixed as he tried to explain to the man who was so close to him that they had lived as brothers these past few years. Defending, guarding each other's back, they had risked their lives for one another. Bryne was his most trusted friend and yet even to him he could not explain the emptiness inside him.

'When King Richard quarrelled with Philip of France and he deserted us, Richard had no choice but to make that treaty with Saladin. We as Christians may thank him that the Holy City is not closed to all those of our faith. Had Richard fought on, all might have been lost.'

'Yet there is no denying that the influence of Christianity hath been much weakened.'

'So we failed,' Alain said and felt the weight of defeat fall on him as a mantle of chain-mail. 'May God and history forgive us.'

'Failed?' Bryne raised his brows. Many men would have been more than satisfied with their accomplishments if they had done as well.

Alain and Bryne had gained personal wealth after the victory at Acre, much of it presented to them for saving the life of the son of a merchant prince. Ali Bakhar's gratitude at having the boy returned to him unharmed had been in the form of priceless jewels, articles fashioned of gold, precious silks and spices. But even more important was the permission to trade freely in the waters between Venice and Cyprus. With that gained they had what many merchant adventurers before them had died for the lack of: the secret of true success in these parts.

Bryne had advised prudence and they had had their fortune transported to Italy, where one of the influential banking families had taken charge of it for them. Bryne had previously arranged that any prize money they won while on crusade was to be invested in his friend's shipping fleet on their behalf.

When King Richard had decided to leave the Holy Land, Bryne and Alain had sailed with him for Cyprus. From there they had gone on to Messina and thence to Rome. Here they discovered that they were both wealthy beyond their dreams, for Bryne's trusted friend had invested wisely and their fortunes had increased a hundredfold in the intervening years. They had left their gold in his charge and carried only enough silver for their journey together with the letters of credit that would buy them whatever they desired, either in France or England.

'Some may believe we failed,' Bryne agreed after a few moments of consideration, for he knew that Alain had no thought of their personal triumphs. 'Had Richard curbed his temper, mayhap history would have had kinder words.'

Alain smiled oddly, shrugging off his mood. 'We fought bravely, but the odds were against us.'

'And now what, my friend?' Bryne's brows rose.

They had lingered some months in Italy, taking time to see the wonders of the country, visiting the great university and medical school at Salerno. They took care to stay clear of Calabria, where King Richard had unjustly seized a beautiful falcon on his journey to the crusades, causing much anger amongst the villagers who had owned it. For a while they had lingered in the lush countryside of Italy's rich wine-growing area, drinking its produce and enjoying the idleness their labours had bought for them.

'Ah, that is the question,' Alain said, and for a moment a merry smile danced briefly in his deep blue eyes. 'For myself, I think I am weary of foreign lands…'

'Aye, I, too, have felt the call.'

'It is years since I saw my mother. She will have despaired of seeing her son again.'

'I wonder if my family still lives?' Bryne frowned as he looked into the distance, an odd expression in his eyes. 'We have all we could ever need here and yet…'

Of late both men had become restless, and as Alain looked at Bryne he suddenly knew what was in his mind.

'So we go home?'

'I left England in the year 1187 to offer my sword to Duke Richard. It was some many months before we set out for the Holy Land, as you know, for King Henry died and Richard was crowned king of England. It is now the beginning of the year of our Lord 1195 and I confess I long for a sight of my own land.'

'Yes, I, too, have felt the need for home and family,' Alain agreed. 'When I left England it was to gain wealth and honour as my brother before me, and perhaps I have achieved a part of what I had hoped for.'

'You are rich and no knight hath fought more valiantly, Alain. What more would you have?'

'Indeed, I have oft wondered.' A wry smile touched his mouth; he could not place a name to that elusive dream. He only knew that it eluded him still. 'Mayhap I shall find it in England. We shall set out for Rome on the morrow, Bryne, and find a ship to take us home.'

The sound of screaming penetrated Alain's thoughts. They had set out early that morning, hopeful of completing their journey to Rome within three days, and had been making good time. Alain's mind had been elsewhere as they rode through the softly undulating countryside. Now, suddenly, he was alerted to danger. That was a woman screaming and she was in some considerable distress. He looked at his companion and saw that Bryne was alert to the situation.

'Over there!' Bryne pointed to their right. 'See, at the edge of those trees. Brigands are attacking three men and two women, and 'tis clear they are outnumbered by the rogues.'

'They are surrounded,' Alain said and spurred his horse. 'Come, Bryne. One last battle before we seek our ship!'

His trusted sword was in his hand as he led the charge, Bryne and the men they had led into many such battles following behind. The thunder of hooves echoed in his head, and he could smell the blood, heat and dust of other fights, remembering the screams of the injured and dying his horse had trampled underfoot in the heat of battle. A wry smile touched his mouth. Had he ever been young and naïve enough to believe that there was glory in war?

He raised his right arm, sword aloft, as he bore down on the first rogue. He was aware of a woman struggling with men who were apparently bent on abducting her and let out a yell that would strike terror into the heart of any warrior. Slashing to left and right, he fought like fifty demons as he hacked his way through to the woman. As always, his sword gave him strength to overcome his enemies. Its magical powers, in which he firmly believed, had carried him through bloodier fights than this. Saladin's soldiers were fiercer warriors than these scurvy knaves, who had already begun to break ranks now that they were faced by Alain's men.

From the corner of his eye he saw that the girl had managed to break free from her would-be captors and was being cared for by one of her own people. It was clear that the fight was over and that the brigands were fleeing into the trees from whence they had come.

Alain gave the girl a smile of reassurance and then turned his head to glance at Bryne. Seeing that his friend had dismounted, Alain did the same. He moved towards the girl they had saved, sword in hand, intending to ask her if she had suffered any harm at the hands of the brigands. He began to speak and then something hit him from behind and everything went black as he fell. He thought he heard the girl cry out, but could not save himself as he sank to the ground at her feet.

'What have you done, Maria?' The Lady Katherine of Grunwald sank to her knees beside the still form of the man lying on the ground. 'You have killed him and he saved me from those wicked men.'

'Oh, my lady—' the older woman looked at her in dismay '—he had his sword ready. I thought he meant to kill you.'

'You foolish woman!' Katherine laid her hand on the knight's forehead. He had such lovely golden hair and was beautiful to look upon. She thought that she had never seen a man so fair. 'Now his men are angry and will likely punish us.' She looked up as a tall, dark knight stood over her, sensing his anger. 'Forgive my woman, sir. She did not realise what she was doing.'

'I saw what happened,' Bryne said, glaring at her. 'Your woman hath done what all Saladin's army could not, lady. Pray that he is not dead, for I pity you both if he—'

Alain's eyelids flickered, his long lashes shadowing against sun-bronzed skin for a moment before he opened them and gazed into the anxious eyes of the girl bending over him. His first thought was that she was no more than a child, thin and pale, her dark eyes large in a face that was interesting rather than beautiful. Behind her he could see Bryne's angry stance and realised in a moment what was going on.

'No, don't murder the child, Bryne,' he protested, sitting up and groaning slightly as his head spun. A wry smile touched his mouth. 'It was not the child that hit me, I swear.'

Katherine looked at him apprehensively. Was he angry? He

did not look angry. Indeed, it seemed he was amused. She gave him a look of apology.

'It was Maria who struck you and she is very sorry. She thought you were one of those wicked men who attacked us.'

'The brigands?' Alain groaned again, feeling the back of his head gingerly. 'Maria hath the arm of an armourer to hit so hard. I vow 'tis a wonder that she did not crack my skull open.' Despite the pain in his head, his blue eyes were bright with mischief as he looked at the older woman. Her face was a picture of rueful indignation and it made him want to laugh long and hard, something he had not felt like doing in many a day. 'What did you hit me with, woman, a mace?'

'It was naught but a moneybag,' Maria said, glowering at him. She was a large woman with big strong arms and a heavy build. 'It is money for the ship to carry my lady home to her family—but you may take it if you let us go on our way.'

Alain was on his feet now. He looked the woman over, taking in her belligerent stance and fearless gaze. She was like a she-wolf defending her young, prepared to fight for the child she loved.

'Fear not, Maria,' he said and smiled at her, amused and somewhat touched by her devotion. 'You and the child have nothing to fear from us. We came to help you and will go on our way now that the brigands have gone.'

'Maria is truly sorry,' the girl said, recalling his attention. He saw that her eyes looked startled, somehow pleading, like a young deer caught in a hunter's trap in the forest. 'Please do not desert us, sir. I believe we have some leagues to travel as yet and, as you saw, we are not able to protect ourselves.'

'You were foolish to travel with such a small escort, child.'

She raised her head then and he saw a flash of pride in her

eyes. 'I am not a child, but the Lady Katherine of Grunwald—
and I had no choice. My father was killed by brigands only
days ago and most of his men with him. Maria and I escaped
because we had stopped to buy food from a village.' She
caught back a sob and he saw that she was fighting the tears
that threatened to spill over. 'These men are all that remain
of my father's people.'

Alain looked about him. The men were old and of little use
in a fight. He frowned as he saw the pleading look in her eyes
and realised that she was in a perilous situation. The brigands
he and his men had driven off were not the only ones she
would meet with on this lonely road. He could not abandon
her to her fate.

'I am sorry for your loss, lady. You are returning to your
home. May I ask where you live?'

'In France, sir—at least, that is the home of my uncle,
Baron Grunwald. My father bid me go to him if anything
should happen to him.' She struggled to hold back a sob and
failed. 'My poor father was a scholar, sir. We have been on a
pilgrimage to the Holy Land these past seven years, for he
wished to see the place of our Lord's birth, but he did not realise how hard the journey would be.'

'He was unwise to bring a young girl on such a journey,'
Alain said and saw her frown at the criticism. 'But I cannot
know his reasons. It may be that he had no choice.'

Katherine looked into his eyes. 'My mother died just before we left home, sir. Since then my father has relied on me
for many things—and I am seven and ten years. Not so very
young, I think?'

Alain's good-humoured smile broke through as he saw
that he had touched upon her pride. 'No, indeed, my lady. I

thought you no more than four and ten, and must beg you to forgive me if I have offended.'

Katherine gave him an odd, shy look. 'No, I am not offended, sir, but my father taught me it is always best to say straight out what you mean.'

'Your father sounds a good man, my lady. Once again, may I say that I am sorry. You have lost much.'

He felt a surge of protectiveness towards her. She was alone in a country that was not her own, with very little money and no one fit to protect her.

'Thank you. I miss Father terribly.'

'Yes, I can understand that.' Alain looked at her with compassion, understanding that grave, serious look in her eyes. To be alone in the world was a terrible thing for one such as she. He thought wistfully of his own happy childhood at Banewulf. He had chafed at the bonds of love then, but sometimes felt an aching need to see his mother and father again. 'I have not seen my family for nigh on eight years now, and I sometimes wonder if they have forgot me.'

Her dark eyes dwelled on his face. 'You have been with King Richard in the Holy Land perhaps?'

'Yes, that is so,' Alain confirmed. 'We had his permission to return home this many months ago and we have delayed in this land of warmth and plenty, but we are now on our way to the coast to find a ship to carry us either to France or, if we are lucky, to England.'

'We, too, are on our way to Rome in the hope of finding a ship.' She looked at him earnestly. 'I do not believe I have thanked you for saving my life, sir. Nor do I know your name.'

'I am Sir Alain de Banewulf—and this is Sir Bryne of

Wickham. We are as brothers and our men fight as one, for we have more strength by sheer force of numbers that way.'

Katherine curtsied to him and then to Sir Bryne, her elegant manners belying the poor quality of her gown and accoutrements. She was clearly well-born, but did not look as wealthy as her position as a nobleman's daughter might suggest.

'I thank you for your kindness in coming to our aid, good knights—and beg that you will allow us to join your party. I promise that we shall not slow you down, and we have money to pay for your services.'

That they had sufficient coin for their journey was evident from the lump forming on the back of Alain's head. He touched it repentantly, looking at the girl and her dragon of a companion. Despite her promise, Katherine and her fierce guardian would hamper their progress, for they must stop more often so that the women could rest. However, neither he nor Bryne could leave the women to the mercy of brigands. They were sworn by their oaths as knights to protect and honour any ladies they found in distress, and their own honour would allow no other course.

There were many lawless bands roaming the countryside on the journey they must make, both here and when they reached France. Some of them were men who had set out for the crusades with high ideals, burning with religious fervour, only to become disillusioned and bitter amongst the stench of death and disease in the Holy Land. Sickness had claimed the lives of too many, and putrid wounds rendered others helpless cripples for as long as they should live. Those fortunate enough to receive the attention of the Hospitallers, as he himself had been when his arm had been injured by the slash of a sword, oft recovered, but the men who had devoted themselves to such work could not treat everyone. Too many had died of sickness and neglect.

Alain had felt the taste of defeat bitter after King Richard was forced to abandon the struggle for Jerusalem, and he understood why some men might take to the roads rather than return home. He had wealth and position and, if God had been kind, a family to welcome him home, but many had nothing to take back but memories that would haunt their dreams.

At Acre King Richard had offered gold to any man brave enough to take away the stones of the tower beneath a hail of enemy fire. His call had been answered eagerly, and the death toll had mounted rapidly as the reckless and the brave rushed to answer his challenge. Such acts of defiant bravery had won them the city where others had failed, but at a terrible cost in life. Now some of those same men had found an easier way to earn their gold—by robbing unwary travellers. Such was the harshness of the world they lived in, and to abandon this girl to her fate would be a sin.

'We have no need of payment,' Alain told the girl, who had been watching him with her big solemn eyes. A wisp of dark hair had escaped her wimple when she was struggling with the rogues. It looked thick and curled about her brow. 'Neither Bryne nor I could allow you to continue without a proper escort, lady. It will be our pleasure to see you safely to your ship.'

'You are a truly honourable knight, sir,' Katherine said and her heart fluttered oddly as she looked into his eyes. How very blue they were! 'Maria and I are grateful for your kindness.' She glanced at her companion meaningfully. 'Say thank you, Maria.'

Maria muttered something, but the look of disapproval did not leave her eyes. It was clear that she had not yet made up her mind that he was to be trusted with the care of her darling.

'I thank you for your confidence in me, lady.' Alain bowed to Katherine and threw Maria a mocking look, which made her frown deepen. 'You will excuse us, ladies. I must speak with my men, make sure that none has been seriously hurt.'

He moved away to join Bryne.

'Before you say anything, my friend—what else could I do? She and that dragon of hers will undoubtedly cause us more trouble than they are worth. Yet we could not abandon them.'

'Her father should never have taken her on his travels if he could not protect her.'

'Indeed, he should not. I agree with you, Bryne, that the journey to the Holy Land was no venture for a young girl, though other women have braved it—Richard's queen, for one. Yet hers was a different case; she had the whole of England's might to protect her and her women. However, a female in distress cannot be ignored. We should be unchivalrous indeed to send them on their way now.'

'You are right,' agreed Bryne with a wry grimace. 'But that one is going to cause trouble. I feel it in my bones.'

'Do you mean the child or the dragon?'

Bryne laughed. Despite the years of war, the hardships, anguish and grief, Alain had retained his sense of humour. He was no longer the pretty youth who had been so eager to join Duke Richard. Instead, he had matured into a man of some stature; a man others admired and respected for his fearlessness in battle. Even his brother, the great knight Sir Stefan de Banewulf, had not been more respected.

'I meant the lady, Alain. Make no mistake, Katherine of Grunwald is not a child. Small and slight she may be—but she hath a woman's mind and heart.'

'You say that as if you disapprove?' Alain arched his brows.

'Something about her worries me,' Bryne confessed. 'I am not sure that I believe her story.'

'Why should she lie?' Alain recalled the grief he had seen in the girl's eyes. She seemed innocent and vulnerable to him, tiny and fragile like a bird. 'What could she have to hide?'

'I do not know, but I would swear there is more that she hath not told us—and that she will cause us trouble before too long.'

'You are too suspicious,' Alain said, dismissing his friend's words lightly. 'She is naught but an innocent child…'

'You worry too much,' Katherine told her companion when they were alone. She smiled at Maria, who had been friend, comforter and stalwart supporter these past years. Without Maria she could never have borne the years of hardship and discomfort, the day-to-day endurance of constant travelling that had been her lot for more than seven years. 'Why should they suspect anything? Besides, I have not lied. What I told them was true. I just haven't told them the whole story.'

'What happens if they discover the truth?' Maria looked at her anxiously. Sometimes her beloved child was too reckless. 'You must be careful, sweeting.'

'How can anyone know? My father entrusted his secret only to me and I have shared a part of it with you. Neither of us is likely to tell anyone.'

Maria shook her head at her. 'Someone else knows. The Baron was killed for his secret. If what he believed is true, you carry a precious treasure, Katherine. Men would kill for it. And these men are no exception.'

Katherine's eyes narrowed in thought. 'I do not believe Sir Alain would kill for gain, Maria. I liked him and I trusted him. Sir Bryne, too, seems a man one can trust.'

'Men are seldom worthy of a woman's trust,' Maria muttered darkly. 'Be wary, my dove. You know I care only for you.'

'Yes, I do know that, Maria,' Katherine said and gave her a smile of rare sweetness.

Her smile lit up her face from inside. She was not a pretty girl. Even her much-loved father had never pretended that she was a great beauty for her features were unremarkable. But when she smiled there was something about her that touched the heart of most who saw it. It came from the goodness of heart and the generosity that were so much a part of her character and had endeared her to those who truly knew her. She had a keen mind and had been educated by her father as if she were the son he had never been granted. In truth there was at times a purity about Katherine that made her almost angelic, and yet coupled with the innocence and the goodness was a mischievous nature that loved to tease and play.

'You may never marry, Katherine,' her father had told her once as they talked of the future. 'Unless I can discover a great treasure, I cannot give you the dowry you deserve.'

'You mean I am too plain to attract a husband without a huge bribe?' Her eyes had twinkled with naughty humour; she had no illusions concerning her appearance. 'Do you hope to pay someone to take me off your hands? For shame, Father!' She laughed as he protested. 'Nay, nay, I know you love me, and think only for my sake. Do not fear, my dear Father. Why should I want a husband when I have you?'

'You know I love you completely,' he had told her with an affectionate pat of her cheek. 'But you are too like me, Kate. In looks as well as all else. Had you been like your mother…'

She had seen the pain in his eyes as his words faded on a sigh. His statement did not distress her as it might other young women. She remembered her beautiful, gentle mother with love and regret. It was all too true that she could never match the Lady Helena for looks or sweetness of nature.

Helena of Grunwald had been a fair beauty with deep blue eyes, her features as perfect as her complexion. Katherine was dark haired like her father, her eyes a deep melting brown. They were her best feature, especially when laughter lurked in their depths, which it often had until the shock of her father's death.

Katherine had seen her reflection once in a hand mirror of burnished silver, and she had thought herself plain. Not exactly ugly, for her features were not misshapen, just unremarkable. Her nose was too short for beauty and turned up a little. She had always admired straight noses. Queen Berengaria had a perfect nose. Katherine had seen King Richard and his queen in Cyprus a few months before the triumph at Acre.

A little shudder ran through her as she recalled the terrible wounds she had witnessed at the time of Acre. Men lying helpless as their lifeblood gushed out from gaping wounds; men with their bodies torn apart, their limbs shattered. And sometimes women and children dying in pain, from wounds they had received helping their loved ones. One memory of innocent men and women being slaughtered in the street had lingered in her mind, causing her nightmares long after their suffering had ended.

Maria, Baron Grunwald and Katherine herself had worked with others tirelessly to help the poor soldiers and civilians who had been injured. It was after Acre was conquered and the King had left for Jerusalem that they, too, set out on their last fateful journey.

Baron Grunwald had been determined to discover some

wonderful treasure. There were many relics to be purchased in the Holy Land, but he believed most of them false, and had set himself the task of discovering something of far greater worth. To this end he had spent months studying old scripts and maps, even hieroglyphs on stone tablets that came his way as he bargained with merchants and hunted in the markets. Katherine had never believed that his search would be successful, but he had by chance discovered something so wonderful, so magnificent, that his excitement had known no bounds.

'Our fortunes are made, daughter,' he had told Katherine one morning when they were alone in the pavilion they shared. It was a large pavilion with partitions for sleeping and they had been in the front, which was used for sitting and eating when the heat of the day was too fierce to be outside. 'Every prince in Christendom would like to own such a treasure. It is priceless.'

Katherine had thought she heard something outside their pavilion, but when she looked there had been no one close by. At first she had welcomed her father's excitement, but as he began to tell her more she had been aware of a coldness at the nape of her neck.

'But do we have the right to sell it, Father?' Katherine asked when her father finished speaking and she learned what the treasure was. 'It is a holy thing and should surely be given to the church freely.'

'You shame me, daughter,' he had confessed, much struck by her words. 'My first thought was for its worth—but you remind me that greed is unworthy. It was you I thought of, Kate. You would have had a splendid dowry and I would have been able to restore Grunwald.'

'Perhaps you will find something else, Father. Some treasure that does not have such importance to our faith.' Katherine almost wished she had not spoken her thoughts for he looked so weary, so disappointed. She knew that the gold he might have earned would have brought ease and comfort to his declining years. 'I would not have you do something unworthy, something you might regret. As for myself, I have no wish for a great dowry. If ever I married, it would be to a man who would have me for myself, not my fortune.'

'Your mother should have had a fortune but she was cheated of it by her brother,' the Baron said and sighed. 'I wed her because I loved her, Kate, but the money would have stopped our home from crumbling about us.' Katherine sighed and shook her head over the memory and her father's sadness. It was a sorrow he had carried for years. 'But you are right, my daughter. No man hath the right to sell such a thing. I am privileged to be its custodian until I can give it to the person most fitted to be a true guardian.'

Katherine's father had conquered his greed, but had soon learned to his cost that others were not prepared to accept that his treasure was not for sale.

She had never known how Baron Hubert of Ravenshurst had discovered that her father had the precious treasure but, as they began the long journey that would take them home, they had become aware that they were being followed.

At first Baron Grunwald had refused to believe that anyone could know that he had discovered the secret that men had been searching for since our Lord's crucifixion.

'I have told no one but you, Kate. And I know you would never have breathed a word outside our tent.'

'You know I would not, Father—but the Lord Hubert's men have been following us since we left Cyprus.'

'He cannot know…' Katherine's father had shaken his head anxiously. It was impossible for the English knight to know what he carried, and yet there was little doubt that his ship had followed close on the heels of theirs. And now that they had landed in Italy, the Baron's men were again following them, discreetly and from a distance, but always there. 'It is impossible, Kate. We make something of what can only be coincidence.'

Yet the next morning they had had a visit from Hubert of Ravenshurst. At first he had been charming, offering to buy the treasure for a huge amount of gold. Had they accepted his offer, it would have made them rich, but Katherine's father had denied all knowledge of the object the English knight sought.

'It is better to pretend to know nothing,' he'd told her after their visitor had departed. The Lord Hubert had made no threats, but his manner had shown them that he was angry at being refused. 'Remember that if you should become the custodian of our treasure, Kate.'

'What can you mean?' Katherine's eyes widened in fear. 'You are the custodian, Father.'

'If something were to happen to me, you must go to your uncle. You know that he hath been the steward of Grunwald in my absence. If I die, he will become the rightful owner. You will have nothing, Kate, but he will take you in for my sake. Besides, there is no one else you can trust.'

'I pray you will not speak of dying! I would rather you gave the…treasure to the Lord of Ravenshurst.'

'Never!' Her father's eyes had glinted with unaccustomed anger. 'I would rather die than give that devil such a precious thing, Kate. His very touch would despoil it. No, it must go to the church, as you said, for all men to see and revere.'

'Oh, Father…' She had looked at him helplessly. Was it pride that made him speak so foolishly?

She wished that she had argued further. She had been against selling the treasure, but, realising the threat to her father, she would have done anything to be rid of it. Anything except hurt him.

Now she wished that she had thrown his precious treasure into the river, but it was too late. Her father was dead and the burden had passed to her, for it was a burden. She knew that she could not simply give it up. Her father had made her promise the day he placed it in her care that she would do all she could to see that it was taken to a place of safety. She must carry on as he would have wished, no matter her own feelings.

Maria knew only that she carried something precious on her person. Katherine could not burden her with the whole truth. If she had been able to reconcile her conscience, she might have rid herself of it, for her father's death had made it hateful to her, yet she knew deep within herself that she could not do such a wicked thing.

What she carried belonged to the whole of Christendom. It must be placed in a great church, somewhere worthy of its significance where it could be seen and appreciated by those who needed it most. Her father had spoken of approaching the Pope himself. They had been so close to achieving what they set out to do, but now her father was dead and she did not believe that the Pope would listen to her. She would probably not be granted an audience and she would share her secret with no other, for even amongst the priests and cardinals there was greed and corruption.

Her father had bid her go home if he died, and in her troubled mind she saw it as the solution to her problem. Somehow she must get her sacred trust home to France. Once she was at her uncle's manor in France, she would be able to decide what must be the fate of this precious thing. Her uncle was Baron Grunwald now. Surely he would know what to do? Yes, she must see the cup safe before she thought of her own future.

What were a few small lies in such a cause?

Katherine's thoughts turned towards the knight with the merry blue eyes, remembering the way her heart had raced when he opened them to look at her. How fair he was to look upon! No man had ever caused her to feel that way before and she smiled at her own foolishness. To let herself dream of this man would be folly indeed. He had thought her a child, and that she had not been in many years. Not since that terrible night at Acre, when she had seen people she loved as friends hounded from their homes and killed like rats in the street.

Her father had told her that such things happened in war, that even the best of men might behave badly when the blood-lust was raised in him, and she knew that what the knights did that day was a part of war. Yet it had haunted her dreams for months and even now she was not completely free of the memory.

Because of that memory, she was vaguely uneasy about telling the whole of her story to the knight who had charged so valiantly to her rescue. She was grateful for what he had done for her, but she dare not trust him with the complete truth.

Something of the importance and value she carried might turn the minds of even the most honourable of men.

Chapter Two

Alain was strangely restless as he woke with the dawn. He had not slept well and it was not simply that both he and Bryne had sensed they were being followed the previous day. As yet there had been mere glimpses of a horse and rider in the distance. At times they had travelled through steep valleys hemmed in by towering hills to either side, at others their way lay through dense woods or past small villages, where they bought food. At no time had the secret watchers attempted to come closer—but why were they there? Perhaps more importantly, what did they want?

The previous night they had camped close to a river. Alain was thoughtful as he walked down to a secluded spot where he intended to bathe. A brief swim in its cool waters would help to clear his mind and cleanse his body. He liked to bathe more often than was the custom in England, a habit he had learned from Arab friends in Palestine. For, despite his desire to free the Holy City from Saladin, he had found it possible to make friends with men of all faiths and nationalities. Indeed, he had found the Arab culture of peace and learning pleasant, and, had it not been for his strong faith, might have stayed happily amongst them.

He was feeling out of sorts with himself this morning as he flexed his muscles, easing off the ache of lying on the hard ground, though he did not know why. But perhaps the act of bathing would relieve the tension that had built in him of late, the feeling that he was missing something, that his life had no real purpose.

'You are a fool, Alain de Banewulf,' he told himself with a wry smile as he walked to the nearby river. 'What is it that you want of life? Why can you never be satisfied?'

The answer was something that still eluded him, as it had for years past. It was as if he searched for something that might never be his, a sense of fulfilment and of peace.

Stripping off his clothes, which were the simple tunic and close-fitting hose of a soldier, and did not include the suit of chain-mail he wore for battle, Alain plunged into the river. He came up gasping and gave a shout of pleasure. The water was cold, but wonderful. How good it was to feel young and alive! His mood was shaken off and he was glad that he had chosen to slip away for these private moments.

He swam across the river with quick, powerful strokes, enjoying the energy that surged through him, then turned over on to his back, floating lazily as he let himself think about the things that had played on his mind during the night.

What was the Lady Katherine of Grunwald up to? And what secret was she hiding? He had thought Bryne too suspicious at the start, but after two days in the lady's company he had changed his mind. For certain she had something on her mind—something she did not wish to share with her companions.

Hearing the sound of someone splashing in the water a little further downstream, Alain turned his head to look for the source. Now he could hear laughter. Evidently, someone was enjoying the water as much as he was.

He could hear voices calling to one another—the Lady Katherine and the dragon, if he were not mistaken. His keen senses told him that they were just past the bend in the riverbank, hidden from his view by the fronds of a weeping tree.

'You should not take the risk, my lady.'

'I am safe enough, Maria. Sir Alain is an honourable knight and his men would not dare to anger him. Besides, I needed to bathe. I felt so dirty.'

'Well, you are safe enough with me to watch over you, for I would kill any man who dared to spy on you.'

Alain smiled to himself, amused by the force of this avowal. He would put nothing past the dragon. His head had been tender for some hours after the last time she'd hit him and he would not want to risk it again.

He would not frighten them, he decided, and swam carefully back to the bank, pulling on his clothes quickly as he felt the chill of the early morning air. He was just fastening his low-slung sword belt when he heard the scream.

Katherine was in trouble! He ran towards the sound and then stopped in surprise as he saw something totally unexpected. A woman was struggling with two ruffians, but it was not Katherine. This woman was taller, older, more voluptuous and very beautiful with long blonde hair tumbling down her back.

Alain did not stop to consider. Drawing his sword, he gave a roar that had oft sent shivers running through Saladin's warriors. As he descended on the three, the men gave him a startled glance and let go of the woman. They then ran off towards a group of three horses and, seizing the bridles of two, mounted and rode off into the woods.

The woman looked at Alain, gave a cry and swooned as he reached her. Sheathing his sword, he knelt beside her on the dry earth and laid his head against her breast, listening for her heartbeat. Thank God she lived! Even as her eyelids fluttered open, Alain felt a heavy blow across his shoulders from behind. It sent him reeling and he lay winded for a moment, then as he pushed himself over on to his back and looked up, he saw Maria standing over him, moneybag in hand.

'You should be shamed to treat a lady so!' she cried, her eyes flashing with righteous fury.

'You hit me again!' Alain said and sat up. 'Be damned to you, woman! You are too hasty with that weapon of yours. I was merely trying to decide if the lady was breathing.'

The beauty was sitting up. She looked far from pleased as she stared at Maria, her full red lips forming a sulky pout.

'Foolish wretch!' she cried, clearly none the worse for her adventure. 'This brave knight hath rescued me from those rogues who were trying to abduct me. You might have killed him.'

'Nay, no matter,' Alain said. For some reason the obvious hostility between the two women made him want to laugh out loud. Maria's look was enough to frighten the dead and the other's was…puzzling. He would swear that she had been thwarted in some way. He was on his feet now, offering his hand to the damsel so recently in distress and now evidently recovered. 'You must forgive her. Maria thought she was protecting you from my wicked intent—is that not so, Maria?'

He got nothing but a scowl from the dragon, but the beauty accepted his hand gratefully, rising a little unsteadily and giving a sigh. For a moment she swayed as though she might swoon and then she smiled. Alain felt breathless of a sudden. He could not recall ever having seen such a smile or eyes that shade—they were such a deep blue that they might almost have been the colour of violets. He knew a fleeting but urgent desire to lie with her.

'I am the Lady Celestine De Charlemagne,' she said, her fingers trembling in his. 'My husband was Baron De Charlemagne…' A deep sigh escaped her soft red lips, a single tear seeming to escape from the corner of her eye. 'My lord was killed at Acre and many of his people with him. I—I am in some trouble, sir. For I have no one to protect me, though I have family who would take me in if I could but reach France.'

'Celestine…is that truly you?' Alain turned his head as he heard another voice and saw that Katherine had joined them. He noticed that her hair was wet, as was her tunic, which clung to her and revealed the budding curves of her young body, curves that had previously been hidden from his gaze. For the first time he was aware of her as a woman. Bryne had been right; she was not a child despite her appearance. But she was looking at the Lady of Charlemagne and she did not seem pleased to see her. 'What are you doing here? I believed you had accepted the protection of—of the Lord Hubert of Ravenshurst.'

'Katherine!' Celestine gave a little scream of delight and ran to her at once. 'My dear child. How are you? Everyone thought you dead. We heard of your poor father's tragic demise and believed…but I am so pleased to see you.'

'Celestine?' Katherine gave her an uncertain look. 'Why are you here?'

'I was forced to escape,' Celestine said and bit her full bottom lip. 'I must tell you that I was terribly deceived in Ravenshurst. He can be charming, but I vow he is an evil man. I have heard such things… No! I must not speak of it, for if he knew I had heard his secrets he would kill me. Pray do not ask me, Katherine, for I cannot bring myself to think of such things.'

Katherine was silent. Celestine had once been her friend, for they had worked together to tend the wounded during the terrible siege of Acre. Then, when Celestine had chosen to become the Lord Hubert's companion, she had wondered if it was from her that he had learned of her father's treasure. She could not be certain that Celestine had known, but she believed that it was possible. Celestine may have heard her father speaking to her or even caught a sight of his writings concerning his discovery, for they had often been left lying on his couch in their pavilion, and the older woman, being a trusted friend, had come and gone as she pleased.

'How did you know where we were?' Katherine could hear the suspicion in her own voice and regretted it as she saw Sir Alain give her a questing look.

'Come, my lady,' he chided softly. 'This lady is in some distress, as you were when I rescued you. The least you may do is to take her to our camp and make sure that she has whatever she needs for her comfort.'

'Yes, of course,' Katherine said, her cheeks warm. He thought her unkind and harsh, but he could not know her reasons—nor could she tell him. She bit her lip and looked at Celestine once more. 'You have no baggage with you?'

'Only a few items I was able to conceal on my person,' Celestine said. 'For I should not have been allowed to leave the Baron's camp had he known what I meant to do. You must not fear me, Katherine. I am not your enemy, though I know

Ravenshurst may have been your father's. I believe there was some quarrel between them, though I do not know the truth of it.'

Katherine nodded, but made no reply. It was difficult to judge whether she ought to trust Celestine or not. What she said might be true, yet there was something false about her. However, since she was here, and Sir Alain had clearly decided to take her under his protection, there was little she could do other than accept her. At least, she must appear to do so, though she would remain wary.

Sir Alain was leading Celestine's horse back to camp, leaving her to bring her erstwhile friend. Katherine noticed that a small leather pouch was slung from the horn of the saddle. Obviously Celestine had not left the Baron's camp empty-handed. She must have planned her escape carefully—but that did not make her guilty of treachery. Besides, how could she have known where to look for Katherine?

'Where are you going?' Katherine asked as she turned to look at Celestine. She wondered uneasily if some of her hostility towards the other woman was because of the way Sir Alain had been staring at her. He'd looked as if he were mesmerised, as if he had been struck by love for Celestine—an arrow from the gods of ancient mythology, perhaps?

Surely she was not jealous? Katherine looked into her heart. Celestine was very beautiful. Even Katherine's father had remarked on it. He had found her charming, but Katherine had not minded their friendship. At one time she had hoped that they might make a match of it, that her father might find happiness with a second wife, but then Celestine had become the Lord Hubert's companion. Some might call her his mistress, though Katherine's father had preferred to think otherwise.

'Celestine would not be so foolish. The Baron is not a man to be trusted, Katherine. Celestine has been left alone in a strange land. She has merely accepted his offer to be her escort on the journey home.'

That had been in Cyprus, before they had sailed for the shores of Italy. It had not surprised Baron Grunwald at first that the English lord had followed them, for they were all bound in the same direction—but then in Italy had come the offer to buy his treasure and his death had swiftly followed his refusal.

'I hope to find a ship to carry me back to France,' Celestine told her now in answer to her question. 'I have dower lands there, Katherine, for my husband settled them on me when we married. Where will you go now that your poor father is gone?'

Tears stood in those wonderful eyes and she looked genuinely upset. Katherine's suspicion eased a little. Perhaps she had misjudged the other woman. Indeed, perhaps she was a little jealous. It was unkind of her to harbour such thoughts against Celestine.

'Why did you leave us to join Baron Ravenshurst?' asked Katherine, thinking it best to have the matter straight between them.

'I have asked myself that question many times,' Celestine replied and sighed. She shook her head sorrowfully. 'I fear I am a foolish woman and his smiles and promises turned my head. A woman in my position must marry, Katherine. I could reside quietly on my own lands for a time, but there would always be men who sought to wed me for what I might bring them. I believed Hubert to be the kind of man with whom I might find content—but it was not so. All men are greedy, but some have a code of honour by which they live. I fear Baron Hubert of Ravenshurst is not one of them. He is ruthless and cruel and I was unhappy in his company.'

'Do you believe all men greedy?' Katherine frowned. 'My father was not—and nor, I think, is Sir Alain.'

'I spoke as a general rule. You are innocent, Katherine, and have truly known only your father. Therefore you cannot judge. I have lived amongst men and know more of their true natures. Most are greedy, ambitious fools.'

Her tone and the way her mouth had gone hard and sour shocked Katherine. She was not such an innocent that she did not know such men existed; indeed, she had met several of that ilk on her travels with her father. She had also met good honest men, such as Sir Alain and Sir Bryne. She believed both were generous, decent men of honour. Sir Alain's was the sweeter nature, though she had noticed that his commands were instantly obeyed, which might mean that he could be very different if he chose. However, she did not think him either greedy or foolish, though perhaps he, like many other men, was blinded by Celestine's beauty. They did not see beyond her charming smile to the devious nature that lay beneath.

'Perhaps you are right,' she said slowly. She would keep her thoughts to herself, just as she would reserve judgement on Celestine for the moment.

'But you are right to think Sir Alain better than most,' Celestine said with a thoughtful glance at her. 'I am sure we can trust him to get us safely to the ship. But you did not answer my question, Katherine. Where will you go when we reach France?'

'To my uncle. He is the Baron now, but he will do his duty by me.' Her eyes clouded with grief too recent to have become muted. She did not dislike her uncle, but he was a gruff, blunt man with none of her father's sensibilities. She would find it hard to live under his roof, but she had no choice. She had no other family and no dowry. 'There is nowhere else for me.'

'But of course there is,' Celestine said and smiled at her. 'If you chose, you could come and live with me as my friend and dearest companion. No, do not refuse me now, sweet Katherine. We have time enough ahead of us and you may tell me when we reach France.'

Katherine smiled, but made no answer. Celestine seemed genuinely to want to help her, but somehow she could not quite believe in her.

'You begin to make a habit of rescuing damsels,' Bryne said with a wry smile. He glanced towards the two younger ladies, who were walking together in the morning sunlight. 'But this one is undoubtedly beautiful.'

'What do you think of her story?' Alain asked and smiled for Celestine's beauty was overwhelming. 'Would you say she is telling us the truth—or doth the mystery deepen?'

'It seems a little odd that the ladies know each other,' Bryne said. 'But as yet I have not had the opportunity to observe the Lady Celestine.'

'And Katherine?' Alain's brow wrinkled in thought. His first sight of Celestine had taken his breath away and yet somewhere in a tiny corner of his mind instinct was telling him to be watchful. 'Is she the key to this affair, think you?'

'I have suspected something from the beginning, as you know,' Bryne said. 'There is something she is concealing, some secret she does not confide in us. I would swear it. Yet I do not think there is malice in her. As for the other one…'

he shook his head '…I shall reserve judgement. We are but two hours from Rome, and may consider our duty done once there.'

'Yes, perhaps,' Alain replied but looked uncertain. 'Yet I would not have harm come to her…'

'Of whom do you speak?' Bryne asked and then smiled as he watched the direction of his friend's gaze, believing he knew. So the wind blew in that quarter, did it? Well, the woman was certainly beautiful, though not to his own taste. 'You think to see them on their way to France? Or is there something more on your mind?'

'I should feel happier if certain things were made plainer,' Alain replied. 'But we shall see what the ladies have to say when we reach Rome itself, Bryne.'

Alain was thoughtful after he left his friend. It could surely not be mere coincidence that Celestine had ridden their way. And if it had been planned…the lady would bear a little careful watching.

It was not Katherine's first visit to Rome. She and her father had stopped for a few weeks in the beautiful city on their outward journey to the Holy Land, visiting some of the ancient sites of interest. They had walked along the Via Appia and by the banks of the River Tiber, which was the very reason for the city's existence.

'It was this way that our Lord was forced to carry His cross on the way to His crucifixion,' Katherine's father had said in reverent tones as they walked in Christ's footsteps. 'And here that Nero sent the early Christian martyrs to their deaths,' he had told her as they gazed at the stone arches of the Colosseum.

Now she returned alone. Katherine's heart ached for her loss. Her father had been a man of great learning, highly respected amongst those who knew him, but a dreamer and hardly suited for a long pilgrimage. Even before he was killed he had developed a bad cough, and she knew he had feared for her future, often bewailing the fact that he had no fortune to leave her.

'I do not know what will become of you, Kate,' he had told her once when in a reflective mood. 'I have neglected my duty, been a bad father to you.'

'You have been the best of fathers,' she had replied and kissed him fondly. Indeed, she would not have changed her life these past years, but she longed for him now, for his wisdom to guide her. 'What should I do, Father?' she asked softly, wishing that he stood beside her. 'Should I seek an audience with the Holy Father? What am I to do for the best?'

Now they were approaching the waterfront, where the ships from many countries often rode at anchor in the sunshine. There were but three in port that day, and Sir Alain had told the ladies that he would make inquiries as to their suitability, arranging passage on their behalf if possible.

Katherine stood on the quayside, gazing out over the water. The last time she had stood here was with her father. She had been but eleven years, still suffering from the loss of her mother and feeling the responsibility of becoming her father's companion. She had known that he needed her, for her mother had told her to care for him as he was often too lost in his studies to remember to eat. A heavy responsibility indeed for a child, but one she had accepted willingly out of her love. The prospect of such a long journey had seemed exciting to her then, an adventure to be shared with the person she loved most in the world. And so it had proved despite the hardships, danger and suffering she had witnessed at firsthand.

On that day so many years ago, the port had been busy with many ships loading and unloading their cargoes, but on this day it was quiet with only a few people walking or standing in conversation. Turning her head to look about her, Katherine saw that Celestine had been speaking earnestly to a man. Realising she was observed, she left him and walked towards Katherine. The man seemed to look hard in Katherine's direction for a moment before turning away.

What had they been talking about? And why had the man, who was a stranger to Katherine, been so interested in her?

'It seems there are no ships bound for France at the moment,' Celestine said when she came up to Katherine. 'One of those you see is bound for Cyprus, another for the shores of Byzantium and the other for England. A French ship may not be here for some weeks to come.'

'I do not want to linger here so long,' Katherine said anxiously. 'Our money will dwindle and may not then be enough for our passage to France.' In fact, she had wondered if her small purse would see them safely home. Most of their goods had been lost when her father was attacked and killed, supposedly by brigands.

'Here comes Sir Alain now,' Celestine said. 'We may hear what he has to say.'

'I fear the news is not what you would wish to hear,' Alain told them as their anxious eyes beseeched him for the news he could not give. 'A French ship is not expected for some time. There was a terrible storm last month and two French merchant vessels were lost at sea. The English ship you see anchored cannot sail for another week at least. It, too, was caught in the storm, and though it managed to limp to port it has sustained damage that has not yet been repaired.'

'Then we have no choice but to remain,' Celestine said and there was a gleam of something that might have been satisfaction in her eyes. 'Do not fear, Katherine. I have sufficient money for the three of us. I shall take lodgings and—'

'No need for that,' Alain assured them at once. 'Bryne has friends here and we have all been invited to make use of the Villa Maderno, which lies in the hills just above us. Bryne has gone on ahead to make sure that everything is in readiness for our arrival.'

'But we cannot trouble you…' Celestine began, faltering as she saw his frown. His manner told her that he would brook no interference with his plans. 'Surely you will travel on the English ship once it is repaired?'

'Yes, that is our plan,' Alain told her. 'Had a French ship been the only one available, we should have taken that and found an English berth when we reached Marseilles. The voyage to England will be longer and perhaps less comfortable without a sojourn in France to break the tedium, but we shall take passage. I think it might be best for you to accompany us, Katherine. The Lady Celestine also, if she wishes?' He raised his brows to her and she smiled at him, her long lashes fluttering against her cheeks.

'Thank you. May I have time to consider?'

'I have taken the liberty of booking passage for all of us,' Alain told her. 'If you would prefer to remain here, that is your privilege, but I fear it might be months before you could be sure of finding a ship that can carry you home. You would find it much easier to purchase a passage from England—and the expense of travelling to England will not fall on you as

I have contracted with the English captain for our whole party.'

'You are very kind,' Katherine said, and then, taking a deep breath, 'But I had hoped I might gain an audience with the Holy Father while we are in Rome.'

'An audience with his Holiness!' Celestine exclaimed. 'My dearest Katherine, what reason can you possibly have for making such a request? It is certain to be refused. Pope Innocent III is a busy man and hardly likely to give his time to a young girl.'

'I dare say his Holiness might find time to see you, Katherine,' Alain said, seeing her expression, which was a mixture of distress and embarrassment. 'However, I happen to know that he is not in Rome at this time.'

'Oh…then I shall not…' Katherine sighed. 'I had hoped, but it is obviously not meant to be.' She looked at him. 'Then I think I shall accept your invitation to accompany you to England, sir. I do not see what else I can do.'

'Is there something I may help you with, my lady?' Alain asked, sensing that she was deeply worried. 'Anything I might do that you cannot do yourself?'

Katherine hesitated. It would be so good to share her burden with someone she could trust. Her instincts told her that Sir Alain de Banewulf was an honourable man, but still she did not dare to share her secret with him.

'I thank you, but, no, there is nothing, sir. It was merely that my father had spoken of a meeting with his Holiness, and I would have liked to give him…something.'

'Could you not leave it with one of his cardinals?' Alain asked. 'I am sure I could arrange that for you if you wished, for I had an audience with his Holiness when I was first in Rome on my return from the Holy Land.'

'You are very kind, but, no, I shall not trouble you,' Katherine replied, though she did not know why. It would have been easy to hand over both the treasure and the provenance that her father had documented so faithfully. Or what was left of it, for so many of her father's notes had been lost with his baggage.

She turned away from Sir Alain's penetrating gaze to find that Celestine was looking at her with barely concealed eagerness. Katherine felt annoyed with herself for saying so much. If Celestine had somehow learned of the treasure Katherine carried, she might try to steal it, either for herself or for the Lord Hubert, with whom she professed to have quarrelled.

Was it unkind of her to suspect her erstwhile friend? Katherine felt that it was unworthy to be so suspicious, yet she could not help it. She almost wished that she had confided the whole to Sir Alain and left it to him to solve her dilemma.

But he was telling his men to mount up and the moment had passed. Perhaps, after all, it was best to keep the secret a little longer. Soon she would be in England and from there she could find a ship to take her to France and her uncle's home.

Until then, she would just have to carry her burden alone.

'Is this not a beautiful villa?' Celestine asked as Katherine met her after having been able to indulge in the luxury of a proper bath in scented water, something she had not done since leaving Cyprus. 'My room is next to yours, and charming. I think Sir Bryne's friend must be very wealthy to own something like this, Katherine.'

'Yes, I believe you are right, for I understand that he owns several homes, both here and in the wine country to the north and in Salerno. It was from one of his estates that Sir Alain and Sir Bryne were coming when they met us.'

'My home in France would seem dark and bleak compared to this,' Celestine told her. 'Sometimes I wonder if I truly wish to return—and yet I might if I had a companion to make me smile.'

'I dare say you will marry again.'

Katherine felt uncomfortable; she knew that Celestine was trying to coax an answer from her and she did not wish to give it, though she did not know why. A return to her own home was not appealing. In truth, the more she thought about returning to Grunwald, the less appealing it became. She had grown used to living and sleeping in her pavilion, though that had been lost with her father's baggage, and she had been forced to sleep under the stars until they met Sir Alain and were given shelter in his own camp.

Like Celestine, she was impressed by the villa, which had many light and airy rooms and was very beautiful with marble mosaics on the floor and white pillars to support the arches that led from one part of the villa to another. There were statues of women clothed in flowing drapes, couches with soft cushions where one might sit or lie to take one's ease and a bathhouse with a bathing pool filled with cool scented water.

Katherine had never experienced such luxury, and knew that it was unlikely she would again. She made up her mind to thank Sir Alain for bringing her here when she saw him next, and perhaps to confide in him at least a little of her secret.

'Shall we walk in the garden for a little before we dine?' Celestine asked her. 'It is very beautiful and I think there is a wonderful view out over the sea.'

'Yes, why not?' Katherine asked. She felt relaxed by the peace and serenity of her surroundings, and a little guilty for having suspected Celestine of wanting to rob her. 'It is such a lovely night and we shall not see its like when we reach England, for I know it will be cold there.'

'I have never been to England,' Celestine confided, taking her arm and smiling. 'Have you, Katherine?'

'No, but I know something about it—my mother was an Englishwoman.'

'Ah…' Celestine nodded wisely. 'Baron Grunwald told me that she was very beautiful, and ought to have been an heiress through her own mother—but her brother withheld the dowry because he did not wish her to marry.'

'She fell in love with my father and the match was made with the help of King Henry II, but my mother's brother did not approve and he would not pay her dowry. Even when she died he refused to pay what was due to her from an inheritance.'

'That was not kind of him, for I believe your father was not a wealthy man?'

'No, indeed. His estate is poor and the castle of Grunwald in bad repair. He had hoped he might find riches on his travels…' Katherine sighed and stopped, for she had almost been led into giving too much away.

'And did he find nothing?' Celestine was struggling to hide her eagerness.

'No, nothing that he might sell,' Katherine said and looked at Celestine. 'Have you heard otherwise?'

'I know nothing of your father's affairs,' Celestine replied. 'Though I did hear the Lord Hubert speak of some treasure…' She waited for Katherine to reply. 'But perhaps it was stolen?'

'If there had been a treasure, it would have been taken when his baggage was stolen,' Katherine said. 'But my father had nothing he might sell.' She sensed Celestine's disbelief and was

almost certain that she had been the one who had discovered
Baron Grunwald's secret and spoken to Ravenshurst of it.

'Then you have no choice but to throw yourself on the
mercy of your uncle—unless you come to me. Have you
given some thought to the matter, Katherine?'

Was she genuine, or did she still believe that Katherine carried a precious treasure? Katherine wished that she could be sure.

They were standing now on a hill, gazing out at the city
below and beyond it the sparkle of a blue sea. A sob rose to
Katherine's throat as she wished that her father might have
lived to stand by her side and see this wonderful vista. How
she missed him, and how alone she felt!

'Do not cry, sweet Kate,' Celestine said and reached out to
take her into her arms. 'You have friends. You are not alone.'

'Thank you, but I was not going to cry,' Katherine said and
avoided her embrace. 'Excuse me, the evening grows chilly.
I think a storm is brewing. I shall return to my room and find
a mantle to wear for supper.'

'No—' Celestine stopped, her cheeks flushing as Katherine looked at her. 'I mean, let me come with you.'

'Thank you, I shall go alone.'

Katherine turned and ran from her, feeling close to the
tears that might shame her. She did not know why she should
feel so distressed. After all, she had always known that she
would have to return to Grunwald one day, and it had not upset
her before. Perhaps it was this beautiful place, making her
aware of the changes in her life? The years of travelling had
been hard in many ways, but they had also been glorious.

Her feet carried her swiftly towards her room, but as she
approached she heard a cry of surprise and anger, swiftly followed by a scream and then the sight of two men running

away. They saw her, but turned aside and sped through the garden, obviously in a hurry to escape. As she entered the room that had been loaned to her and Maria for the next few days, she saw that her baggage had been opened and her things strewn all over the floor. Maria was lying on the floor, and Sir Alain was kneeling beside her, helping her to rise.

'What has happened here?' Katherine asked. 'Maria—are you hurt?'

'No, I am not harmed, though those rogues did their best to render me an injury,' Maria muttered. 'I discovered them ransacking your things, my lady, and they attacked me. Had this knight not come to my rescue, I might have been murdered.'

'You were taken by surprise, Maria,' Alain told her. Having ascertained that she was no more than bruised and shocked, he had a merry twinkle in his eyes. 'I dare say your trusty weapon was not to hand.'

'You should not mock her, sir,' Katherine said as Maria scowled at him. 'She has had a fright.'

'I do not think they took anything, my lady—nothing important,' Maria said as she sat up and was helped to her feet by Sir Alain. 'I disturbed them before they had time to do more than begin their search.'

'Do not fret, dearest,' Katherine told her. 'You are more important to me than anything they might have taken here.'

'But your father…' Maria began and was quelled by a warning look from her mistress. 'Forgive me…'

'May I ask what they were looking for?' Alain asked, glancing from one to the other. 'It is clear they think you have something important, Katherine. They took a risk in coming here—this place belongs to one of Rome's foremost citizens and they could face execution for what they have done this evening.'

'My—my father gave me something to look after the morning he died,' Katherine said. 'Until that time he had carried it within his own baggage, but because he suspected that he might be robbed, he gave the trust to me.'

'My lady…Katherine,' Maria warned, 'be careful of whom you trust…' This knight seemed to be all that he should, and she was grateful for his help, but, when it came to her darling's safety, she trusted no one!

'I think we have no choice,' Katherine said. 'My father discovered something, sir—something that hath no intrinsic value of its own, but which is valuable because it was once used by our Lord himself. It is something that is important to Christendom and ought to be placed in the care of the church.'

'So that is why you sought an audience with his Holiness?' Alain frowned as Katherine nodded. 'And you are not willing to entrust it to any other than the Pope himself?'

'I—I do not know,' Katherine admitted. 'My father believed there was much corruption in high places, amongst both kings and churchmen. He wanted it to be placed where all can see and perhaps be healed by the experience of having seen such a relic.'

'What exactly is it that he discovered?' Alain saw her quick frown and shook his head. 'Nay, do not tell me if you prefer to keep your secret, though I vow it would be safe with me. Like your father, I would never seek to gain personal gain from something so valuable to Christendom.'

'Then you are rare amongst men,' Maria muttered and glared at him. 'Not all Christian knights have your scruples, sir. I vow there are those only too keen to steal it for themselves.'

'What mean you?' Alain's eyes narrowed as he looked from her to Katherine. 'Has this something to do with the Lord

Hubert of Ravenshurst? Was it his men who came here? I recall that you spoke of him when the Lady Celestine joined us.'

'Yes, I spoke of him,' Katherine said as she realised that
she could no longer hold back such important information.
'Somehow he learned of my father's discovery. You must
know that my father wrote down the provenance of…his discovery, for without it he could not prove that the treasure is
what he believes it to be. There are many holy relics for sale
in Palestine, and indeed in Rome itself, but my father's discovery was made by painstaking research over many months
and years.'

'There are always holy relics wherever you travel,' Alain
agreed, 'and many of them are false. I dare say that some,
which have been made into shrines, have no true provenance,
but something of the importance that your sacred trust entails
would need proof if it were to be accepted as the true—' He
broke off and looked at her, and she saw a gleam of excitement begin in his eyes. 'If it is what I think…men have been
searching for it from the time of the crucifixion.'

Katherine felt a quiver of alarm. She had known that even
the most trustworthy of men might be tempted by her treasure, perhaps not for greed, but for the glory that such a find
could bring them.

'I have not told you what it is, sir,' she reminded him. 'It
may be that my father was mistaken…'

'Would you let me read his writings?' Alain asked. His eyes
were steady on her face but held warmth, a concern that made
her heart race. For a moment she thought that his feelings towards her were more than mere courtesy. 'If I gave you my
solemn word that I will return them to you when we reach England, would you trust me?'

Katherine hesitated, and then nodded. Instinct told her that if she could not trust this man, then she could trust no one. She crossed the room to where a plant in a great earthenware pot stood in an alcove and lifted it, revealing a flat leather pouch. Hesitating but a moment, she picked up the pouch and handed it to Alain.

'You will find my father's writing hard to decipher, sir, for he had a small neat hand, and in places he has used his own code. From these you will not learn the nature of his treasure, only the details of his research. There were fuller descriptions of his work, but they were lost with his baggage. I believe there is enough left to give credence to his discovery, but you may study these and give me your opinion.'

'I thank you for your trust in me, Katherine,' Alain said and hesitated, then reached out to touch her cheek. It was the merest graze of his fingers, but it sent tremors running through her, and his smile made her blush. 'You may be certain that I shall keep the nature of your secret to myself—though I am bound by friendship to tell Bryne that the Lord of Ravenshurst is your enemy.'

'I dare say Sir Bryne is a man you can trust,' Katherine replied, for, if he was Alain's friend, how could he be otherwise? 'You may tell him as much as I have told you should you think it right.'

Alain inclined his head. 'In future I believe you should take care in walking alone, Katherine. At least until we are in England.'

'I am grateful for your kindness, sir, and for the opportunity to confide in you. It is a heavy burden I carry, and I confess that I do not know what to do for the best.'

'Will you allow me to help you once I have read and

thought about your father's work? If I am convinced that his discovery is truly important, I would count it an honour to see it placed where it might be of benefit to all of our faith.' His eyes met hers in a gaze that held her fast. 'The question is— will you trust me, lady?'

Chapter Three

'It seems that I already have, sir,' Katherine replied and her heart skipped a beat as his look seemed to caress her. There was something about the curve of his mouth and the expression in his eyes then that made her feel that she might trust him with more than her secret. When he looked at her in that way she was ready to swoon. She could almost believe that he might feel more than friendship towards her. No, that was mere wishful thinking on her part and foolish. 'In truth I believe I have no choice.'

Alain reached out to take her hand, holding it for a moment as he gazed into her face. 'I thank you for that trust, Katherine, and do swear to assist you in your task to find the right home for your father's treasure.'

'But where should that be?' Katherine asked. The question had exercised her mind all too often. 'In a great church or in the house of some powerful king?'

'That is a weighty question and not one that can be answered immediately,' he replied. 'And now, my lady, may I take you to supper? It was for this purpose that I came, fortunately in time to hear Maria's screams.'

'Yes, I thank you,' she replied and laid her hand on the arm he offered. She could see from Maria's expression that she believed she had spoken too freely to Sir Alain—but what else could she do? She must trust someone, for it seemed that the Lord of Ravenshurst was determined to steal her treasure no matter what.

She had told Sir Alain nothing of her suspicions of Celestine, Katherine realised, as they went into the banqueting hall and discovered that Celestine was already there, sharing a glass of wine with Sir Bryne and a tall, handsome gentleman. Celestine was smiling invitingly up at the newcomer, seeming to enjoy his attention. Observing his manner for a moment, Katherine guessed that he was the owner of the villa.

Marcus Aurelius Calabria had returned to Rome from his travels and was delighted to find he had unexpected guests. Especially one as beautiful as the Lady de Charlemagne.

He turned as Alain approached, greeting him with evident pleasure, his eyes moving over Katherine without registering interest and returning to Celestine almost immediately.

'It was the most delightful surprise to discover that we had company,' he murmured. 'I do trust that you are to remain with me for some time?'

'For a few days only,' Sir Bryne replied as Celestine merely fluttered her long lashes at him. 'The ship we travel on is making repairs and should be ready to sail within the week—but, for myself, I intend to return to Rome often. With the opportunities for trade that have opened to us, I think I may make a home in Venice one day. I would see England and my family, but I think the climate there too dark and dank to hold me forever.'

'It is often the case with those who have seen other lands,'

Marcus replied with a smile. 'I have visited your country, Bryne, as you know, and formed friendships with your father and others—but I would not care to live there. It is a dark, gloomy place, too full of mists and frosts for my liking.'

'Indeed, I wonder if I shall find my home too gloomy,' Celestine said and fluttered her long lashes at him. 'Especially after seeing your beautiful home, sir. I had not known such places existed.'

'I thank you for your compliment,' he said and inclined his head to her. 'We live much as our ancestors in ancient Rome, lady, for my family have a long tradition. In the north we have a castle as dark and cavernous as any you might have encountered, for my uncle is Duke of Ferencia and guards his lands as best he may. I have been visiting with him for a time, but here in my summer home I enjoy the simple life. In Rome we have no enemies and may walk freely as we will.' He saw Alain's frown and raised his brow. 'Something troubles you, my friend?'

'I would have a few private words with you, Marcus,' Alain replied and drew him away from the Lady Celestine. In a moment Marcus was heard to exclaim and look angry and then he and Alain left the room together, deep in conversation.

'What has happened?' Celestine asked, startled by such a change in her host's behaviour. She was slightly annoyed, for she had felt that she was making a favourable impression upon their host.

'Sir Alain drove off two men who were searching my room,' Katherine told her. 'They had knocked Maria down and might have killed her had he not arrived in time.'

'God have mercy!' Celestine had gone pale and crossed herself. 'Thank goodness you were in the garden with me, otherwise you might have been hurt, Katherine.'

Katherine frowned. The older woman seemed concerned for her and it would be churlish to suspect her of having asked her to walk in the gardens merely to get her away from her room. She noticed that Bryne's eyes had narrowed, that he was looking very thoughtful. What could have brought that expression to his face?

'Yes, I was fortunate,' she said. 'But my poor Maria might not have been had Sir Alain not chanced to hear her cry.'

'Maria is a servant—' Celestine began and then realised her mistake. 'But of course I know that she is dear to you. Yet I cannot help be thankful that it was she who discovered the villains and not you, Kate.'

Katherine gave her a cold look. 'Maria is my friend, not a servant. Please remember that—and I would prefer that you call me Katherine. Only my father called me Kate.'

'Forgive me. I did not mean to offend.'

'It is merely a preference...'

Katherine was ashamed of the coldness in her voice, but she could not help it. Deep down inside her, there was something telling her that Celestine's friendship was false and she could not dismiss the warning.

Sir Alain and Marcus had returned to the company now. They spoke briefly to Bryne, and then Marcus clapped his hands and the servants began to serve supper.

As in ancient times, when the Romans held their great banquets, the company sat on benches or silken cushions piled on the floor and ate with their fingers from low tables. Finger-bowls of silver and gold had been provided for washing the hands, and music was played to entertain them while they ate and talked.

This was not a great banquet, merely a gathering of a few

friends, but the food served was rich and there was what seemed to Katherine to be an endless stream of exotic dishes. She ate sparingly, enjoying most the fruits and dates. Occasionally, she dipped her fingers in the scented water and wiped them on a soft cloth to dry them. The wine was heavy and potent. She drank, as sparingly as she ate, from a wine cup, which was fashioned of silver and studded with precious jewels on the foot. Through the open arches that led out to the gardens floated the scent of night-flowering blooms. The sky was dark, but the stars were sprinkled generously across the velvet blackness.

'It is the stuff of dreams, do you not think so, lady?' Sir Bryne asked as he leaned towards Katherine. Celestine was laughing with their host and Alain seemed to be lost in thought. 'Marcus and his family know how to enjoy life, do they not?'

'It is certainly most pleasant,' Katherine replied. 'Do you truly intend to make your home in Venice one day, sir?'

'It is the greatest trading nation on earth,' Bryne replied, looking thoughtful. 'A man of enterprise might become wealthy there beyond his dreams, and powerful—especially when he has good friends. I have certainly considered it, but I must see my home and family once more before I decide.'

'Have you a large family?'

'My father was elderly when I left England and may not be still living, but I have elder brothers and they have wives and children. I hope to find some of them alive and well on my return.'

'You have no wife, sir?'

'No.' Bryne frowned. 'There was a lady once…but she married another, richer man and I put all thoughts of marriage aside and determined to make my fortune. Yet I suppose I may marry one day, if only in the hope of a son to follow me.'

'And Sir Alain…?' Katherine asked and then blushed as his brows rose. 'Forgive me. I ask too many questions.'

'I believe he has not thought of marriage as yet, lady.' Sir Bryne smiled at her and Katherine lowered her eyes. She must be more careful of her words or she would give herself away, and that would be embarrassing. 'Though with such a man it is not always easy to know what is in his mind.'

Sir Alain seemed to have shrugged off his reflective mood and was now laughing and talking to Celestine, apparently enjoying the pleasure of her company. It was clear that he found her attractive, which was natural, for she was very beautiful. Feeling a tiny pang of disappointment, Katherine scolded herself for allowing the green-eyed monster of jealousy into her heart. She could not blame Sir Alain for finding Celestine fascinating. The older woman was both beautiful and charming…even if Katherine did suspect her of being false.

But perhaps she was letting her emotions blind her. She had no right or cause to be jealous. She must put aside these foolish ideas and thoughts that had begun to creep into her mind, plaguing her whenever she was unwary enough to let them.

Sir Alain had turned his head and was looking at her now. Katherine glanced quickly away, for she could not meet his gaze, which was concerned and thoughtful, but not the kind of look he bestowed on the lovely Celestine.

She knew he thought her a mere child, and perhaps she was compared to Celestine. Yet she felt like a woman, and her heart ached for the tenderness she was developing towards this man, foolish as it might be.

'Our host was telling me of a shrine in his garden,' Alain

said now. 'This villa was built on the site of others that had been here since the great days of Rome. There was once a temple to the goddess of love here, and a shrine still remains.'

'How very pagan,' Celestine said, 'and rather exciting. I should love to see this shrine—would not you, Katherine?'

'Yes, perhaps,' answered Katherine a little uncertainly.

'The time to see it is at night when the moon shines, for the goddess loved the moon,' Marcus Aurelius told them. 'If it pleases you, I shall show you now, for the moon hath come out from the shadows and will light our way. It is said that, if you please the goddess, your heart's wish will come true.'

'Oh, we must see this shrine,' Celestine exclaimed. 'Do say you want to see it, Katherine!'

'Very well, if you wish it.'

Katherine rose reluctantly, but it was clear that Celestine was eager to see the shrine of the goddess of love. She was walking with her hand upon her host's arm, teasing him with smiles and words as they walked just ahead of the others.

'Are you offended by the thought of a pagan goddess?' Alain asked Katherine. She gazed up at him for a moment, her eyes wide and serious, before shaking her head. 'Then is it the Lady Celestine that offends you?'

'Neither,' Katherine replied. 'I am a Christian by faith, sir, but my father was a great scholar, as I have told you, and we discussed other forms of religion. I dare say there is merit in many of them, but I would not put my faith in anything a pagan goddess might reveal to me.'

'Would you not?' Alain gave her a wicked smile, which made her catch her breath. Something inside her made her feel as if she would melt in his warmth. How handsome he was when he smiled like that! And how foolish she was to let it affect her this way. 'Not even if you might gain knowledge of your heart's desire?'

'I have no desires, sir,' Katherine replied with commendable dignity in the face of his provocation. Her heart was racing like the wind, but she would give him no indication of the confusion his teasing aroused in her. What was this strange feeling inside her—was it what they called desire? If so, she had no right to feel it for a man who had no such feelings towards her. 'I am not like to find a lover nor yet a husband, for I have no fortune and my face is unremarkable.'

'You are not a beauty,' Alain said, looking at her seriously now. 'But you have something about you, lady, that many would find attractive.'

Katherine laughed merrily. 'You are kinder than my father, sir, for though he loved me dearly he never thought me other than plain. He told me that I was unlikely to wed without a large dowry and I have no thought of it.'

'Are men such fools that they must have either a pretty face or a sack of gold?' His brows rose, but the expression in his eyes puzzled her since she did not know what lay behind it.

'I do not believe that all men are fools, sir. Indeed, I would not think either you or Sir Bryne a fool—but still I do not believe that I am likely to find many suitors…and perhaps no one I would care to accept. I would prefer to remain unwed rather than make an unhappy marriage.'

'That is your choice, of course.' He hesitated, his eyes making her heart thud in her breast as she felt something stir inside her—a feeling so sweet, like warm honey—and was almost breathless. 'But what of love and the fulfilment of your destiny?' His brows rose as he teased her and her foolish heart leaped. Why did she feel so light-headed—almost as if she could walk on air?

'If I found love, that would be another matter,' Katherine said and her smile lit up her face, though she managed to retain her appearance of cool dignity. 'But I fear my destiny may be to remain unwed until I die.'

'That would be a sad destiny for one of your nature,' Alain said and the soft tone of his voice set her insides churning. She was hot with something that she suddenly knew for desire. This was how a woman felt about the man she loved, and Katherine could no longer deceive herself. She had for her folly fallen in love with Sir Alain de Banewulf!

She glanced aside, for she could not bear that her own expression should give her away. It was surely unmaidenly to have such desires. Besides, he had given no indication that he felt anything of the kind for her. He was kind and concerned for her welfare, but nothing more. To reveal her foolish passion would humiliate and shame her.

Fortunately for Katherine they had reached the shrine and, after some exclamations from Celestine, the small group fell silent. It was a beautiful spot in a small grove. The shrine was just a pile of stones that most would ignore, but it was surrounded by fragrant shrubs and vines that sheltered it from prying eyes, and there was a quietness about the place that touched the soul.

Katherine was very aware that this was a holy place. As a Christian she could not worship the deity that had been consecrated here, but she felt its power and its goodness. There was no evil here, just a benevolent kindness that seemed to reach out and envelop her—the feeling of love so strong that she found herself wishing for something so ridiculous and smiled to herself.

Foolish, foolish Katherine! Sir Alain would never love her as she loved him.

'What must I do to please the goddess?' Celestine asked of her companion and broke the feeling of reverence that had held them all until that moment. 'Shall I give her my silver bangle?'

'In ancient times women gave her gifts to learn the secrets she knew,' Marcus Aurelius replied. 'But I have been told that the gift must come from the heart—and a simple thing will find more favour than a rich jewel.'

'Then I shall not give her my bangle,' Celestine said. 'For it is one of my most precious possessions. I shall think of something else and visit her another day—for I would not have you hear my demands of her.' She gave him a mocking, inviting look.

Katherine turned away with a little shiver of disgust. It seemed that Celestine used her smiles indiscriminately on all men to get her way with them. She had seemed to entice Sir Alain with her inviting looks, but now she was more interested in their host.

Katherine noticed that Sir Alain was watching and frowning, and she felt her heart contract with pain for him. She was sorry if Celestine had hurt him, for he was a gentle and true knight and she did not want him to suffer a broken heart.

'I shall take you back to the villa,' he told her, turning his back on Celestine. 'Come, lady, I would see you safe and the hour grows late. I shall not see you in the morning—I have some business I must attend before we leave Rome.'

Katherine made no reply, simply turning with him and allowing him to lead her back to her own room. He said goodnight to her, made her a courtly bow and waited until she was inside the villa before turning away.

Would he return to the others—or would he prefer his own

company? He seemed to spend much time in thought and she wondered what kind of a man he was inside. In truth she hardly knew him. Perhaps it had merely been the moonlight that had played such a trick on her? How could she love a man she did not know?

Smiling at her own impudence, she went to perch on a stool and sat dreaming as Maria came to free her hair of its covering and brush it so that it flowed over her shoulders in soft waves. Now, if she had but known it, with that look upon her face, a gentle smile curving her lips and her hair reflected in the moonlight, she was truly as attractive as Alain had told her. But she had no mirror to see her own reflection, nor would she have believed it had someone shown her. In her own mind she believed herself plain and nothing could change that long-held opinion.

The night was too beautiful to allow for sleep. Katherine was restless and rose from her bed, looking out at the moonlight. The scent of the wisteria that hung on the villa walls was strong and made her somehow wistful. Perhaps it was the full moon that kept her from sleeping—or was it something else?

There had been a sound… There it was again, the soft tinkle of a woman's laughter. Celestine was in the garden. Now Katherine could hear the deeper laughter of a man. Two figures had come into view. They lingered for a moment in the moonlight, the man drawing the woman into his arms to kiss her.

Katherine watched as Celestine arched her head back, her manner that of surrender to his desire. It was an intimate moment and private. Withdrawing from her window, Katherine felt hot and ashamed of spying on the lovers.

She had not been able to see them clearly enough to know

who the man was, but she suspected that it was their host. Celestine had been doing her best to tease him all evening. And now it seemed that they had an understanding of an intimate kind. Perhaps she would stay in Rome with him.

Feeling even more restless than before, Katherine returned to her bed and lay down. Seeing the lovers entwined in that passionate embrace had made her more aware of all that was missing in her life. Would she ever know that kind of intimacy? It was unlikely, for who would want to lie with her? She had thought that she could face a life without love, but that was before she had looked into a pair of blue eyes and seen a smile that made her heart beat faster.

She knew that once she had parted from Sir Alain her life would seem emptier than before—but there was nothing she could do but accept her fate. To sigh for the impossible would only bring her unhappiness.

'Are you thinking of staying here for a while?' Katherine asked Celestine as they walked in the villa gardens the next morning. 'Our host has said that we are welcome and you have expressed doubts about returning to your dower lands.'

And she had seen that kiss in the garden the previous night!

'It would suit me to live here as the wife of such a wealthy man,' Celestine admitted. 'But our host already has a wife. They live apart for much of the time, but there is no chance of another taking her place. I dare say I might be his mistress if I cared for it.'

'I see…' Katherine glanced at her curiously. Had that kiss meant nothing to Celestine? 'Are you attracted to Marcus Aurelius?'

'As much as I am to most men,' she admitted and laughed

as she saw Katherine's look of inquiry. 'Do not be shocked, my sweet Katherine. When you have been married you will understand that all men are much the same and desire only one thing of a woman. Understanding that is the key to getting what you need from them. For as long as you keep them wanting, they will do anything to please you. But their passion soon tires.'

Katherine was shocked at the cold calculation she saw in the other's eyes. 'But what of love?' She echoed the question Sir Alain had asked of her the previous night. 'Does that mean nothing?'

'It is a myth,' Celestine said mockingly. 'Do not believe those sweet songs the bards sing, Katherine. They are meant to lure the unsuspecting woman into a trap. Men use courtship to gain what they most desire. Once they tire of their pleasure, they care not what becomes of the woman they once professed to love.'

Katherine was silent, though her mind denied Celestine's words. She knew it was not true. How could it be? Her father had loved her mother until the day he died. Her memory had been as a shrine to him and he had never despoiled it. Perhaps such a love was rare, but it did exist and Katherine knew that she could never be satisfied with anything less.

'No, no, I shall return to France,' Celestine said as though making up her mind. She turned her coaxing smile on Katherine. 'And I hope to persuade you to be my companion, dearest girl. Have you made up your mind?'

'Not yet,' Katherine confessed. 'Whatever happens, I must see my uncle first, Celestine—and then who knows?' In her heart she knew that she would never want to live with this woman, but it might be best to let her believe otherwise.

Celestine had as yet given her no reason to suspect her of treachery, and yet she could not trust her.

'Why so pensive?' Maria asked as she dressed Katherine's hair that evening. 'I hope you are not being foolish, my dove?'

'What do you mean?' Katherine avoided her faithful nurse's searching gaze. 'No, do not tell me. I am in no mood for one of your scolds.' She had not seen Sir Alain all day and had discovered that she missed him almost more than she could bear.

'It will end in tears.' Maria shook her head at her. 'He thinks you a child. 'Tis the other one he lusts after, mark my words. That one will have them all running after her like panting dogs.'

'Maria! I will not have you say such things.' Katherine turned away from her angrily. She did not care to hear Maria's words, though she knew they were said for her benefit. Had she mistaken the look she'd seen in Sir Alain's eyes? It had been brief, yet she had thought for one glorious moment that he might care for her—but Maria's words had made her doubt. Why should he look at her, slight and plain as she was, when he might have another, more beautiful woman if he chose?

Donning her mantle, she left her chamber and walked through the gardens towards the banqueting room. It was such a lovely night and her heart yearned for something—for love.

She smiled and shook her head over her own foolishness. It was the memory of that pagan shrine and the way it had reached out to something inside her, making her feel that she, too, might know the sweetness of love. She must be sensible. She must remember who and what she was, and that love was not for her.

Hearing laughter ahead of her, she stopped as she saw a man and a woman walking towards the house. They had clearly been strolling in the gardens and she realised that it was Celestine and Sir Alain. He had returned from his business and sought out Celestine, not Katherine.

Celestine was smiling up at him, and he was laughing, clearly enjoying her company. They looked so well together, and Sir Alain seemed to find Celestine amusing company.

Katherine turned away, the pain of seeing them in such intimacy striking deep. Maria was right! She would be a fool to hope for anything more than friendship from Sir Alain. To dream of him could only bring her pain.

Was it he Katherine had seen kissing Celestine the previous night in the moonlight? She had thought it someone else, but now she could not be sure. The image of Sir Alain kissing Celestine…making love to her…was too painful to be borne and Katherine dismissed it, forcing a smile to her lips as she went to meet them.

She had no right to expect anything. No right to be jealous of the intimacy between Sir Alain and Celestine.

'Ah, there you are, dearest child,' Celestine said and gave Katherine a false smile. 'We were just talking about you. This sweet, foolish man was worried about your safety, but I told him you would find your way to supper without his help—and now you see that I am right, Alain.'

'Marcus has posted guards to prevent another unpleasant occurrence,' Alain told Katherine. He looked at her gravely and her heart sank. Was she merely a burden, a duty to him? 'But I would have come for you had you waited a little, lady.'

Katherine's head was held high, pride in every line of her

body. 'I am perfectly able to find my way to supper alone, sir,' she said. 'Nor would I want to deprive you of your pleasure.'

She walked past them and into the house, the sound of Celestine's tinkling laughter following her. She was a jealous child, Katherine admitted to herself as she fought for composure. It was a fault in her and something she must conquer. Yet she could not deny that she felt resentment against Celestine for taking so lightly something that Katherine desired too much. Yes, she was jealous. Why else would she let herself be so affected by the sight of Sir Alain and Celestine together?

Tears pricked behind her eyes, but she fought them back. She was not going to cry, no matter how much it hurt!

Alain stood looking out at the moonlight. It was a glorious night, too beautiful to be alone. He did not know why he could not sleep, yet his thoughts had kept him restless. It was a night for lovers. He would not see many of its like once he returned to England. Yet he had chosen to keep his own company.

It would be pleasant to walk for a while. At least then he might settle himself, put his mind at rest. Something had been bothering him for the past few days. Something to do with Celestine, with the sly look he had caught in her eyes at times— or was it Katherine who bothered him? The two seemed bound together in his mind, both part of the puzzle that plagued him.

Celestine was undoubtedly beautiful, a woman that any man might crave in his bed, and, for a short time, he had felt desire for her—but there was something about Katherine that made him want to protect her. She was vulnerable, in need of his help, and sometimes when he looked into her eyes, a strange desire to sweep her up and ride off with her, to protect her all his life, came into his mind. It was foolish, for she was not at all the kind of lady he had thought to make his bride.

He walked as far as the end of the garden, gazing down at the city below, which was for the most part in darkness. The moon had been obscured by clouds and for a moment the sky was almost pitch-black. But he could hear voices—a man and a woman arguing. The man sounded angry and impatient.

'You make little progress, my lady. My patience grows thin. If she gets clear to England…'

'I have done what I could. Your men had their chance. You should blame them, not me. I did my part in the affair.'

'Have you seen nothing of it? She does not confide in you?'

'I am trying to win her trust. These things take time, sir. You are too impatient.'

'If I thought that you had betrayed me…'

'You would kill me?' Celestine's laughter was soft and mocking. She was clearly unafraid of his threats. 'Where would that get you, my friend? Without me she will cling more closely to our gallant protector—and I do not think you have the courage to challenge him.'

'Damn you!' There was a growl of anger, swiftly followed by a curse. 'I swear I'll kill you one of these days, Celestine.'

'But you love me—you love what I do to you, my sweet, don't you? I can make you purr like a kitten if I choose, do not forget that. I think you protest too much. Was it not I who—?'

Her words were cut off abruptly and the sounds became more intimate. Alain had no doubt of what was happening somewhere in the darkness. Celestine knew this man well, that much was certain. She had met him here by appointment rather than chance.

He frowned as he turned and walked back towards the

house. Just what had he overheard? Was Celestine plotting with someone to steal Katherine's treasure? And, if so, who was that person? Ravenshurst—or another?

Alain had heard enough to put him on his guard, though not enough to give him proof of the suspicions he had been harbouring since Celestine joined them.

It was true that she was one of the loveliest women he had ever seen. Her smile had taken his breath away, making him desire her, but almost at once he had begun to wonder what lay behind the mask. Her story did not ring quite true and he had seen a look in her eyes at times that had put him on his guard. And now he was sure that his instincts had been right. She was no friend to Katherine, for all her pretence.

Yet he could not be certain of what he had heard. Those few whispered words might mean anything. It was of a surety that the Lady Celestine must be watched, and closely. And he must be very careful. If he showed too much kindness towards Katherine, Celestine would be on her guard and he believed she had a clever, devious mind. His only chance of discovering what she plotted was to flatter her, make her believe that he was charmed by her—and that meant she must not suspect his true feelings for a moment.

'Did I not tell you that the lady would cause us trouble?' Bryne said the next morning when they were visiting their warehouse to inspect a new cargo of silks and spices that would be worth a small fortune once it was transported to England or France. Alain had told him of what he'd overheard the previous night and of his half-formed suspicions. 'If Hubert of Ravenshurst is involved in this, he will stop at nothing to get what he wants.'

'You think he will pursue her even to England?'

'I think it likely.' Bryne frowned. 'Do you believe in this story of the Holy Grail? Stories of its whereabouts abound, Alain. Legend has it that it was brought to England long ago, and Arthur's knights searched for it in vain. Yet now it seems it was in the Holy Land all this time. How can anyone be sure where it has been all these years?'

'That is the problem. To prove it is the precious cup is a task that may take a man his lifetime…'

'A man would have to be very certain to follow such a cause, Alain.'

'Katherine hath not named the treasure she carries, but it is the one item that men have searched for ceaselessly—think of it, Bryne. The cup that our Lord drank from on that last night. Think of the satisfaction there would be in giving that to Christendom.'

'One of the most holy relics imaginable,' Bryne said and frowned. 'If Ravenshurst believes she has it—I think him capable of any crime to obtain it. Have you thought what it would be worth? There are those who would pay a king's ransom to have it in their possession.'

'Ten times as much as many kings could pay, I dare swear,' Alain agreed. 'But Katherine believes it should be given freely to the church and I agree with her. It should not belong to one person, but to the whole of Christendom.'

'Indeed, I agree,' Bryne said, looking thoughtful. 'Yet men go to war for far less. I dare not think what trouble such a relic could cause, for if it were given to one church others would claim it as their right.'

'I think Katherine wanted to give it to the Pope had he been in Rome.'

'She will give it to no other but his Holiness?'

'She says not,' Alain replied with a frown. 'She is determined to take it with her, perhaps to ask her uncle's advice. Which means it will probably go to King Philip of France... He is a good Christian knight—but think you he is a proper guardian for such a treasure?'

'She hath the right to do as she pleases if her father discovered it.' Bryne's gaze narrowed in thought. 'Do you believe it to be genuine and not one of the relics that anyone may buy on the streets of Palestine and Rome?'

'I do not know for certain that it is the cup Christ used at the Last Supper. It might be something of less importance—but I may know more of its provenance when I have read Baron Grunwald's writings.'

'You have not finished your study of them?'

'Hardly begun. The lettering is small and not easy to decipher, and indeed some of it is in code. I dare say Katherine's father wished to protect his discovery.'

'It is a dangerous burden she carries, Alain. You realise what this means, of course?'

'It means that I must stay by her side until the treasure is no longer in her possession. To desert her would almost certainly mean her death. Whoever was with Celestine last night was determined to have it, no matter the cost.'

'Have you told Katherine that?'

'No, for she would likely deny me the right to protect her. The lady is more spirited than most.' Alain smiled at his own thoughts. In appearance Katherine seemed little more than a child, but as he came to know her he saw that she was brave and true, and had a fierce pride.

Bryne chuckled. 'And her guardian a veritable dragon. I

think Maria trusts no one, including me. Yet even so she and
Katherine are no match for the like of Ravenshurst—and if
he knows of the treasure then others soon will, for he in-
dulges too often in his wine and in his cups runs loose at the
mouth. It is a pity that this treasure, whatever it may be, was
not left where it had lain since that time.'

'Yet think of the good it might do in the right hands.'
Alain's eyes lit with fervour. The Holy Grail was a prize beyond price, something that any true Christian must venerate.
'Think of it, Bryne—the cup that Christ used just before his
death.'

'That is true,' Bryne agreed with a frown. 'The pilgrims
would travel far to pray at such a shrine—but where does it
belong, my friend? Who hath the most right to own it? Methinks it is too valuable for any man to possess. It would be
a burden rather than a blessing.'

'Yes, for some.' Alain nodded. He could see Bryne's point
of view, though for him it was a find of such wonder that he
could only marvel at it. 'Always supposing that it is the cup
men have sought since the crucifixion.'

'Sometimes rumour is enough. A story of tears from a
statue will bring the desperate flocking in their droves to
pray—think what this cup would do,' Bryne replied. He
smiled crookedly at his companion, but there was a look of
determination in his eyes. 'Methinks we may rue the day we
met with the Lady Katherine—yet, I am of your own mind,
Alain. We must stay with her until the treasure has been placed
in safer hands.'

'I had thought you wanted to spend some time in England?' Alain raised his brows.

'It was my intention and remains so—but my own concerns

may wait until this matter is ended. I would have no harm come to Lady Katherine by my neglect. I respect her too much to have her fall prey to that rogue. Ravenshurst shall not lay hands on her while I breathe, though I would beg you to keep all I have said in confidence. Speak nothing of this to anyone, including Katherine. I believe she finds my company pleasant and perhaps feels some warmth towards me—indeed, I have hope for the future—but it is too soon to speak of more.'

Alain said nothing, merely nodding his head in agreement. Bryne had been disappointed in love as a young man—he must truly care for Katherine if he was now thinking of taking a wife.

'It is agreed then,' he said and smiled at his companion. If it was in Bryne's mind to marry the lady, he would not stand in his way. Yes, he, too, cared for Katherine, but he was not yet certain of his feelings. His need to protect and care for her ran deep, but he did not know if it was what men called love or merely friendship. If she loved Bryne and he her, then Alain must accept it, even if it caused him some pain. 'Our duty is to the ladies. We shall protect them against Ravenshurst or others of his ilk.'

Chapter Four

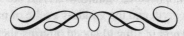

Katherine did not know what had brought her back to the shrine of the pagan goddess, except that it had seemed such a peaceful place that first evening. That morning the sun was shining and the garden was filled with the scent of blossoms and the sound of birdsong. She stood for a moment looking out over the sea, and then, turning, found her way to the sacred grove.

A sense of peace fell over her almost at once, and for some reason that she could not fathom she found herself laying a perfect rosebud at the foot of the pile of stones. It was the kind of offering that Marcus Aurelius had said the goddess liked best.

'I do not ask you for anything,' Katherine whispered. 'Your faith is not mine, and yet I believe that you were good and true—and I have found peace here. I thank you for that gift and want no other.'

She stood for a moment in silent contemplation, and was smiling as she began to retrace her steps towards the house. A restless night had caused her to examine her heart and to reach some sort of settlement within herself. In a few days they would begin the voyage to England, and after that she would part from Sir Alain. She must make up her mind to it and forget the foolish thoughts that the sight of him aroused in her.

'Ah, there you are.' Celestine's voice hailed her as she drew near to the house. 'I thought you must have gone for a walk. I had thought of visiting that shrine we saw the other night, but I have decided against it. It is all nonsense anyway. Love is but a myth and the goddess a relic of pagan times. It would be a waste of time to lay an offering there.'

'Yes, I am sure you are right,' Katherine replied. It was silly of her, but she hoped that Celestine would not visit the shrine. 'Besides, you are so beautiful that you do not need the goddess to help you.'

The older woman smiled complacently. 'It is true that many men have loved me—but I have found none that I truly love. They are such shallow, selfish creatures. They think only of their own needs and desires—but we are too clever for them and brute strength does not always win the prize.'

Katherine made no reply. She did not understand Celestine's meaning. The older woman often seemed shallow and selfish to her, but perhaps she was judging her too harshly.

'Yet you said that you would marry again?'

'For position, for the life that I would lead as the wife of a wealthy man,' Celestine replied with a toss of her head. 'I do not care to be poor nor to hide myself on my dower lands. I want a man with influence at court—for such a man I would be willing to marry.'

Celestine could choose her own husband, thought Katherine, an unworthy pang of envy passing fleetingly through her mind. For Katherine marriage was something she knew to be unlikely.

'Have you seen Sir Alain this morning?' Celestine asked, wrinkling her smooth brow.

'No. I believe he had some business.' Katherine held back her sigh. Soon, Sir Alain and the way he made her feel would be merely a memory. For a time she had thought he might truly care for her, but of late she had noticed a certain reserve when he spoke to her. Yet she could not think what she had done that might have offended him.

'I dare say he has many business affairs for he is a man of some influence and wealth...' Celestine seemed to be thoughtful. 'More wealthy than I had imagined at the start.'

'Yes, I suppose he must be. I am sorry, I cannot tell you where he is.'

'Well, no matter. We shall no doubt see sufficient of each other on the voyage to England,' Celestine said with a complacent smile. She looked about her. 'We must make the most of this sunshine, Katherine, for it will be much colder in England...'

'Yes, I expect it will—and yet I shall be glad to leave Rome.'

Katherine had been slightly uneasy while they stayed in Rome, for she could not forget what had happened that first night at the villa, when, but for Sir Alain's timely interruption, her faithful Maria might have been seriously harmed and the treasure stolen. There had been no further attempt to search her room, nor to abduct her since that first time, and Katherine understood that Sir Alain had conspired with their host to make certain she was well protected.

Nevertheless, she was relieved when they boarded the ship bound for England. Sir Alain had chartered it for his exclusive use, which meant that no one else could travel with them, and since there were no other ships in port that could follow them immediately, she believed she must be safe. Perhaps the threat was over now, for the Lord of Ravenshurst would scarcely follow her to her home in France.

With the threat ended, at least for the next several weeks, Katherine was able to let down her guard. She had begun to recover a little from her first sharp, tearing grief, though she would always miss the father who had been so dear to her. However, her spirits gradually lifted as the days passed, for she was more fortunate than Celestine, who was forced to spend much of her time in the cabin with Maria to tend her.

Katherine herself did not suffer from seasickness, even when the weather was choppy, the waves battering fiercely against the ship. She came up on deck as often as she was able, and spent many pleasant moments talking either with Sir Bryne or Sir Alain.

She was on deck the morning they hailed a French ship, which was making its way to Italy, and saw the exchange of messages by flags hoisted on each vessel.

'What are they saying?' she asked of Bryne as he came to watch with her at the prow of the ship. 'I know the flags all stand for something, but I cannot read them.'

'They are merely to assure the captains that there is no need for alarm,' Bryne told her with a smile. He had come to like the young woman very much, and to admire her inquiring mind. 'As you know, King Richard and Philip of France quarrelled on the way to Jerusalem, and some say that the French have conspired with Richard's captors to hold him hostage these many years. But these ships are merchantmen and have no quarrel with each other, and that is the message they signal to one another.'

'But did Richard not also quarrel with Duke Leopold of Austria?' Katherine asked. 'I have heard that a ransom hath been on offer for some time but that the King will not agree to it.'

'We heard this in Rome from Marcus Aurelius,' Bryne agreed. 'But I believe some mischief has been afoot to keep Richard a prisoner longer—perhaps at the instigation of the French king, perhaps on the part of Richard's brother.'

'You speak of Prince John?'

'Yes. Richard made him the guardian of his kingdom when he left for the Holy Land, and there are some who would say that was unwise. I have heard that John hath tried to usurp his brother's throne. Unfortunately, the people suffer for his harsh rule. And while Richard is a captive of the Holy Roman Emperor, there is none to deny him.'

'Richard is the bravest of men,' Alain said, coming to join them in time to hear Bryne's words. 'But I believe none ever called him the wisest. And the way he treated the hostages at Acre was both terrible and unjust. Yet it is his right to rule England and I would not have him languish in captivity and his brother on the throne in his stead. We must pray for his speedy release.'

'Amen to that,' Bryne said. 'Excuse me now, for I would speak with the captain.'

Katherine smiled as he left them, standing silently beside Sir Alain. He was silent also, gazing out over the white-crested water for a moment before he turned to look at her.

'You seem better in spirits of late, Katherine. The voyage suits you, I think?'

'Yes, I believe it does.' Katherine looked away from his intent gaze for fear that he would see too clearly into her mind.

A part of her recovery was, she was sure, due to the pleasure she drew from his company. 'I like the feel of the wind in my hair and the spray on my face.'

Alain nodded his approval. 'You are a better sailor than the Lady Celestine. She has spent most of her time in her cabin since we came on board.'

Clearly he was missing the lady's company. Katherine's heart sank. She had thought he spent time with her because he liked her, but now she saw it was only because Celestine had not been able to come on deck. Perhaps he sought her out for news of the woman he cared for.

'She is sick much of the time,' Katherine said. 'Maria and I do what we can for her, but she is fretful and hard to please. She vows she will never go on board another ship, but indeed she must if she is to return to her home in France.'

'Yes, I fear it cannot be avoided. I would ask the captain to put you ashore in Marseilles, but then you would have a long and difficult journey by land. Despite Lady Celestine's discomfort, I believe it will be best for you to continue to England with the ship.'

'We should be more vulnerable on land,' Katherine agreed. 'If another ship bound for France has reached Rome by now, the Lord Hubert of Ravenshurst may follow sooner than we thought.'

Alain did not answer immediately, looking at her thoughtfully.

'I have deciphered much of your father's work,' he told her at last. 'Some of it remains elusive; as you warned me, it is writ in a code of your father's devising and I have not been able to break it.'

'Do you believe my father has discovered a great treasure?' Katherine's eyes were dark and intent as she gazed up at him.

Alain replied in measured words. 'It is certain that he believed so. He refers to many documents that he studied before setting out on the final stage of his search. If we had those, we might be better able to say for certain that the…treasure is genuine.'

'My father was no fool, sir,' Katherine said quietly. 'He would not have searched so long or worked so hard to find something that was not genuine.'

'I do not doubt him, nor after reading his work could I have anything but respect for the late Baron Grunwald,' Alain assured her. 'But there are those that will—men who would doubt anything unless it can be proved absolutely.'

'My father was aware of that,' Katherine told him and sighed. 'That is why he made so many notes. What I have given you is but a fragment. The rest was lost when his baggage was stolen.'

'Do you believe that it was at Ravenshurst's instigation that your father was attacked and his possessions stolen?'

'I have wondered,' Katherine admitted, her brow wrinkling as she thought about it. 'Especially since I was almost abducted a few days afterwards—and then my things were searched at the villa. I do not think common brigands would have dared so much. And Ravenshurst wanted the cup very badly. Yet I find it difficult to believe that a Christian knight could be so evil.'

'There are many who fought with the crusades for a common cause that I would not care to call friend,' Alain told her with a frown. 'I have had little contact with the Lord Hubert of Ravenshurst, but Bryne knows of him. Their fathers quarrelled once over some land that Ravenshurst claimed, and Bryne says the son is a worse rogue than his father.'

'Then I must be on my guard,' Katherine said, looking anxious. 'The sooner I am rid of my burden the easier I shall be in my mind. Indeed, I would give it to the Lord Hubert if I could bring my father back to life—but to lose it now would be to despoil his memory. He was proud that he had found such a valuable thing.' She sighed and met Alain's eyes, knowing that she could no longer keep her secret. 'I dare say you have guessed what my father believes he has found?'

'The cup that our Lord used at the Last Supper?'

'Yes, that is what he believed,' Katherine said and wrinkled her brow. 'Yet even I have wondered…'

'You doubt it is the Holy Grail?'

'It is such a simple thing,' Katherine replied. 'When people speak of it, when they depict it in drawings or manuscripts, 'tis always as a precious thing fashioned of silver or some rich metal. The cup my father found after his studies is a plain thing, of no value in itself.'

'Ah…' Alain nodded his understanding. 'Now I begin to understand some of what puzzled me in your father's writings. A cup of obvious worth might have been discovered long ago, but something simple, of little or no value in itself, could have lain unnoticed for centuries—or been discarded as worthless.'

'It was my father's belief that the cup was of the kind commonly used by ordinary people of the time. After all, most of Christ's disciples were poor men that He called to Him from their work. He himself had no wealth, for did He not despise money, so should the cup He used at supper be anything but a plain thing? My father discovered a document that seems to confirm that one of the disciples took the cup away with him, perhaps as something to remember a pleasant evening, and that after the crucifixion he carried it with him until he was able to place it where my father found it.'

'And may I ask where—?' Alain began, but broke off as he saw Celestine approaching them. He saw at once that she was annoyed, and knew the cause. She did not like to see him in close conversation with Katherine. He smiled at her, holding out his hand to acknowledge her presence on deck, for he knew it was the only way to placate her. Celestine demanded homage for her beauty, and he would give it until he was sure of her mind. 'Well met, my lady,' he said, his expression one of genuine concern as he saw how pale she looked. She had, after all, been ill. 'It was brave of you to come on deck; I believe you have suffered gravely.'

'I thought I should die,' Celestine said and clutched at the ship's rail to steady herself. 'I have never been so ill in my life. I swear it was not thus when we travelled to the Holy Land.'

'The weather has not been kind to us,' Alain said as she came to stand by his side. He bestowed a smile on her that would capture the heart of almost any lady. 'I am sorry you have suffered so much.'

'I still feel very unsteady,' Celestine said and gave him a wan smile. 'But I shall stay on deck for as long as possible, sir. I believe the air may do me good…' She gave a little sigh and appeared to sway slightly on her feet. 'Would you be so kind as to lend me your arm so that I may walk about a little?'

'Yes, of course. It will be my pleasure.'

He offered her his arm, and, with a wan look for Katherine, she walked away, leaning on him and sighing.

Katherine was aware once more of a pang of jealousy. Sir

Alain was always kind and courteous to her, and she knew he was genuinely concerned to help her deliver her trust to its final destination, yet he did not look at her the way he looked at Celestine. Yet how should he when she was a plain creature, thin and unwomanly, and Celestine was beautiful?

He had become more attentive to Celestine since they came on board ship, and she was very much afraid he was in love with her. Katherine's heart ached for it, as much for his sake as her own. Celestine did not truly love him as he deserved to be loved. She would use him to suit her purpose, whatever that might be.

'Do not look so sad,' a voice said and she turned to see that Sir Bryne had come up to her unnoticed. 'She is not worthy of him. For the moment he may be besotted, but it will pass. In time he will realise that she is shallow and he will be free of her spell—for it is a kind of witchery that she casts over men. Marcus spoke of it and I have felt it myself, though her powers cannot bind me. I once loved another woman of her kind and know that her smiles mean nothing.'

Katherine smiled bravely, hiding her hurt. If Bryne spoke of his friend being besotted, then it must be so. She had not imagined the look in Sir Alain's eyes nor the power of his smile when he spoke to Celestine.

'It is not for me to judge one way or the other,' she said quietly, trying valiantly to hide her feelings. 'But Sir Alain has been good to us and I would not see him hurt.'

'Nor I,' Bryne admitted, his mouth grim. He was angry with his friend, for he had never known Alain to be taken in by a pretty face before and could not understand why he showed Celestine so much attention. Unless he was playing a deeper game than any of them understood? That might be the case, and, if so, it excused his behaviour of late. Yet he did not care to see Katherine hurt and so he spoke more harshly than he ought of his friend. 'If he were not a fool in matters of love, he might see that you are worth ten of her, Katherine. I vow a man could not choose better than to have you as his wife.'

Her cheeks felt warm as she saw the admiration in his look. 'You are kind to me,' she said shyly. 'I have no mirror, sir, but if I did, I know that it would tell me Celestine is far more lovely than I could ever be.'

'You are not pretty,' Bryne told her, his eyes serious as they dwelled on her face. 'But there are times when you are certainly beautiful. It is a kind of beauty that the Lady Celestine cannot match.'

Katherine's beauty was of the soul, and came from within, but it was not something that Bryne could put into words. A simple knight, he was not given to flattery and could only speak from the heart.

'Now you flatter me!' she cried and laughed, her eyes lighting up with mischief. In that moment Bryne's words were proved true, though she would never know it. 'Even my father told me I could not expect to find a husband without a great dowry. It was for this reason he sought so hard to find a treasure…' She sighed and the laughter died. 'I have wished that he had never discovered it, for he might still have lived.'

'Ah, do not look like that for it breaks my heart,' Bryne said. 'Your father was wrong, Katherine; you see before you a man who would willingly offer you his name and his home.'

'Oh, Bryne…' she said in a voice hardly above a whisper. His simple words had touched her heart. 'You do me such honour, but you know…you know I cannot accept, don't you?'

'I understand that your heart is given to another,' Bryne replied and smiled at her gently. 'But I wanted you to know that you need never be alone. If you have need of me, I shall always come to you—wherever you are.'

'You must not make such a promise,' Katherine answered. She had learned to like and respect this knight and felt guilty that she might be the cause of some disappointment to him. 'I would not have you waste your life, sir. You should take a wife who will love you and bear your children.'

'I shall take only one woman as my wife—and until I see you happy, Katherine, I shall wait and hope…' His words trailed away as Alain brought Celestine back to them. 'It is good to see you recovered, lady.' He bowed formally to the older woman.

'Thank you, sir. You are very kind.' Celestine could not resist giving him an inviting glance. It seemed that she must play her games with any man who spoke to her. 'But I am feeling unwell again and must seek my rest once more. Katherine, will you not come with me? I feel I shall fall if I go alone.'

Celestine waited expectantly, almost as though she thought one of the men would offer to take her to her cabin. Neither spoke and she took hold of Katherine's arm, clinging to her as if in need of support.

Katherine saw that a little smile of satisfaction played about her mouth as they walked away from the men, and as Celestine let go of her arm to go into the cabin, she realised that she had achieved what she had set out to do. She was not as ill as she had pretended, but it had irked her that Katherine was able to go on deck when she could not, and her next words confirmed it.

'It is unseemly of you to go on deck alone, Katherine,' she

said with a sour look. 'What would your father have said? And, more importantly, what will others think of you for behaving in such a loose manner? You will have no honour or reputation left if you continue like this. Truly, I am shocked that you could behave so carelessly. It is not becoming in a young woman.'

'I have done nothing wrong,' Katherine replied defensively. Travelling with her father, she had been used to more freedom than was usually permitted a woman, for her father had perhaps been careless in his care of her. 'I but talked to Sir Alain and Sir Bryne. I was in full view of everyone on deck the whole time. I do not know how you can accuse me of behaving immodestly.'

'Nevertheless, I feel responsible for you,' Celestine said. 'You have no guardian to protect you, and if I am to assume that duty you must promise to be more careful in future.'

'I have no need of a guardian,' Katherine replied. She was tempted to say that Celestine was in no better case, but held her tongue. Their relationship was still strained and would not be improved by a quarrel. 'Maria usually accompanies me. I shall ask her to do so in future.'

Celestine pulled a face. She had no lady of her own to attend her and had grown used to ordering Maria as if she owned her. It did not suit her to be reminded otherwise, but having made her point she merely groaned and clutched at her middle.

'I feel ill,' she said. 'Do not regard me if you require Maria's services. I am sure I would not want to deprive you of your pleasure.'

She had made it impossible for Katherine to leave her. Despite her distrust of Celestine, she could not leave her to suffer alone—and perhaps she had been thoughtless. It would be better if she took Maria with her when she went on deck, but until Celestine was well enough to be left, that was impossible.

Why did the older woman want to make sure she could not go on deck without her? She could not be jealous—not when Sir Alain was so courteous and attentive towards her?

Yet she had plainly come on deck to oblige Katherine to return with her. Katherine did not believe that it was concern for her modesty that had prompted her, so what else lay behind her stratagem?

Katherine did not curtail her visits to the deck completely, but Celestine had made her aware that she might be laying herself open to a charge of immodesty, so she spent less time talking with her friends.

She saw the puzzled look in Bryne's eyes and hoped that he did not think she was avoiding him because of the offer he had made her. Indeed, the kindness with which he had done so had made it impossible for her to feel embarrassment and she welcomed his friendship as much as before. Sir Alain was as unfailingly courteous as always, always the perfect knight, but gave no sign that he had noticed anything different in her behaviour. There was certainly nothing of the lover about him, no hint that he might feel for her as she did for him. She must have imagined that look she'd seen in his eyes in the garden of Marcus Aurelius.

Katherine was saddened, but it did not surprise her. He still thought of her as a child, his warmer feelings directed at the beautiful Lady Celestine. When at last the weather became calmer and Celestine began to venture on deck more often, he spent most of his time at her side rather than with Katherine.

Well, why should that distress her? Katherine scolded herself for allowing it to make her heart ache. She had always known that her feelings for him were folly. Why, then, should she feel hurt that he showed preference for Celestine?

She was heartsore as she watched them together. She had thought him both intelligent and noble; indeed, he was all that a knight should be, but if he were truly besotted with Celestine, as he appeared to be, then Katherine would be a fool to love him.

Were all men blinded by a woman's beauty? And yet she had now and then seen something in his face that made her wonder. Sometimes his eyes had such a steady, thoughtful look—was it possible that they saw beyond mere beauty? Was it possible that Sir Alain played a more skilful game than she could imagine?

Such thoughts went some way to easing her pride, but not her heartache. Watching them together, the way that Celestine smiled confidently up at him, her smile clearly inviting, was too painful to be borne. Katherine wept inside herself, but tried hard not to let them see how their intimacy was hurting her. Even Bryne's constant presence at her side could not ease the pain that was growing inside her each day. She thought that her despair must be making her ill, for she had begun to feel unwell despite the fact that the sea was now calm, the storms having blown themselves out.

But Katherine's illness was not seasickness, it was a draining lethargy that had stolen over her unawares. She was feeling unusually tired and her head throbbed so much at times that she hardly knew how to bear it. Perhaps she was sickening for something?

She would be glad when they were in England. Once they

had parted company with the two knights, she would no longer have to see *him* every day or to watch him making a fool of himself with a woman who merely sought to use him for her own ends. It could not be long now, a day or so only if the weather were kind.

'I have persuaded Sir Alain that he should accompany us to France,' Celestine told Katherine the morning that the cliffs of Dover came into view. 'Was that not clever of me?'

Katherine looked at her, feeling sick as she saw her self-satisfied expression. Was it not enough that she had had to endure watching them these past weeks? Must the torture continue until she reached her uncle's house?

'Do you think it necessary?' Katherine asked. Her head had been aching since she woke that morning and she felt a little strange in herself. Twice that morning she had been dizzy, though she had tried to hide it from the watchful eyes of Maria. Oh, how glad she would be to reach her uncle's house! She was tired of Celestine's self-satisfied looks. 'I think Maria, my father's servants that remain to me and I will be safe enough in France. My home is not far from Calais—so I shall not need an escort.'

'Then we shall part company there,' Celestine replied with a little curl of spite about her mouth. 'If you persist in this foolishness, Katherine, I can do no more for you.'

It was on the tip of Katherine's tongue to ask what service Celestine had performed for her. Indeed, it was she who had had to lend the older women some of her best things because she had brought so little with her when she escaped from Baron Ravenshurst's camp.

'I have never asked anything of you,' Katherine replied

with dignity. 'And I can make my own way to my uncle's house, thank you.'

It was the closest they had come to a quarrel and Katherine felt the other woman's eyes on her, narrowed in anger and dislike. She was sorry that she had made an enemy of Celestine, though she could not bring herself to trust her.

'Then you may go to perdition for all I care!'

Celestine turned on her heel and walked away.

'Be careful, my lady,' Maria said from just behind her. 'That one has the tongue and the sting of a serpent. She will make a bad enemy.'

'You are right,' Katherine replied and sighed. Maria was suspicious of everyone, but in this case her instincts were true. Yet her head was aching so much and she felt so very unhappy that she hardly knew how to keep on her feet. 'I suppose I must beg her pardon, for she believed she was helping me. It's just that—' She broke off for it was too painful to explain exactly why she had been sharp with Celestine. 'I shall be glad when we are home, Maria.'

'It will not be as it was when you were a child,' Maria said, giving her an odd look. 'Your uncle is a weak man, my lady. He could not protect you as these English knights have done. If I were you, I should accept their offer to escort you to Grunwald. It may be best to see how things stand there before you part company with such good friends.'

'Why, Maria!' Katherine laughed merrily. 'I believe you have changed your mind about them.'

Maria shook her head at her. Even if she did have a secret respect for a certain knight, wild horses would not have dragged it from her! 'Now don't you start your games, Katherine. I may have acted hastily in the past, but I would do so again if I feared for your life and honour.'

'You are my best, my dearest friend,' Katherine said and, laughing, kissed her cheek. 'If I have no others to care for me, I am rich in your love, Maria.'

'Nay, stop that,' Maria said, her face suffused with colour. 'I'm your nurse and 'tis my duty to have a care for you. No nonsense now, my lady! Besides, there are others who might care for you given a chance.'

'You mean Sir Bryne, I suppose? He would wed me if I chose—but he does not love me, Maria. He merely wants a wife to give him sons. Any gentle woman would do as well.'

Maria gave her a hard stare, hands on hips. 'And what's wrong with that? There's many a woman would be glad of the chance to wed such a man. Be careful you do not disregard your one chance of a better life.'

Katherine said no more, merely smiling. She knew that Maria was right to warn her that she ought not to part company with the knights too soon, for how could she know what awaited her at Grunwald? Supposing her uncle did not want her there? Where else could she go? Perhaps to an Abbey to spend her life in prayer... For a woman with no dowry and little else to recommend her, there was no other option.

If only her head did not ache so very much! Perhaps then she might be able to think more clearly. She was beginning to feel very unwell, but she would not give into her illness.

Watching the play of emotions on her face, Alain thought that he had never seen anyone who displayed their feelings so openly. He felt a stirring of something deep inside him. She was like an open book to him, her sadness, grief, pleasure and merry smile different pages, and each as intriguing as the next.

Unlike the Lady Celestine. He frowned as he thought of his most recent conversation with her, when he had told her that he intended to accompany Katherine to her home.

'If you do not wish to come with us to Grunwald, I can arrange for an escort for you when we reach England,' he had told her. 'My father and brother have resources I may call on until I can settle my own affairs. I should see to it that you are well protected, lady.'

'But I would not dream of leaving Katherine until she is safely settled at her home,' Celestine had replied with a lift of her fine brows. 'Surely you do not think me so heartless?'

'Heartless? No, I do not think you that, lady.'

Celestine pouted her full, sensuous lips at him. 'Sometimes I believe that you do not think of me at all—your concern lies in another direction, does it not?'

Alain frowned, sensing her pique. 'If you mean the Lady Katherine, then, yes, I am concerned for her. She hath no one else to protect her and has been in some danger. I would see her safe with her family.'

'And what of me? I have no one to protect me, sir. My lord was killed at Acre; though I have family, there is none I truly care for. Will you not offer me your escort once Katherine is at Grunwald?'

'I shall make sure that you are not unprotected,' Alain replied. 'But I have business in England, and must return there as soon as I may after seeing the Lady Katherine to her home.'

He had realised his mistake almost at once, for Celestine's eyes had narrowed to spiteful slits. Damn it! All his careful work might have been destroyed in a moment. He should have made some flattering remark as had been his wont, but something in her manner had pricked him into an unwise answer. If Celestine realised that he had merely been humouring her all this time, had not the slightest interest in her as a woman, he had wasted his breath paying court to her. He must be more careful in future—at least until he knew that Katherine was safe.

His frown deepened as he saw Bryne go up to Katherine, watched the ease in her manner, saw her laughter and the way she laid her hand upon his arm. There was a difference in her manner towards him, for she seldom relaxed these days, though sometimes she would smile or laugh and then…then her face lit up from inside and she was truly lovely. Yet she had few smiles for him of late.

And that might be his fault. He had been careful to show her only the courtesy due to any lady, for something had told him that if he were to reveal his true feelings she might be in danger.

Was it possible that she had formed a deep and lasting attachment to Bryne? He was almost certain that his friend was in love with her. If that was the case, he must stand aside and wish them happy, but for the moment he was concerned only with making certain Katherine was safe from her enemies.

He walked towards them, saw the glow fade from her eyes, watched the uncertainty begin and wondered what he had done to make her doubt him. She had not been thus at the start. His heart twisted with sudden pain, and his expression hardened, for he must show no warm feelings towards her.

'We must prepare to disembark shortly,' he told her, unaware that he was frowning. 'When we go ashore I shall make inquiries about a passage to France.'

'You are very good,' Katherine said, blinking to keep back the foolish tears. Why must her head ache so? And her throat had begun to hurt. She wondered if she might be sickening with a fever, for she had been prone to take them as a child, though not for some years now. 'Celestine says that you are to escort us to Grunwald. I must thank you for your consideration, sir—but are you sure that we do not keep you from your business?'

'It is true that I have affairs to settle,' Alain replied. 'But my business may wait a few days. If we can charter a ship almost immediately, you will be with your family in less than a week.'

'Yes…' Katherine felt a pang of regret and realised that, painful as it was to see him and speak to him, it might be worse to part from him forever. 'If your affairs are pressing, I do not mind a delay. You have done so much for us that I would not be a burden to you.'

'Perhaps…' Alain suddenly felt reluctant to deliver her to Grunwald too swiftly. He wanted to be with her, to make sure that no harm came to her. 'I shall make inquiries and see how things lie. Now, if you need anything to take with you, you should fetch it from your cabin. Your baggage will be sent on afterwards.'

'I have all I need with me,' Katherine replied. She had her father's treasure hid close to her body, and nothing else seemed to matter for the moment. Her head was feeling rather strange, as if it were not quite a part of her body. 'Everything else may come with the baggage.'

'Then perhaps we should leave,' Alain said and smiled at her. 'The boats are ready to take us to the shore. Come, I shall help you…'

He went over the side, standing on the rope ladder a few rungs beneath the ship's rail while Bryne helped to steady her at the top. For a moment her feet tried and failed to find the first rung and she gave a startled cry as for a brief second her head whirled, but in a moment Alain had secured her foot for her.

'Do not fear, Katherine,' his voice reassured her. 'You shall not fall. I am here and will make sure you come to no harm.'

'I am able to manage now. It was only a moment of uncertainty.'

When they reached the boat below, Alain was waiting for her. He took her hand, helping her, catching her as she almost missed her footing again, holding her close to steady her for a second. She caught her breath as her heart raced, and, looking up into his face for a moment, she knew a longing to be kissed. Surely he felt something—his eyes seemed to caress her. Oh, how she wanted to be held in his strong arms, to be kissed, touched…to know the love that blossomed between man and wife in their marriage bed…but she should be ashamed of such wanton thoughts! Her head was going round and round and she did not know what possessed her.

Katherine's blushes were saved as a shout from above warned them that Bryne and Celestine were on the way down, Bryne supporting the lady much as Alain had done for Katherine.

Celestine's smiles were all for Bryne, the look she gave Katherine cold and accusing. Katherine wondered if she could see into her mind, if she had guessed her secret. She prayed that it was not so—she could not bear that the other woman should know how vulnerable she was in the matter of Sir Alain.

He was kind and considerate towards Katherine, but it was Celestine he found irresistible, Celestine he desired in the way that Katherine longed to be desired. She was too thin and plain, and…she loved a man who would never love her.

Oh, how ill she felt. Her heart was breaking and pain and fever racked her body. If only she could die, then this pain might cease.

At last her feet were on dry land, and after so many days at sea she felt rather odd, as if the ground were moving beneath her feet. It was quite common for those unused to sailing to feel that way, she knew, and she was not alarmed, though she still felt unsteady. Once again Sir Alain's strong arm was there to steady her, and she smiled at him gratefully.

'It will pass in a few minutes,' he assured her. 'I know how you are feeling, for it happened to me on my first voyage to France.'

'I am better now,' Katherine assured him, though she still felt a little strange. 'How kind—' She gave a gasp of dismay as the earth suddenly whirled about her and the next second she was falling.

It was Alain who caught her, sweeping her up in his arms before she could reach the ground. He knew a moment of panic as he looked down at her; her eyelids were fluttering against her pale cheeks as a soft moan escaped her. Why had the foolish girl not told him she was ill?

'This is more than finding her legs again after a voyage,' he said and Bryne came anxiously towards him. He glanced at Celestine and then at Maria, who had gathered round. 'Has she shown any sign of feeling unwell of late?'

'No, said Celestine, her mouth a thin line of annoyance.

'Yes,' said Maria with a worried frown. 'She complained of a headache when she woke this morning, but told me not to fuss because she felt better almost immediately.' Laying her hand on the girl's brow, she looked at the two men. 'I believe she hath a fever.'

'Indeed, I believe you are right,' Sir Alain said and his concern showed in his face. 'We must get her to an inn and quickly, for she needs the attention of a physician.'

'Forgive me, sir,' Maria intervened. 'But I do not trust physicians. They will bleed her and apply hot irons to her body and the poor love will suffer terribly. I have nursed her through many fevers. If you will but find us a good clean bed where she may lie in peace and I may tend her, I believe we can manage without the ministrations of a physician.'

Alain looked at her doubtfully, but her tone was so urgent, her pleading so persuasive that he was moved to agree.

'You will need herbs and medicines,' Bryne said. 'Tell me what you need, Maria, and I shall fetch them myself.'

'I thank you both,' Maria replied. 'I shall give you a list of things I may need, sir. My master taught me to write and I keep a list of my ingredients always with me in case of need.' She took out a much-folded and worn scrap of parchment upon which the script was faded and hard to read, but with some discussion between them, Bryne was apprised of all he needed to know.

'It may take me some hours to find an apothecary who has all that you need,' he said. 'But you may be sure that I shall return as soon as I am able.'

All at once, things began to happen. Sir Bryne took the horse that one of his men had procured for him and set off at a gallop. Sir Alain's men had somehow commandeered a wagon from a passing freeman, and Katherine was laid on a pile of blankets that had been found for her.

One of Alain's men was detailed to look after Celestine,

who was disgusted by the way things had changed so suddenly, for now it was Katherine who was receiving the attention she believed was her due. Yet she did her best to hide it as the small cavalcade started off.

Sir Alain, his men and Celestine rode on the horses that had been hired for them from a hostelry nearby when the ship reached harbour, while Maria rode in the wagon with Katherine. She had already administered a few drops of a potion she carried in a small *flacon* at her waist, but for the moment there was no change in Katherine's condition. She lay with her eyes closed, her skin dry and hot with fever, unmoving and unaware as they arrived at the inn.

She did not stir as Alain carried her into the inn and up the stairs to the chamber his men had bespoke earlier. He had planned to spend only one night at the inn, which was clean by the standards of most, but still a poor place to stay. It was more usual for travellers to seek out a monastery, where the monks would provide a clean, comfortable bed and good food, but, poor as it was, this would just have to do for the time being.

Laying his burden down, Alain stood gazing at Katherine's pale face for a moment, until he was given a look by Maria that told him he must leave.

Yet still he lingered, unwilling to leave Katherine, for he believed she was gravely ill. 'You will let me know when she is better?'

'Yes, sir,' Maria replied. 'But for the moment I must be alone with her. There are things I need to do for her—and 'tis immodest for you to be here.'

'Forgive me,' Alain said. 'I have been thoughtless, but it was merely my concern for her. I shall go and leave you to care for her—but you will call me if you need me?'

'Yes, sir. Please go now. I must try to cool this heat or she may die.'

'God forbid!'

Alain turned at once, leaving Maria to do what she could for her mistress. He discovered that his feelings upon the matter were much stronger than he had imagined. His feelings for Katherine had become a warm, deep affection that he might perhaps feel for…his sister? Yes, that must be it, he reasoned. This anxiety, this desire to keep her safe and to protect her were right and natural if he thought of Katherine as a sister. He smiled as he remembered Marguerite, who was his true sister. The last news he had had of her was that she was about to be betrothed to a man called Orlando, who was Stefan's close friend.

For a moment he allowed himself to dwell on pleasant memories of the past, but then he found that he was anxious and restless again. In the parlour downstairs, which the landlord had cleared of undesirables once he discovered the quality of his visitors, Alain was offered food and drink, but discovered that he had no appetite.

He ordered that his men should be housed and fed to the best of the host's ability, and was told that his men had been given accommodation in lofts above the stables and a barn that was used for fodder. They would do better in their own pavilions, Alain thought, and wondered if he should send some of them ahead of him to Banewulf.

Yet he might need them if Ravenshurst were to somehow follow them to England. In the morning he would send someone to find an open stretch of countryside where they could make camp, but for this evening the stables and barn must do.

'Give my men ale, bread and meat,' he told the landlord.

'You shall be paid well for your trouble, though we may have to stay here longer than I had expected.'

''Tis an honour to serve your lordship,' the landlord said and bowed in a servile manner. 'Is it your lady that was taken ill so suddenly?'

'No, merely a lady I have pledged to see safely home to her family,' Alain replied with a frown. Yet even as he answered, he wondered if he deceived himself, for a part of him wanted to lay claim to her, to declare that she was indeed his. Yet he had no right; Bryne had a prior claim on her affections and she must remain as a dear sister to Alain. 'But I have great respect for her and she must be given every comfort.'

'That is more than I have been given,' Celestine said, entering the parlour at that moment. 'My bedchamber is so tiny I can hardly breathe.'

'It is my third-best chamber,' the landlord said. 'The best was given to his lordship...'

'Then you may have mine, lady,' Alain said at once. It was merely chivalry to give the better room to a lady, but he could see that Celestine was angry and he wished to placate her. When they first met, he had thought her beautiful and charming, but now he was aware that her lovely face hid a scheming mind. It was because of his suspicions that he had gone out of his way to please and flatter her and it was perhaps even more important now. 'A place on the floor will do for me, if need be. Bryne can have your chamber when he returns.'

'All this fuss for nothing,' Celestine said and blushed as she realised her mistake. 'I am sure Katherine will recover in a short time. She seemed perfectly well on board the ship. I dare say it is just tiredness or some such ailment. I, too, have been ill…' Her tone seemed to imply that no one had been concerned when she was suffering in her cabin.

'I was concerned for you,' Alain assured her at once, because it would not do to allow her to see into his mind. If she played a devious game, then so must he. 'But we knew what ailed you, and, unpleasant as it was, we did not fear for your life. The Lady Katherine is suffering from a fever and we cannot tell how serious it may be.' Many fevers were deadly and more died than survived them.

'We must hope it is not contagious.' Celestine pulled a face. 'This will mean a serious delay for us all…'

'But there need be no delay for you,' Alain said at once. 'Should you wish it, I can spare some of my men to escort you to your home as soon as a ship is available.'

Celestine frowned. This was not at all what she wanted!

'I could not abandon Katherine while she is ill. No, no, I was merely thinking of you, Sir Alain. I dare say you long to see your home and your family.'

'I shall not deny that my thoughts have turned homeward several times of late,' Alain told her. Now what game did she play? This sudden concern for Katherine was false if he had judged her right. He must be doubly careful now. 'However, it is my duty to see the Lady Katherine safe, and this I shall do.'

'Then I must stay with her,' Celestine said. 'It would be immodest for a young girl of Katherine's innocence to travel alone with you and Sir Bryne—even though I know you to be honourable knights.'

'She has the dragon,' Alain quipped and then smiled inwardly as he saw that Celestine did not understand the jest. 'I meant Maria. She protects her mistress as fiercely as any dragon. I do not think she trusts any man where her darling is concerned.' Or woman either, he thought, for he knew that Maria disapproved of Celestine. She might not have voiced it in his hearing, but it was there in her eyes when she least knew it.

'Then why did you not say so?' Celestine's eyes snapped with temper; she had no sense of humour and suspected that she was being mocked, but was not sure what lay behind the expression in his eyes. She had thought him just another knight of little depth, believing she could wind him around her finger as she did other men—but perhaps there was more to him than she had previously imagined. 'Maria is merely a serving woman. She cannot protect Katherine's modesty sufficiently. It is my duty to protect Katherine from the vicious spite that might otherwise destroy her reputation.'

And who will protect your modesty? The quip was on the tip of Alain's tongue, but he did not speak his thoughts aloud. He knew that he had already upset Celestine that day, and it would not do to mock her too openly. Particularly now that Katherine was ill.

He inclined his head towards her, making no further comment. She glared at him and went out, clearly still upset by the day's events. He must do what he could to restore her good humour, Alain realised. He began to pace the floor of the small parlour, restless and anxious for the girl who lay above.

As a young boy his mother had often cured him of fevers, Alain remembered. He wished that she were here with them, for he was certain she would know what to do for Katherine. Banewulf was but hours away if the messenger made all speed! If he sent word his mother would surely come, for she would be overjoyed to see him again.

Feeling the relief flow over him, Alain called for writing

materials and penned the note that would bring his loving mother to his aid. His letter finished, he took it out to one of his most trusted men and gave it to him, commanding him to make all speed.

'Give your letter only to my mother, the Lady of Banewulf,' he said. 'And make haste—I need her help most urgently.'

'I shall not stop, my lord,' the soldier said. 'Your letter shall be delivered as swiftly as it may be done.'

Alain thanked him and went back inside the inn to wait. Pacing the floor, he found himself unable to relax, and, after sending once more to see how Katherine was, sat down to pen another letter.

His business in England was of some importance, though he had dismissed it lightly to Katherine. He must not neglect it despite the anxiety that hung over him like a black cloud.

Chapter Five

'How is she?' Bryne asked as he met Alain in the inn-keeper's small parlour the following evening. The hour was late and it had grown dark, the night sky lit only by a sprinkling of stars. 'Has there been a change? It took me so long to find an apothecary that could help me that I feared I had been away too long and should be too late.'

'Indeed, I feared it, too. Maria has been out of her mind with worry for the herbs she carries have had no effect in lessening the fever.'

The tallow candles spluttered in their sconces, the stink of them pervading the air. Used to the luxury of wax, Alain took his friend by the arm out into the night air.

'That is better. I swear I thought the stench of that place could get no worse, but I was wrong. I would take Katherine elsewhere but I fear she is too ill to be moved for the moment. Maria says she has managed to cool the fever a little, but Katherine is still as she was when you left us, neither worse nor better.'

Bryne cursed. 'We are such fools not to have seen she was ill before this!'

'How could we have known? She did not say she was ill, and she seemed in good spirits.' Alain frowned—Bryne was right, they ought to have seen the signs. He had wondered at the girl's quiet manner, thinking that she had some reason for it, that perhaps she might be angry with him, but now thought it may have been the sickness coming on. 'I have written and asked my mother to come to us. She hath some skill with healing and may save Katherine where others might fail.'

'Should we not summon a physician?' Bryne could not hide his deep anxiety. 'I would not have her die from our neglect.'

'We must give Maria and my mother a chance first,' Alain replied. 'I remember that my mother had no faith in physicians, for she said that many of them were charlatans who had little skill or knowledge, but pretended to know everything and did more harm than good.'

'But if she should die before—' Bryne broke off as there was a commotion behind them and then a small party swept into the inn yard, the clatter of hooves and the rattle of wheels breaking the silence of the night. As they turned, a woman was being helped down from her horse and came immediately towards them, a smile upon her face.

'Alain!' she cried, relief and pleasure in her voice as she saw him. 'Is it indeed you, my son? God be praised! I could hardly believe it when your messenger arrived last evening. So many years without a word and then to know that you were here!'

'Mother?' Alain stared at the woman in stunned disbelief, though he knew at once that it was she. She was older, of course, her beauty matured into something softer than he remembered, but still she was exceptionally lovely, her smile as warm and loving as it had always been. Overwhelmed by a sudden surge of emotion, he strode to meet her, sweeping her into his arms in a hug that made her breathless. His throat tightened and he felt the sting of unmanly tears. 'My dearest Mother! It is so long since we have seen each other, though you have oft been in my thoughts. But how came you so quickly?'

'Marguerite was about to make the journey to London and when I received your message, I decided at once to accompany her. I could not miss this chance to see you, Alain, and to bring the help you requested of me. We have lost no time upon our journey, for your letter sounded urgent.'

'I bless you for your promptness, Mother, for I have sore need of you.'

'My beloved son,' the Lady Alayne said, tears of happiness at seeing him again streaming down her face unashamedly. 'It is three years since we have heard aught of you and we feared the worst.'

'I sent word when we reached Italy,' Alain said apologetically. 'My letter must have been delayed or lost. I am sorry that you have been distressed, Mother—but as you see I am alive and well.'

'God be praised for it, my son.' She gazed up at him, her eyes glowing. 'You have grown, Alain. You are almost as broad in the shoulder as your brother Stefan now.'

'But what of you? And my father—and Marguerite?'

'Marguerite is with me,' she replied, and, as he looked round eagerly, 'She will come to greet you, but for the moment she has taken her son to a chamber the innkeeper has reserved for her, because he has been fretful on the journey. I fear he tires her at times.' A shadow passed across Lady Alayne's face. 'Your sister was widowed last year and has not yet recovered from her grief. Your father does well enough, though he did not accompany us. You must know that he seldom leaves Banewulf now. When are you coming home? Your father would dearly love to see you again.'

Alain took her arm. 'Come into the inn, for it is cold out here. I fear it is but a poor place, Mother, but there is a fire and some mulled ale to warm you.'

'I know the inn for I have used it before, but I always bring my own comforts with me. We shall have wax candles and our own linen on the beds.' She smiled at Alain as they came into the parlour and the light made it possible for them to see each other more clearly. 'It is good to see you again, my son.'

'Mother…' A woman in the full flush of her beauty came into the room, a small child clinging to her hand. 'It seems that there has been a muddle about the bedchamber I had ordered—' She broke off as she saw Alain, a look of delight dawning in her eyes. 'Brother—is it truly you? Your man said that you were here, but I could not believe it after so long.'

'Marguerite.' He went to embrace her, looking down at her lovely face, seeing the shadows beneath her eyes, witness to her grief. 'Mother told me about Orlando. I am sorry…' He glanced down at the child clinging to her hand. 'And this is your son?'

'I named him for his father…' Shadows flitted over her lovely face as she looked with love at her child.

'It is a sad thing to lose your father so young.' Alain's hand caressed the child's head for a moment.

'Orlando was gravely ill and at the end it was a relief,' Marguerite replied calmly, though grief worked in her face. She lifted her head, letting pride carry her through. 'I believe you are the culprit in the matter of our rooms, Alain. It seems that your party has taken all the best chambers. There is none left for us.'

'You may have mine and welcome,' Bryne said instantly and the women turned to him; in the emotion of their greeting they had not noticed him standing quietly by.

'This is my friend Sir Bryne of Wickham,' Alain told them as his mother and sister looked curiously at the man who had spoken. 'Katherine has the best room for she is ill…it was for that reason I sent for you. And the Lady Celestine…' He broke off as Celestine came into the room. Her expression showed that she was displeased about something. 'Mother, Marguerite, this is the Lady de Charlemagne, who is occupying your room, I think.'

'The landlord told me that I must move into the small chamber!' Celestine cried, clearly too angry to hear what he had said to her. 'It seems that my room is needed for other guests.'

'Lady Celestine,' Alain said, 'this is my mother and sister and I fear we have taken the chamber that was reserved for them. If you are agreeable, they may share the larger chamber…'

'Your mother and…' Celestine's eyes narrowed as she looked at the women. One had clearly been a great beauty, for she was still lovely even in her middle years, and the second was one of the most beautiful women she had ever seen, with pale golden hair and bright blue eyes, so lovely, indeed, that she felt a pang of jealousy. Having been told that she must return to the smaller chamber, she had been furious at her treatment, but now saw that she must accept or appear churlish and ill mannered. 'Then I must give way, of course,' she said and smiled graciously. 'I did not know that you had arranged rooms for your family, too.'

'Nor did I,' Alain replied. 'My mother's arrival was a surprise and a most welcome one.' He turned to his mother, his face betraying his anxiety as he recalled why he had sent for his mother. 'There is a young woman I would have you see, Mother. Her name is Katherine of Grunwald. I fear she is very ill and I pray that you can help her, for I know you have some skill with healing.'

'Only a very little,' Lady Alayne replied. 'But I shall be pleased to see this young woman, for I can see you are anxious for her.'

'I shall take you to her myself, for she is guarded by a dragon who might otherwise refuse to let you near her darling.' Laughter lurked briefly in his eyes and it gladdened the heart of a mother who had carried the memory of her son's merry smile for many years.

He went out into the hall again and she followed him up the broken stone steps that led to the upper chambers. A strong smell of spilled ale and cooking odours pervaded the air and he wrinkled his nose in distaste. He had forgotten how bad the inns could be in England, for he was used to the outdoor life and the homes of noblemen.

'You intrigue me—a dragon, Alain?'

'Indeed, and a fierce one.' He laughed, the shadows leaving him for a moment. 'Maria is Katherine's companion and devoted to her. I call her the dragon because she has twice felled me with her moneybag, and if looks might kill I should have been slain long since.'

His mother's eyes twinkled with amusement. 'I believe you would make a great bard, my son, for you spin a goodly tale. Now tell me, where did you discover this odd couple—and why did the dragon fell you with her fearsome weapon?'

'You may mock,' Alain said, 'but I had a lump the size of a hen's egg the first time she hit me. It was in Italy that I rescued the lady and her companion, from brigands that were attacking them. She may be in some danger of further attack and so I have promised her my protection until she reaches the safety of her home.'

'Ah…' The Lady de Banewulf's eyes saw more than her son would tell and she smiled to herself. 'I see there is more to this story than you wish to tell me for the moment. Perhaps we may talk further another day?'

'Nothing would please me better, for I have been too long away,' Alain replied. 'But Katherine's story is her own and I may tell you only a part of it—unless I have her permission.'

'Then we must see what we can do to help her.'

Alain knocked and then entered the chamber, followed by his mother. Maria was standing by the bed, soothing Katherine's heated brow with a cloth wrung out in cool water. She looked round as he entered and it was plain to see that she was desperately worried.

'Is there no change?'

'None,' Maria said and there was a sob in her throat. 'I spooned a little of my fever mixture into her mouth, but she is still so hot.'

The Lady Alayne went over to the bed and looked down at the girl lying there. She was aware of surprise—the woman seemed little more than a child and was very ordinary to look at, not the beauty she had been expecting after seeing the older woman downstairs. As she reached out to touch Katherine's forehead, the girl moaned and opened her eyes to look at her.

'Is it you, Mother?' she whispered, a smile of such sweetness on her lips that Alayne instantly understood why her son had become so anxious for this girl he hardly knew. 'Have you come to take me to Heaven with you and Papa?'

'It is not time for you to join your loved ones, Katherine,' she murmured softly for she was instantly drawn to the girl and addressed her as she would a daughter. 'You are young and must look to the future. You will fall in love and marry and have children of your own one day.'

'No…' Katherine muttered and moved her head restlessly on the lumpy pillow. 'He will never love me…never love me…'

'I think that many people will love you, Katherine,' Alayne said soothingly. 'Do not fret so, my poor child. I am here now and with your good woman's help we shall make you well again.'

'Mother…' Katherine caught at her hand, holding it tightly as the fever held her. 'Please stay with me…please do not leave me alone. I am so alone…' Tears trickled from the corner of her eye. 'So alone…'

Alayne's heart was touched. Now she wanted to make Katherine well for her own sake and not just to please her son. She bent and kissed her feverish brow.

'You shall not be alone now, dear Katherine. I shall be here and my son is your friend. You shall be as a daughter to me and I shall make you well again. Do not weep, for you have many to love you.'

Katherine gave a sigh and released her grip. Her eyes had closed again and she had lapsed back into the state of unconsciousness once more.

Alayne straightened up and looked at the girl's devoted companion. She had no need to be told who the woman was, for she could tell at a glance that her son had judged right. Maria's fierce manner hid a tender devotion to her mistress, therefore she would treat her as a friend, address her by name and not as a lowly servant.

'She is very ill, I fear. Tell me, Maria, what have you given her thus far?'

'A mixture I make of herbs,' Maria replied, surprised but pleased to be spoken to in such a friendly manner by a great lady. She bobbed a respectful curtsy for she was aware that this lady was truly noble, both by breeding and by character. ''Tis but a simple cure, my lady, but it has helped her in the past.'

Alayne asked for the names of the herbs she had used and nodded.

'You have given her a mixture I use myself for relieving fever. It is well enough for chills and such ailments, but this child needs something more. I have a mixture in my travelling box, which I believe may help her. I shall make it up and give her the first dose myself—after that you must give it to her exactly as I show you. Too much and you may do more harm than good, do you understand me?'

'Yes, my lady. I know there are stronger cures than mine, but I have never dared to use them for the Lady Katherine.'

'You can do no harm if you follow my instructions. You will trust me in this, Maria?'

'Yes, my lady, for I can see that you are a good woman— a true healer.'

'What makes you say that?' Alayne looked at her closely.

'I have met another such as you long ago,' Maria said. 'It was she who taught me to make the simple cures I know—but I do not have the learning or the gift for the healing you do.'

'Yes, perhaps it is a gift,' Alayne replied. There was a smile on her lips, though shadows of remembrance lingered in her eyes. Once, a long time ago, she had been named a witch because of her healing powers. It had made her wary in her dealings with others. 'Though there are some who would not call it thus…'

'I am not one of them. If you can help Katherine, I shall be always grateful, my lady.'

'I see that you love her. We shall nurse her together, Maria. I shall have my own sheets and pillows brought to make her more comfortable, and wax candles perfumed with flower oil so that the air is sweeter in here. We shall both pray for her and in the meantime I shall make my special cure for her.'

Alayne smiled at her son as she went out. He was looking anxiously towards the bed, and she touched his hand in passing.

'Go back to your friend now, Alain. Your place is not here and Katherine is in good hands. Both Maria and I will do our best for her—the rest is in God's gift, not yours or mine. Have you no business to keep you from fretting?'

'Yes, there is something I must do. You do well to remind me, Mother,' Alain said and looked at Maria. 'There are things I must attend that will take me away from this place for a few days. Some of my men will remain to guard you. Tell me, is all safe?'

'Yes, my lord,' Maria replied. 'You may rest easy in your mind.'

'Then I shall go, for if I stay…' Alain shook his head and went out leaving his sentence unfinished.

His mind was in some confusion, half-formed thoughts lingering in his head. Why did he feel so desperate for Katherine to wake up and smile at him, the way she had smiled when in her fever she had believed her mother had come to her? Why did he feel as if he might be about to lose something precious, something he had not even known he had? If Katherine were to die, it would leave a strange void in his life—but why should that be?

He shook his head over his muddled thoughts, finding them impossible to understand. She was but a child, and these feelings of tenderness he had towards her were naught but the concern of any man for a woman he would protect…and love? The thought popped into his head, but he dismissed it at once. Affection, concern, a need to protect, all these things he would allow himself—but love was not for him. He had other purposes in life.

Alain shook off his doubts and fears as he spoke to Bryne for a few moments and then left the inn. In Rome he had been charged with a mission that he must fulfil if he could, a mission that would take him to London and to the court. He did not want to leave Katherine unprotected, for it was possible that Ravenshurst might follow her to England, and it was agreed that Bryne should stay to guard her for the time being. After all, if she recovered her senses, it was Bryne that she would most want to see. It was to Bryne that she talked easily, for Bryne that she smiled most often.

Bryne had no notion of the task Alain had set himself, but was more than willing to see that no harm came to Katherine while he was gone.

'You know I care for the lady,' Bryne said. 'I have promised to serve her should she need me.'

'You would wed her, I think?'

'If she would have me,' Bryne agreed.

Alain nodded, wondering why that simple answer should be as a knife struck into his breast. Katherine could not do better than to wed such a loyal and generous knight, and he should be happy for her. Yet there was a tiny voice in his head that denied it. It was a good match—why could he not be pleased for her? Why did he want to protest that she was his and no other's?

He crushed the thought ruthlessly. He had work to do—important work, and Katherine was but another sister to him…

Katherine had never felt so ill. She was aware of cool hands touching her, of kind voices and faces she did not know. Sometimes she thought that her mother was with her, and at others she believed she was in hell. The pain was unbearable, her body racked by a terrible fever that made her wander in her mind and cry out, revealing more than she knew to the women who cared for her. Time and again one name was on her lips as she lay in her fever, her piteous cries wrenching the heart of the women who tended her so devotedly.

'I wish Alain had not left the inn,' his mother said to Maria, as Katherine's condition seemed to worsen. 'When I sent him from her chamber I did not mean that he should leave altogether. He was plainly anxious over her condition, and I thought he would be better employed in training with his men—I did not expect him to disappear. Do you know where he has gone? She cries for him so piteously, and it might ease her to hear his voice.'

'He said that he had things he must do, my lady.' Maria looked at her doubtfully. She had feared this and, for all her love of Katherine, thought it a hopeless cause. 'You will not tell him what she has said? I beg you not to reveal her heart to Sir Alain, my lady. He is kind to her, but it is the kindness of a friend, of a good man. We both know that it is unlikely he feels the same passion for her as she feels for him, and I would not have her shamed in his eyes.'

'My son would not be so unkind as to mock her for her love,' Alayne replied. Yet even as she spoke she was not sure. How could she know her eldest child after so many years apart? The boy she had loved so dearly had gone and there was a man in his place, a man she did not know at all. 'Does he guess nothing of her feelings for him?'

'I do not believe so, my lady. He thinks her a child—and besides, he seems to favour the Lady Celestine.'

'That woman?' Alayne was surprised. 'I would not have thought it. She is very beautiful, but I find her cold—and selfish. Yet men are sometimes blind where beauty is concerned.'

'It hath always been so, my lady.'

'But where has he gone?'

'Please…water…'

The words were faint, but they drew the attention of the ladies who cared for Katherine, and they both turned towards the bed.

'The fever hath broken, my lady!' Maria cried. 'God be praised!'

'Yes, we must thank God for giving her back to us,' Alayne said as she came to stand by the bed and look down at the girl. Katherine's eyes were open now and she gazed up at them, seeming bewildered, but she drank gratefully from the cup that she was offered.

'Just a sip at a time,' Alayne warned for she knew that the girl was very weak. 'You have been very ill, Katherine.'

'Who are you?' Katherine asked as her eyes began to focus and she saw the woman's face clearly for the first time. 'I thought sometimes that you were my mother or an angel, but I seem to know your face though not your name. Have you been nursing me?'

'Maria and I have cared for you together. You needed watching all the time, for we feared we might lose you. I am Lady Alayne de Banewulf. Sir Alain is my son and was named for me.'

'Yes…I see the resemblance.' Katherine smiled weakly. 'That must be why—' She broke off and looked about the room. Her eyes were eager, but then the light died and she blinked as if the disappointment was almost too much to bear. 'I thought once that he was here with me…'

'He was here for a while,' Alayne assured her. 'He was worried for you, Katherine. I sent him away because it was not proper for him to be in your bedchamber—and he had business he said would take him a few days, but as yet he hath not returned, though it is time enough.'

'Oh…' Katherine's hand trembled on the bedcovers, but she fought her desire to weep and won, though her eyes misted. 'How foolish I am, but I feel so very weak. If I cry, you must forgive me.'

'You may weep if it makes you feel better,' Alayne told her with a smile. 'I am not surprised that you feel weak, my dear. You were very ill and have lain in this bed for more than nine days.'

'Nine days…' Katherine looked at her in horror. 'I have been in a fever for nine days? 'Tis a wonder I did not die of it.'

'You might have died if it had not been for this lady,' Maria told her. She looked at Alayne with a rare approval, for there were not many who earned her respect. 'I do not think that my cures would have helped you this time, my love.'

'Oh, Maria…' The tears that Katherine had tried so hard to control trickled down her cheeks. ''Tis no wonder that Sir Alain grew tired of waiting for me to recover.'

'He said he would be only a few days,' Alayne told her. 'He has stayed away longer than I imagined. Yet he knew that I would not leave you while you needed me. And Sir Bryne was here to watch over us if we had needed him, though I have my own servants and we are well protected.'

'Oh, I do not reproach Sir Alain,' Katherine said as she recovered from her tears. 'He has already done much for me and I have no claim on him.'

'It is not like Alain to desert his friends. I have begun to wonder if he has come to harm, for he took only a few men with him—' Alayne stopped as she saw Katherine's face pale. 'No, no, I am a foolish mother. I am sure he will return just as soon as he may.'

'He may be in danger because of me…' Katherine cried in anguish, her hands plucking at the bedcovers. 'I should never have asked for his help. If anything happens, it will be my fault.'

She was so distressed that Alayne did not ask what troubled her. Instead, she offered her another drink, this time a soothing draught that made Katherine's eyelids seem heavy.

'Rest now and you will feel better when you wake,' Alayne told her soothingly. 'Perhaps my son will have returned to us by the time you are well enough to leave your bed.'

She watched as Katherine drifted into sleep, feeling cross with Alain for staying away so long. He had not made plain his intentions towards this girl. Were they to think of her as his future wife? Maria had told her that she was not entirely friendless, for she had an uncle in France, but it was clear that she had formed a deep attachment to Alain. It was very remiss of him to simply ride away and abandon her.

Alain cursed the time spent kicking his heels, waiting for Prince John to see him. He had brought a message from the moneylenders of Italy regarding the ransom that was being demanded of King Richard. It was an assurance that help was available, if needed, to obtain the release of the King.

When Prince John had finally agreed to an audience, he had refused to listen to Alain's words, dismissing the help offered as unnecessary.

'My brother hath made his own bed. If it be made of thorns, let him lie upon them until he rots! I'll not go cap in hand to any moneylender for his sake! Be damned to all the gold merchants, for they are nothing but bloodsuckers.'

'But my lord…' Alain was silenced by the look of hatred the Prince directed at him. 'The King has been captive too long…'

'I did not give you leave to speak.' Prince John's eyes flashed with imperial pride. 'You have delivered your message. Go now and bother me no more or you may rue the day you took it upon yourself to be my brother's lackey.'

Alain bowed his head, leaving the great chamber without another word. His feelings were of anger and frustration. He had wasted his time at court and would have done better to stay at the inn with Katherine. At least he knew she was not dead, for Bryne had sent word that she seemed to be recovering. She was safe and well cared for with his mother and Bryne. She did not need him and he was needed elsewhere, yet it chaffed him to think of her ill and took all his strength of purpose to keep from returning with all speed.

Alain was restless for he had believed he would be free once his message was delivered, but the King's brother had been so dismissive of it that he knew he must find others who would listen. It seemed that Richard's release might hinge on a promise of payment, for the sum demanded was more than England's king could rightly pay and would beggar him and his kingdom.

Yet there were men who would raise coin if need be for the return of England's rightful king, and he must seek them out before he could consider his duty done. All personal feelings must be put aside until he had done all he could to secure Richard's freedom.

'I insist that you come home with me,' Alayne said as she saw how difficult Katherine found it to walk even a short distance. 'You must not think of returning to France for the moment. You are far too weak and the journey would probably kill you.' Besides, from Maria's account, there was no telling what kind of a reception the girl would receive.

'But you were on your way to London with Marguerite,' Katherine said awkwardly. 'You cannot wish to return home for my sake. Perhaps I should just stay here until Sir Alain returns?'

'No, I could not allow that, my dear. Nor is there the least need, believe me. Marguerite is to continue to London with an escort,' Alayne told her. 'She is to stay with Sir Stefan and the Lady Elona, and their children. I shall return home, for my husband will wish to hear my news. Besides, nothing will persuade me to leave you here alone.'

'You are so kind…' Katherine looked at her uncertainly. Indeed, she was still feeling far from well and would have found it hard to manage by herself. 'But what of Sir Alain? What will he think if he returns and finds I have gone?'

'My son shall be told of your whereabouts. It is his own fault if he is anxious.' Alayne frowned. 'Sir Bryne says Alain has sent word to him, to say he has been delayed at court, and I believe that to be true, but he might have spared the time to write a letter to us. It is thoughtless of him and so I shall tell him when we next meet.'

'Please do not quarrel with him on my account. Sir Alain has more important things to attend,' Katherine said in his defence. 'After all, I have no claim on him, and I dare say he will write to you when he has time.'

'My son was never one for letter writing,' Alayne admitted with a wry smile. 'Well, we shall not fret over his absence, for no doubt he thought you safe in my care—and that is why I must insist that you return with me to Banewulf.'

'But…what of Celestine?' Katherine hesitated. 'Is she to come with us?'

'The lady left us this morning quite early,' Alayne answered with a quick frown. 'I fear I spoke sharply to her more than once, for I found her in your room when you were sleeping, and thought she had been searching your things. I asked her to explain and she said she did not care to be accused by me and would stay here no longer.'

'She may have been looking for something she thinks I have.'

'Well, I do not think she found it, for I saw her enter and came immediately. I do not trust that lady. Her beauty hides a sly, greedy nature. And I am glad she has decided to leave us.'

'But where could she go?' Katherine was puzzled. 'I did not think she had friends in this country.'

'She had money,' Alayne told her. 'I was informed that she had taken passage on a ship and was leaving this evening on the tide. I do not know if she spoke truly or if it was a lie— but for the moment she has gone and I do not think she will follow us to Banewulf, for I should not welcome her there.'

'Yes, I believe she had gold and jewels, though she was careful to keep them hidden.' She smiled at Alayne. 'I confess that I am relieved, my lady, for I did not feel easy with her near, though that may be unkind of me.'

'I do not believe she was your friend,' Alayne replied. 'I have met others of her kind, and I believe she cares only for herself.'

'Yes…' Katherine wondered if she ought to tell this kind friend of the treasure she carried, but decided against it for the moment. If Celestine had left them, she must have been convinced that the treasure did not exist. Why else would she have made up her mind to go? Unless she had simply grown tired of waiting for Sir Alain to return. She looked shyly at the lady who had been so kind to her. 'Is it truly your wish that I should return to stay with you at Banewulf?'

'Yes, most truly. I would not otherwise have asked you.' Alayne smiled at her. 'My tiresome son promised you his escort to France, I understand?' Katherine nodded. 'Sir Bryne has offered to take you in his stead, but I have asked if he will escort Marguerite to London and he has agreed. The men Alain left here to protect you will accompany us to Banewulf, and there we shall wait until he chooses to return.'

'It must be something very important to keep him so long—do you not think so?'

'Indeed, I hope it is, for I shall burn his ear when he returns otherwise,' Alayne replied, looking cross. 'This is not the behaviour I expect of my son! It was unkind of him to desert you, and so he shall hear from me.'

'You must not scold him for my sake,' Katherine said again with a smile of such sweetness that Alayne cursed her son for being a fool. Whatever errand he was on could not be as important as this girl! 'If it were not for Sir Alain, I should have died in Italy when those men tried to abduct me. I owe him my life—and now I must thank you for saving me from the fever.'

'Well, we shall forgive him if he has a good excuse...but come, you have not given me your answer, Katherine. You will come to stay with me for a time, will you not?'

'I should be happy to do so—but perhaps I ought to tell you that there could be danger for your family if I do.' Katherine looked at her anxiously. She would be alone if Lady Alayne went home and left her, but her honesty would not allow her to keep secret the fact that there might danger in helping her.

'Why—what can you mean?' Alayne saw the indecision in the girl's face. 'You need tell me no more than you wish. Am I to understand that you have been in danger yourself— and not just from those brigands?'

'There is someone who would take something I have sworn to see safely to its destination,' Katherine answered. 'This knight is called Hubert, Lord of Ravenshurst, and he would steal my...treasure if he could. Indeed, he has tried at least three times, and I believe that Celestine had some part in this affair.'

'Ah, I see.' Alayne nodded her understanding. 'You need say no more. I have heard of the Ravenshurst family—and they are all rogues. You will be safe enough at Banewulf, and you may put your treasure in my husband's strongroom if it pleases you.'

Katherine smiled, feeling relieved. 'I thank you, my lady— and I am grateful for your offer of hospitality.'

'Very well. I shall go now to write to my husband and tell him to expect us. And after that I shall instruct my servants to begin the packing, for the sooner we leave this wretched inn the better...'

Katherine smiled, but the smile faded from her eyes as Lady Alayne left the room. More than two weeks had passed since Sir Alain left her in the care of his friends, and they had had no word of him directly. Was he in some trouble? Was it because of her—because of the treasure she carried?

She had begun to think that instead of being blessed the relic was cursed, and her heart ached with her fears for Sir Alain. She knew that he would never love her as she loved him, but she could not bear the thought that harm might come to him because of her.

She prayed that God would send him back to his home before too long had passed.

Alain came out of the silk merchant's shop, having placed an order for a vast number of the expensive goods he had found on offer there, which would be delivered directly to Banewulf. He had bought presents for his mother and sister, and a warm, fur-lined cloak for Katherine, as he had remembered that her old cloak was sadly threadbare. He was feeling pleased with himself. At least this day's work had not been wasted. And it was good to be home in England at last. The years of war had been long and hard, though he had never regretted his decision to take the Cross. He had fought fiercely and for a cause he believed in, and his only regret was that they had not been able to take back Jerusalem.

Many of his comrades would never see their homes again, for they had died on the battlefield, of fevers and wounds, or been taken hostage on their journey home. To journey so far abroad was a hazardous business and Richard was not the only one to fall victim to treachery, but not all men could count on friends to aid him and raise a ransom.

Alain had done his best to aid the King's return, and could only hope that it was enough. Having pledged money to help pay Richard's ransom and obtained other pledges from men of like mind, he believed that it would not be long before the King was released and on his way home. It would be a bad day for England if Prince John were to gain the throne permanently.

As he hesitated, feeling the bite of an icy wind, he saw a small cavalcade of riders pass by on the opposite side of the street. They had not seen him, but he had recognised at least one of them. Now what was the Lady Celestine doing here?

He heard her laughter, and saw the knight turn to look at her, and in that moment something came to his mind. He had seen the Lord of Ravenshurst only a few times, but he was almost certain that it was he. So the lady had gone back to him, had she? Just what kind of a game was she playing? And why had she left Katherine? Pray God nothing was amiss!

No, no, he reassured himself. Katherine was recovering from her fever and safe with his mother. He need not fear for her. Yet the nagging doubts plagued him as he returned to his lodgings. A little smile touched his mouth as he realised that somehow Katherine had wormed her way into his affections more deeply than he had realised or wanted. Perhaps it was her air of fragility that made him think her younger than she was at the start, Alain reflected, or merely that she wore the most shapeless, ugly gowns he had ever seen. At least his gift to her would enable her to have two or three new gowns.

He smiled as he summoned his body servant and told him to prepare to leave London. It was time he returned to the inn. Katherine would be impatient to leave for France—and yet he was not sure that he would feel easy in his mind about delivering her to this unknown uncle. Perhaps he would wait for a while, discover what he could about Baron Grunwald.

Chapter Six

'That colour suits you well,' Alayne said as Katherine looked at her for approval. 'I thought that Marguerite's old clothes might fit you—they are things she had before she was wed and have been packed in a trunk since then. She will never want them again and I know she would be pleased for you to have them.'

It was surprising the difference the clothes had made, revealing the truth that Katherine was indeed a woman, and not a child.

'It is kind of you to give them to me—if you are sure your daughter will not mind?' Katherine touched the material of the tunic reverently. She had never worn anything so fine, for her father had not been able to afford such luxuries. 'This is beautiful—and I love the colour. I have nothing but brown or grey of my own.'

'Yes, I had noticed,' Alayne told her with a gentle smile. Katherine's clothes were a disgrace, but had probably served their purpose. No doubt her father had sought to keep her looking as plain and childish as he could for her own safety, for they must have encountered men of all kinds on their travels, and had the girl been dressed fittingly her figure would have been revealed as that of a young woman. 'I dare say your clothes were very suitable for travelling, Katherine—but you are a lady, my dear, and you should be dressed according to your rank. Besides, that green is a good colour for you, and brown makes you look like a—a small brown bird. Yes, that is what I see when I look at you in that old brown tunic, sweet Katherine—a *wrenna*.'

Katherine trilled with laughter, for she knew the bird Lady Alayne spoke of. It was the tiniest, most insignificant bird of all that crept along the hedgerows and hid itself whenever possible.

'Oh, you do not need to tell me that I am plain,' she said merrily. 'My father always told me it was so and I know it as the truth.'

'Your father was wrong, my dear,' Alayne said and handed her a mirror of burnished silver. 'Look at yourself and tell me if what you see is ugly.'

Katherine took the mirror uncertainly. The image it showed her was of a young girl with shining hair and eyes, and a soft mouth that looked—yes, it looked quite nice when she smiled.

'Is that truly me?' she asked as she handed the mirror back.

'Yes, Katherine. The new way of doing your hair hath much improved your looks. You are not pretty as some women are, but none can deny that you have some indefinable quality all your own.'

'Marguerite is beautiful. You cannot say that my looks compare to hers!'

'No, nor would I pretend that they do,' Alayne said and laughed because she saw that Katherine was not hurt or distressed by the truth of her appearance. Indeed, her eyes danced with amusement, for she was the least vain of women. 'But you do have a certain sweetness…a charm and innocence that many men would find enchanting. You should not think yourself plain, Katherine. Say rather that you are attractive, and now that you have made up some of the weight you lost when you were ill I think you look very well, my dear.'

'If I do, it is due to you, my lady,' Katherine said. 'You have fed me so well that I could not fail to feel better—and you have given me these lovely clothes. How shall I ever thank you?'

'By being your own sweet self,' Alayne replied. 'You must know that I have become very fond of you these past weeks. I shall be sorry when I am forced to part with you. Can I not persuade you to live with us? Must you return to France? I would be happy to have you here as my daughter and friend.'

'How kind you are,' Katherine said. 'But I fear I must return to France one day. However, if my uncle should not want to take me in…' She faltered, for she did not know what she would do in such a case.

'Then you must return to us. I mean it, my dear. Do not hesitate, Katherine. If you are unhappy at any time, send word and we shall fetch you back to Banewulf.'

'I shall remember what you have said.'

Katherine was warmed by her words. The welcome at Banewulf had been more than she could ever have expected— but all she could think of was what would happen when Sir Alain returned to his home.

Had he thought of her at all while he was away? Sometimes she dreamed of him, and in her dreams he took her in his arms and kissed her, a kiss so passionate and hungry that it made her swoon with delight. When she woke from such dreams her cheeks were warm, for she was shamed by her wantonness.

How could she dream of such things? She was a maiden and these thoughts were not chaste. Indeed, they were wicked. Especially when there was no hope of the man she loved ever having the same feelings for her.

So Katherine had completely recovered and his mother had taken her back to Banewulf with her. Alain was surprised that Bryne had not gone with them. He knew that his friend would have felt obliged to do as Lady Alayne asked and accompany Marguerite to London, but it still seemed strange that he had been willing to leave Katherine to others if he was intending to make her his wife.

Alain was almost certain that Bryne had intended to make Katherine an offer of marriage, which was why he'd done nothing that would interfere with his friend's plans. After all, he was certain his feelings for Katherine were those of a brother for his sister.

And yet there were times when she haunted him; her large, sometimes serious, sometimes merry eyes had a habit of intruding into his thoughts, both waking and sleeping. Of late his dreams had grown stronger, more erotic, and he was shamed by them. He should not allow himself to think of Katherine in that way. Even if she were not the child he had always thought her, she was the woman Bryne had spoken of as his intended bride, and therefore forbidden to Alain.

He was a fool to even consider the possibility of making Katherine an offer himself. He would not harm Bryne for the world, and besides, he was not sure that the girl even liked him. If she did and if by some chance Bryne had changed his mind...but she was little more than a child. She would grow up one day, of course. And she would be an excellent mother for his children. His mother would approve of her.

But Katherine was not the kind of woman he had thought to marry when the time came for him to take a wife. He had always imagined he might marry someone rather like…the Lady Elona. She had been intended as his bride, but he had been too young and too restless to think of marriage at the time—and she had fallen in love with his half-brother Stefan on their journey from France.

Alain had not wanted to marry anyone at that time, for he had been restless and eager to make a name for himself—but he had liked his brother's wife very much. When he occasionally toyed with the idea of taking a bride one day, it had been of someone like Elona he had thought. Katherine was very different. Elona was fiery, full of spirit, while Katherine… He discovered that he did not truly know. Katherine had a kind of spiritual quality, a goodness and innocence that made him feel protective towards her, but he had seen humour in her eyes. Was there another woman inside—a woman she kept hidden from them all?

Katherine was intriguing, he decided. There was a certain mystery about her. In some ways she was still a stranger to him; it would be interesting to know her better.

Women of a certain kind had been eager to share his bed over the years, but he had taken few lovers. He was a natural man, but he was fastidious and would not take a woman lightly as many of the knights did. There had been a beautiful Arab girl he might have had as his wife, for her eager father had offered her to him, but he had seen the reluctance in her eyes and refused the offer. Whores were not to his liking, and it would have been dishonourable to steal a brother knight's wife, so, apart from a few snatched inter-ludes with fresh-cheeked countrywomen, he had lived a life of abstinence.

He had never met a woman he wanted to marry…then why had he thought of offering for Katherine at all? She had no looks to speak of. She was small and plain and brown like a bird, and he was afraid that he frightened her, for she looked at him so anxiously at times.

No, no, it was nonsense. Katherine was too young to think of marriage—to him or anyone else.

'You have been a great help to me today,' Alayne told Katherine as they returned to the house that morning. 'My work is not always pleasant amongst the sick of the village, and it was good to have a companion. You saw for yourself how they suffer if we do not care for them.'

'I was pleased to help you,' Katherine told her. 'My father and I did what we could for the injured at Acre, but I do not have your skills, my lady. I would that I could do more. It must be such a blessing for your people when you visit them.'

'If you truly wish to learn, I could teach you some simple skills,' Alayne told her. 'You may help me in my stillroom if you wish.'

'I should like that of all things.'

'Good.' Alayne gave her an approving smile. Katherine had gained a wide education on her travels, but was ignorant of most things that she would need to know as the chatelaine of a great house. If Alain was thinking of making her his bride, it would be best if she learned something of what would be expected of her. 'It will be pleasant to teach you all that you need to know, my dearest. I grow fonder of you with each day that passes, and in truth I do not know how I shall part from you when the time comes.'

'It will be hard to part from you,' Katherine admitted. 'For you have become the mother I thought you when I was ill.'

Alayne embraced her. 'Perhaps I shall not need to part from you,' she said. 'We must hear what my son has to say when he returns.'

'But when will that be?' Katherine asked. She sighed as her companion shook her head. Sometimes she believed that she would never see him again.

His business must be important to keep him from his home so long.

'So you have returned at last,' Sir Ralph said to his son as they embraced. 'I am glad to see you again, Alain. Your mother told me you had grown into a fine man, and she was right. She was anxious when you stayed away so long, but I told her you would return as soon as you could. Women do not always understand that a man has many calls upon his time that they may not share.'

'Indeed, I ought to have sent word of my intention to return,' Alain replied. 'But I was engaged in important work, and I was reluctant to send letters for fear they should fall into the wrong hands. And I believed that Katherine was in safe hands.'

'Ah, yes, the girl,' Sir Ralph said, an odd expression in his eyes. 'She is a good modest girl, Alain. Your mother is very taken with her, and they have become good friends. I believe it is your intention to escort her to her home in France?'

'It was, but I think we should make inquiries first,' Alain said. 'I would not have her travel all that way only to be turned back if they do not want her. She has an uncle, but there is little money as I understand it and she may be an unwanted burden.'

'That is my own thought,' Sir Ralph said and nodded his appreciation. 'To that end, I have written to the Baron Grunwald and told him that his brother's daughter is staying with us for the moment. We shall wait and see what his answer brings. There is no hurry after all—is there?' Sir Ralph frowned. 'Yet I think there is also an uncle in this country—Katherine's mother's brother. Has she said aught to you of him?'

'Nothing at all, Father,' Alain said. 'But it would not harm to make some inquiries before we decide. Besides, Katherine has been ill and I think another journey…' He broke off as two ladies came into the hall, his jaw dropping as he saw the younger of the two. It was Katherine, but not as he had ever seen her. She was wearing a tunic of emerald green belted with a girdle of gold threads. Her face was a becoming pink, and she was smiling in a way she had seldom smiled in the past. He knew at once that she was happy here and he went forward, his hands outstretched. 'I am relieved to see you looking so well, Katherine. I feared for your life when you were struck down with that fever, but then my mother came and I knew that you would be well cared for.'

Why, she was almost beautiful when she smiled. How was it that he had not seen it before?

Katherine blushed and dipped her head, her cheeks flushed. Alain thought that she would rather he did not press his attentions on her, and moved aside for her to pass by. She went to stand by the hearth, looking at the floor—anywhere rather than him. Her glow of pleasure had faded, and it was clear to Alain that she was not comfortable in his presence.

'Where have you been all this time?' his mother asked, claiming his attention. 'Did you not think we might be anxious for you? Could you not have sent some word of your where-abouts?' There was a sharpness in her voice that he had sel-dom heard from her and he realised that she was annoyed with him. He transferred his attention to her, frowning slightly. Had he done something to displease both Katherine and his mother?

'Forgive me. I would not have distressed you for the world, Mother. I was on an important mission—a secret mission, which is why I did not write to explain the delay.' He heard Katherine's gasp and shook his head. 'No, Katherine, busi-ness of my own. I may speak of it now, for I believe it will not be long before the whole of England knows the truth. I have been told that King Richard has been released and is on his way back to England. It was to help secure promises for his ransom that I was in London. I went first to his Majesty's brother, but gained but a poor response, for the Prince seemed almost to hope Richard would rot in his prison.'

'That man!' Sir Ralph exclaimed. 'Richard was a fool to leave him as Regent here. It is my belief that he has conspired with France to keep Richard a prisoner.'

'I think you may be right, Father—but if what I have heard is true, the King will soon be home again.'

'God be praised!' Sir Ralph said and was echoed by his wife. 'If that was your mission, you owe us no apology, my son. His Majesty has your first loyalty always.'

'The ransom hath been pledged and perhaps some already paid,' Alain told them. 'I myself have pledged some part of my fortune, and others were willing to do the same. Yet I fear that the sum asked was so great that Richard will bear the weight of it for so long as he lives.'

'It was ill luck that took him to Austria and the Duke Leopold's clutches!'

'Aye, that it was. But it was to the Holy Roman Emperor Henry VI that he had to pledge so much for his freedom— and that will not please his temper.'

'Richard is a true Plantagenet,' Sir Ralph answered. 'They have ever been a quarrelsome brood—but Richard is the lawful king and we must uphold him.'

'Aye, no matter what. I would not have that rogue John as my king if I could avoid it.' Alain scowled. 'He is a rogue and deserves to be treated as such.'

'Be careful what you say,' Sir Ralph cautioned. 'John rules here for the moment and such words are treason. If anything should happen to prevent Richard reaching London and being acclaimed as the true king once more—you could be arrested for such sentiments.'

'I know that you speak truly, Father,' Alain replied. 'But there is none but you and Mother to hear me—and Katherine.' He smiled at her and was relieved to receive a shy smile in return. Perhaps she did not find him such an ogre, after all. 'I trust you are recovered, Katherine.'

She looked different. Her cheeks had a pleasant colour in them, but there was something more. What had changed her? Of course! It was the first time she had worn her hair loose like that. Always before it had been tightly braided or hidden beneath a wimple. He thought it suited her hanging loose about her shoulders, that she looked more womanly, older and—attractive. It was thick and shone with health, the ends curling slightly about her face where it had been cut shorter. She had certainly improved in looks and he guessed that his mother had had a hand in the changes in her.

'I have been cosseted and cared for at every turn,' Katherine confessed with a smile for her hostess. 'No one has ever been so good to me as Lady Alayne.'

'But it pleases me to make you happy,' Alayne said. 'I have been trying to persuade Katherine that she must stay with us for much longer. I hope you do not intend to take her away from us too soon, my son?'

'Father agrees with me that we should send word to your uncle. Indeed, he has already done so,' Alain said, looking at Katherine and trying to decide what she was thinking. It seemed that she had grown more adept at hiding her feelings, and he realised that she had changed in more than her appearance. Somehow he no longer saw her as a child, but a young woman on the threshold of life. 'I would not have you make such a journey only to find that your uncle cannot welcome you for some reason. It would be better to wait—do you not agree?'

'You must stay with us for a few months at least.' Lady Alayne added her entreaty to that of her son. 'Please say that you will, my dear.'

Katherine looked into Alain's eyes. They were such a deep blue and they made her want to be in his arms, to feel the touch of his lips on hers, as she had felt it in her dreams. Once she had wanted only to escape the pain of being with him, but now that Celestine was not there to hang on his arm and flutter her long lashes at him, she discovered that she no longer felt so desperate. Indeed, the happiness she felt at his return was something she had had to struggle to hide. Better that he should think her reserved than too eager.

'If I am no trouble to your mother, I shall stay,' she said. 'My uncle will be shocked to hear of his brother's death and will need time to adjust to the news, I dare say.'

'Then we are agreed,' Alayne said and looked satisfied. 'Katherine will stay here with us. Indeed, she must for a time.' She gave her son a forgiving smile. 'And now I must thank you for your gifts, Alain, for they arrived this morning. As I understand your instructions, the material is for my stores, to be used as I see fit, and there is one special gift for Katherine.'

Alain nodded and looked at Katherine. 'I bought you a warm cloak; if memory serves me right, your own hath seen much wear,' Alain told her, bringing a rosy flush to her cheeks. 'And our winters can be cruel, Katherine. I would not have you take ill for the inclement weather.'

Katherine mumbled her thanks, seeming embarrassed by his concern for her, and Alayne sighed inwardly. Why could her son not have simply said that he had bought her a gift? He made it seem that the cloak was a garment meant for convenience when it was one of the finest that even his mother had ever seen. It was clear to her that Alain was not indifferent to this young woman, even if he had not the wit to see it for himself, and for her part she thought that he could not do better than to marry her.

Katherine was sitting on a bench in a sheltered spot in the garden lost in thought when she heard the sound of footsteps and looked up to see Sir Alain coming towards her. For a moment her heart raced and she wanted to run away and hide, but to do so would be rude and she did not wish to offend him. Yet she was afraid of giving herself away, of letting him see that she cared for him more than was seemly.

Oh, why must she love a man who could never love her? Why could she not have loved Bryne, who had wanted to marry her?

'Are you warm enough sitting here?' Alain asked, and as she nodded, unable to speak at first, 'May I sit with you for a moment?'

'Yes, if you wish it.' She found her voice at last. Her hand trembled as he sat beside her and his nearness set flutters of pleasure winging through her body. Yet she gave no sign of her feelings, her expression serious as she asked, 'For I must thank you for your gift. It is a beautiful cloak and I have never owned one like it.'

'Then I am happy to have given it to you, Katherine—but it was not to receive your thanks that I sought you out.'

Her heart fluttered as she saw his serious look. 'May I help you in some way, sir?'

'Will you not call me Alain?' he asked, his eyes studying her face intently. He did not know how it was, but each day she seemed to grow more attractive to his eyes. 'I hope that we are friends, Katherine? You do not dislike me?' On board the ship she had seemed to like him, but now she seemed so reserved that he was afraid he had offended her.

Dislike him! How could he think it when the very sight of him set her heart racing like a mad March hare? Little did he know that his touch made her breathless with a feeling she knew was desire, though she blushed for shame for it. She curled her nails into her hands, knowing that she must be careful. If he guessed that she loved him he would be awkward in her presence, for he could not want such feelings from her.

'How could I dislike you when you have been so good to me, sir?'

'Then why do you not smile for me?' Alain's tone was teasing. 'You smile for my mother and for others—but you look at me as if you thought I meant you harm. On the ship we laughed together, Katherine. Tell me what I have done to offend you. Was it because I left you at the inn?'

'No, of course not. How could you stay when you had important work?'

'I thought of you, Katherine, but I knew that you had others to care for you.' He reached out to take her hand, his thumb gently caressing the palm and making her tremble the more. It aroused such feelings in her, such longings. She snatched it back from him, her cheeks heating. 'You will not let me hold your hand even for a moment. What can I do to make amends?'

It was not possible to explain. She could not say that she loved him, loved the sight of him, the smell of him, the very thought of him. She could not tell him that when she had recovered her senses at the inn and found he had not stayed to see how she fared, she felt as if her heart had been wrenched from her body, that she had been devastated to realise how little she meant to him. How could she tell him that her dreams were full of him, that she longed for him to take her in his arms, to feel the touch of his hands on her body, to be held close to his heart, as he had held her for a moment when she almost fell into the boat taking them ashore? She could not. No maiden could say such things to a man, especially one who had shown no feelings of desire towards her.

'Forgive me…Alain,' she said and smiled at him. For a moment he glimpsed laughter in her eyes but could not know that it was her own impossible thoughts that amused her. 'I would not offend you for the world.' She reached out and touched his arm briefly, before withdrawing her hand again like a shy kitten. 'You saved me from those brigands and my poor Maria from the robbers who broke into my chamber in Rome—and you sent for your mother when I was ill. If it were not for you, I might be dead, forgotten by all and grieved by none.'

'I cannot believe that there is none to grieve for you,' Alain said, ever watchful. 'Is there no one who would wed you, Katherine? You must have a lover?'

'I have no lover,' she replied and her eyes shone with honesty and truth. 'There was someone who offered for me, but I think he was being kind, because he knew I was in need and wanted to comfort me. And, indeed, I did not wish to take advantage of his kindness.'

Alain digested this in silence. Did she not realise that Bryne truly cared for her? Or had she decided that she did not wish to wed him? Perhaps Bryne had been refused and that was why he had left her to his mother's care. If that were so, the field was clear for Alain if he wished to press his suit.

'And what of your family?'

Katherine was silent for a moment, as if the question gave her pain.

'I hardly remember them. When I left France with my father, his brother came to live at the castle as its keeper. His name was Robert and he was younger than my father—but I remember that I did not like him. He seemed a hard, cold man.'

'Has your uncle no wife?'

'I do not know. I believe he had none then, but that was a long time ago. I dare say he has married since then.'

'And your mother's family?'

'I know that she had a brother. His name is Philip of Rotherham, and he is an Englishman. My mother should have received an inheritance from her mother, handed down through her maternal grandfather, when she married. It was a considerable sum, I believe—but her brother withheld it. Had he paid the money he owed my father, we might never have set out on our travels. Indeed, I know my father believed that it was the quarrel with her brother that brought on my mother's early death, though I do not know how that may be. I know that her death broke my father's heart.'

Alain looked at her thoughtfully. How had he ever thought her a child? She was a serious, intelligent, caring and lovely woman. Her beauty was more spiritual than physical, but it was there—in her eyes and in her smile. The kind of beauty that a man would never forget. She was, in fact, a woman Alain would remember all his life, not a fleeting fancy as he might find other women of a more conventional beauty.

'Would you like me to discover what has happened to your mother's inheritance? It might be that I could find a way to recover it for you.'

'Perhaps…' Katherine frowned. 'I do not think Philip of Rotherham would let it go willingly. Yet if my Uncle Robert will not take me in when he has your father's letter…' She faltered. 'My father was cheated of his rights, but he never tried to seek reparation and he might not wish me to do so now.'

'That money is yours by right,' Alain said. 'Would you allow me to discover what the situation is—if I am discreet?'

'I have already caused you too much trouble, sir.' She looked away from him, and he was caught by her dignity and her courage. She was truly a woman a man might want as his wife.

'You have been no trouble at all,' he assured her. 'My only quarrel with you is that you will not call me by my name. I thought we were friends, Katherine? Am I such an ogre? Perhaps you should set your dragon on me again?'

She turned her head to look at him. He gave her such a

wicked grin that Katherine laughed, letting go of the reserve she had carefully kept in place since his return.

'I shall try to remember to call you by your name,' she said and this time the words came from her heart. 'For, indeed, you and your family have been true friends to me. I do not recall ever having been so happy or so comfortable in my life. I loved my father dearly, but he never recovered from his grief at losing my mother, and sometimes he hardly knew I was there. At other times he would remember me and then he would talk to me. He told me about his hopes and dreams of discovering a great treasure—and in the end he did.'

'Ah, yes, the treasure…' Alain remembered why he had sought her out. 'I must tell you that I have shown your father's notes to a priest I trust. He is a man of great faith, a man uninterested in worldly goods or power—and he told me that he does not believe the notes give your father's discovery sufficient provenance for something as important as the Holy Grail.'

'Then we can do nothing?' Katherine gazed at him in dismay. 'My father set such store by his discovery. I feel I would be letting him down if I simply ignored it.'

'We could go higher,' Alain said. 'My friend is but a simple priest and others might think differently—yet I believe you might find it difficult to prove that the cup you have is the one men have sought in vain all these years. You have told me it is but a simple thing, and I think that most fitting—for was not our Lord a simple man? But most think of the Holy Grail as a thing of unique beauty, a precious thing of value in itself, and would see little worth in the cup you told me of. Had your father's notes and the documents that he used in his study not been lost, it might perhaps have been otherwise.'

'The brigands carried off his baggage and the notes with it…' Katherine's brow furrowed. 'If they were under orders from Hubert of Ravenshurst…' She looked at him intently. 'Do you think he would realise what they meant—how important they were—or would he throw them away?'

'Ravenshurst is a bully and a rogue, but I dare say he can read. He would have learned when he was studying for his knighthood, and if he went so far as to set those brigands on your father…' Alain paused to let his words sink in. 'I fear he knows all too well, Katherine—and if he should gain the cup, he would be in a position of great power.'

'Do you think it might be possible to bargain with him for the return of my father's notes? If I could find enough money to buy them from him—with my mother's inheritance?' For a moment her face lit with eagerness and Alain caught his breath. How had he ever thought her plain? He knew an urgent desire to take her in his arms and make love to her, but was afraid that he might frighten her. He reached for her hand, holding it loosely as he idly caressed it. This time she did not immediately snatch it away, though her cheeks turned pink. 'No, of course he would not give them up…' The glow faded from her eyes and she sighed. 'If he has them he must want the cup badly. That is why he has twice tried to steal it from me.'

'You must promise me you will not think of approaching Ravenshurst, Katherine. He is a dangerous man.'

'What do you mean? How could I approach…?' Her face drained of colour as something in his expression warned her of the truth. She withdrew her hand from his. He saw the knuckles turn white as she made nervous fists of her hands, clearly much affected by the news. 'You have seen him—here in England?'

'When I was in London on the King's business,' Alain confessed. 'I am sorry to tell you that the Lady Celestine was with him.'

'Celestine…' Katherine nodded. 'I never believed in her story of escaping from the Lord Hubert's camp. She had brought things with her that must have been noticed when she mounted her horse—and I have always thought it strange that the men who were attacking her that morning did not take her horse when they rode off.'

Alain stared at her for a moment, then threw back his head and gave a shout of laughter. 'I see I have severely misjudged you, Katherine. I thought you a child, but you are not that— nor are you a helpless female. It is clear that you were a better judge of the lady's character at the start than I—for at first I was dazzled by her beauty. It was only after a little time had passed that I began to discover she hath a serpent's tongue and a devious mind.'

'And a sting in her tail,' Katherine said ruefully. Her shyness had dissolved and suddenly she was able to talk to him easily, to relax and be herself. 'I am sorry if she hurt you, sir. I do not believe that Celestine is capable of true love for anyone.'

'Save for herself perhaps,' Alain replied and there was a strange look in his eyes. 'I will admit that I was smitten by the lady's smile for a time—but only a short time. After that I was careful not to make her angry, for all our sakes—but yours most of all, Katherine. I thought that she might take her spite on you, and, like you, I also thought it strange that the rogues trying to abduct her should leave behind her horse and the bag of gold and jewels slung from the horn of her saddle when they made their escape…'

'I believe they plotted it between them,' Katherine said

and looked serious. Her eyes were large and dark and something in them at that moment drew Alain like a moth to a flame. She grew more lovely to him with every moment. 'Celestine and the Baron. She must have thought she could gain my confidence and that I would tell her of the treasure. We were friends for a time at Acre, but I have wondered if it was she who told the Baron of my father's discovery. If she could, she might have stolen it from me, but I carried it with me always. My father thought it might be safer with me, for my clothes were so shapeless that I was able to conceal it easily on my person.'

'Do you have it now?'

'It is in your father's strongroom for the moment. I thought it safer so—until we are certain what to do with it.'

'You are wise for it will be safe there, and we must think carefully over this, Katherine. Even if the provenance is not good enough for the high officials of the church to give it credence, there are others who are not so scrupulous.'

'If only we could recover my father's notes…'

'If somehow we could persuade Ravenshurst to give them up…' Alain shook his head, a glint in his eyes. 'Perhaps we should steal them back?'

'But that would be wrong,' Katherine said. 'The Baron would not give in without a fight and men could be hurt. I would rather my father's discovery was never acknowledged than that it should cause more bloodshed.' She remembered the screams of the family she had befriended at Acre and shuddered. Would the stench of blood and the sight of a child dying terribly never leave her?

'I shall think of something,' Alain said. 'For the moment we must be patient. We have other concerns—your future, for instance. Have you thought what you will do if your uncle, Robert of Grunwald, does not welcome you to his home?'

'No…' Katherine looked down at her hands, feeling a return of unease as his eyes fixed on her. As yet her uncle had not replied to the message sent to him and it was possible that he would refuse to help her. 'Celestine offered me a home with her and was angry when I refused her and—the Lady Alayne has said I might return here to be her companion.'

'Ah, my mother…' Alain smiled oddly. His mother, who saw and understood more than most. 'Yes, that would be better than being at the mercy of someone you did not truly like. And I think you have been happy here?'

'Yes, very happy—yet I must visit my uncle soon,' Katherine said, her brow creasing in thought. 'It is my duty to tell him of my father's death. He is the Baron now and Grunwald belongs to him. It is only right and proper that he should be told.'

Alain thought that after so many years with no word of his brother, Robert of Grunwald probably already thought of himself as the Baron, and of the castle and lands as his own.

'We shall journey to Grunwald in the summer,' he said. 'The travelling will be better then—and there are other concerns. I shall see what has become of your mother's brother and the inheritance that was owed to your father.'

'As you wish,' Katherine said and stood up. 'I think I shall go in now, for it begins to turn cooler.'

'And I have promised to go on an errand for my father, and have been remiss in spending so much time here with you,' he said and smiled at her. 'I find your company all too tempting these days, Katherine.'

He stood up, gazing down at her as she lowered her head. Then he tipped her chin towards him, dipping his head to kiss her on the lips. It was a sweet, brief, gentle kiss, but it set her senses racing. She gasped, hardly daring to move or breathe for fear that he should guess how his kiss had affected her, but he merely smiled, touched her cheek and turned from her.

She glanced after him as he walked away. Now what could he mean by that? His kiss had set her aflame with pulsing desire, but to him it had been no more than a passing fancy. She must never let him guess just how much it had meant to her.

Alayne was reading a letter when Katherine asked if she might enter her solar the next day. She looked up and smiled at the girl standing on the threshold, holding out her hand in welcome.

'Come in, my dear,' she said. 'You know that I am always pleased to see you. I have this moment received a letter from my daughter. Marguerite writes to tell me she is on her way to Banewulf and that Stefan and his wife accompany her.'

'You will be pleased to see them no doubt.'

'Yes, for I love to have company,' Alayne said and patted the stool beside her. 'You did not meet my daughter properly, for you were still ill when she left for London. She asks about you and is anxious to meet you now that you are recovered. Stefan's wife sends her good wishes also and looks forward to meeting you.'

'I shall be happy to see them, my lady—but shall I not be in the way when you have so much company?'

'Of course you will not, foolish girl,' Alayne said and laughed. 'We have room enough for all of you, and I refuse to be parted from you—besides, where would you go? My son tells me that he is waiting for a letter from your uncle before he takes you to France in the summer.'

'I do not know where I should go,' Katherine confessed honestly. 'But I might find refuge in a nunnery for a while, I suppose.'

Perhaps she ought to take refuge with the good sisters. It might be the cure for her sinful desires!

'Think no more of it! Once they had you there, they might never let you go.' Alayne shook her head. 'You know that it is my wish you should make your home here with me. Besides, Alain is to take a short trip to his own estate, which is some three or four days travelling, and Marguerite may have his chamber while he is gone.'

'Alain is leaving?' Katherine felt a sharp pain in her heart. 'He said nothing of it to me.' But why should he? She was merely a woman he had rescued from brigands. Why should he tell her his plans? And yet there had been something in his manner of late, something that made her think he might have stronger feelings for her. No, she was being foolish, allowing herself to dream of a love that was all on her part. He had offered her friendship, nothing more.

'I believe he has only now made up his mind to it,' Alayne told her. 'My husband made certain investments on his behalf when he was fighting in the crusade, and Alain has never seen the estate here in England. The lands that passed to Sir Ralph on our marriage were in France and have been sold to buy more land in this country—an estate that is quite near to the small estate that will belong to Stefan one day. It was while we were staying there last year that we became aware of the opportunity and the purchase was made. However, although Sir Ralph has set some work in hand, he believes more needs to be done on the house, and Alain wishes to see to this himself.'

'I see…' His reason for leaving was clear enough, but she

wondered why he had not told her himself. 'How long will Sir Alain be away?'

'I have no idea, but here he is—you may ask him yourself.'

'I was looking for you, Katherine,' he said and his smile brought a flush to her cheeks as she rose to greet him. 'I wanted to tell you that I have made up my mind to visit the estate my father purchased on my behalf. I shall need a home of my own in the future, for Banewulf is my father's estate and I must have something with which to fill my time now that I am home.'

'Oh…' She allowed herself to meet his gaze as she asked, 'And how long shall you be gone, sir?'

'A few weeks, no more,' he said. 'But I have other news for you, Katherine. I have discovered that your mother's brother is still living and his home is not far from here. I shall visit him while I am away and discover what I may concerning his feelings for you.'

'You are kind to do so much for me.'

'It is my pleasure,' he replied and the look in his eyes set her heart racing. 'I would not leave you did I not know that you were safe with my family. You will have Marguerite and Elona to keep you company soon and will not miss me, I dare swear.'

Was there a note of inquiry in his voice? Katherine could not be certain. She only knew that her heart beat so fast that she could hear it drumming, and she was afraid that he could read her feelings too easily.

'You will always be missed in this house, my son.' His mother answered for her and saved Katherine the need to find the right words. 'Come back to us soon—and be sure to send word. I do not wish to be anxious as I was the last time you said you would be gone but a few days and were absent from us for nearly a month.'

'I shall write most faithfully, Mother,' he said with a wicked grin. 'May I have your permission to write to you, Katherine?'

'If—if it pleases you.'

'It does.' He crossed the room in swift strides, bending to kiss his mother's cheek, and then turned to look at Katherine. For a moment she thought he meant to take her in his arms and her heart missed a beat. Instinctively, she held out her hand to him. He hesitated, taking it in his carefully, as if it were made of some fragile material that might break at his touch. His finger caressed the back of her hand for a moment, making her pulses race frantically, and then he turned it over, bending his head to drop a light kiss in the palm. 'Hold that safe for me. I shall return soon so that you may pay it back to me, Katherine.'

She gazed at him in wonder, but then saw that his eyes were alight with mockery. Indeed, he was merely teasing her as he often did, his merry smile lifting the corners of his mouth as he bowed elegantly to her and then to his mother.

'I bid you adieu, sweet ladies. Know that you will be ever in my dreams ere I return.'

Katherine could not answer him. Was he merely teasing her as the knights did their ladies at the court? This fashion of paying extravagant compliments, of teasing a lady, of dalliance, had begun, 'twas said, at the Courts of Love in Aquitaine when Queen Eleanor ruled there. Katherine believed that it was common behaviour amongst the ladies and gentlemen of the court in France—perhaps England also? Since she had never been anywhere of the kind she had no way of knowing if it was commonplace. Celestine had known how to play the game, but Katherine had no such graces.

'My son is a rogue to tease you so,' Alayne remarked as he went out and they heard his steps running down the stone steps. 'You should give him his own back, Katherine. He does not deserve to win you lightly. I was angry with him for deserting you when you were ill—and even now it ill behoves him to speak in that fashion.'

'I am sure Sir Alain meant no harm.'

'You defend him? But of course you would—you love him. No, no, do not blush so, sweet Katherine. Your secret is not writ upon your forehead. I do not think Alain knows for certain, and that is why he teases you. I have a kind of sixth sense about many things. Sometimes it is helpful to see what others cannot—but at other times I fear it.'

Katherine was struck by her words. 'Have you the sight, my lady? I know that you have the gift of healing…'

'I am not sure that I have the gift of sight as it is called— but there are times when I sense something bad may happen, and too often it does. Yet it is always for others. I do not have it when it affects myself. I had thought Alain almost too sensitive. As a child he seemed to feel things too much, but he seems different since he returned from his travels. I suppose that he is no longer a child.' Alayne sighed. 'I must confess to you that I wish he would marry and settle on his estate. I fear that he will grow bored with the life here and set out for some war in a far-flung land—and that we may never see him again.'

'Have you seen something?' Katherine asked and her voice shook as she experienced a start of fear. How could she bear it if something happened to Alain?

'No, do not fear it.' His mother laughed and the resemblance to Alain was very strong in that moment. 'I am merely voicing a mother's natural fears—something you will understand one day.'

'I am not sure that I shall ever marry.'

'Oh, but I am very sure you will,' Alayne said and laughed softly. 'I have seen you holding your son in your arms. The vision came to me one night when you lay sick. I was close to despair, thinking you beyond my help—and then I saw you with a babe in your arms and I knew that you would recover. I gave you another, stronger dose of my medicine and the fever began to wane that very night.'

'Did you truly see me with a child in my arms?'

'I never lie to those I care for. You will marry and you will bear at least one child, Katherine—that is all I can tell you, for the vision was clear but brief.'

'You have been so good to me,' Katherine said. 'I can never thank you enough for all you have done for me.'

'If you examine my motives, I am not to be thanked,' Alayne told her with a smile as wicked as her son's. 'For if you gain your heart's desire, then so shall I…'

Chapter Seven

❦

'I always enjoy visiting at Banewulf,' the Lady Elona told Katherine as they sat together at their stitching. The sun was shining in through the small window, bringing a hint of spring to the room and making it warmer. They were embroidering a new altar cloth for the chapel at Banewulf and found pleasure in each other's company. 'We visit the court only rarely, for my husband does not like Prince John. Indeed, I think it would be dangerous to go more often, for the feeling is mutual. Stefan says that the Prince thinks himself king and will not lightly yield his place to Richard.'

'Sir Alain feels the same,' Katherine said and frowned. Almost a month had passed and they had not heard from him. Despite his promise to write faithfully, he had sent only one letter to his mother, and a few lines of verse to Katherine. His poem had made her blush and she had hidden it deep in her coffer for fear that someone should chance to see it, for it was wickedly amusing and seemed to hint at things it was surely not seemly for a maiden to know. She would have thought it a love poem had she not been certain that Alain saw her as a child. 'He said he would be only a short time before he returned to us.'

'Stefan said the same when he left me here,' Elona told her and smiled oddly. 'Have you not guessed it, Katherine? It is quite simple—they have both slipped off to help Richard take his crown back from the usurper.'

'Alain and Stefan have gone to join Richard…' Katherine stared at her, an icy trickle of fear sliding down her back and making her shiver. 'But how can this be? I did not know that the King had returned to England.'

'I think only a few know of his return,' Elona told her. 'Stefan thought he had kept it from me for fear that I should worry, but I know him too well not to realise when something is going on. I was aware that he had received a letter from his brother and I heard him talking to other men of like minds.

'There are many in England who have suffered beneath John's rule, even become outlaws. I believe because they stood up for the rights of the common man that John would suppress. His tax collectors bleed the people dry, taking everything they have so that they would starve if men of right thinking did not help them.

'Stefan believes that John has tried to usurp his brother's throne and would cheat him of it if he could—so he has gone to meet with others who will fight to see that Richard is acclaimed as king again. I know he believes that the people will rise to support their rightful king.'

'Yes, perhaps that is so.' Katherine looked at her keenly. 'You have not told Lady Alayne where they are gone?'

'I would not dream of it,' Elona said and smiled at a distant memory. 'Before Alain went off to fight in the Holy

Land, he fought in single combat for his brother's sake. King Henry had accused Stefan of treason, for my husband was always Richard's man, but he had been badly gored by a wild boar in the forest. He was determined to prove his innocence by trial of combat, but he was weak and might not have won.

'Three men offered to fight in his stead—his father, Sir Orlando, who was his friend and became Marguerite's husband, and Alain. Stefan chose Alain, for he feared to offend his brother, who had not proved himself at that time—and Alain won. Indeed, Stefan said that he had seldom seen a man fight so well, and he has proved himself many times since, for we have heard of his bravery at Acre and other battles.'

'I know that he fights bravely, and he is a true knight, generous and steadfast in his friendship—but I wish that he had told me the truth.'

'Would you not have worried for his sake?'

'Yes, of course,' Katherine said and laughed at herself. 'I am a foolish woman. He would not tell us because he knew we should be anxious. Yet I have noticed that Lady Alayne has been quiet of late. Do you think she knows more than we do?'

'She will have felt it without understanding if they have been in danger,' Elona said. 'She always feels these things— sometimes she has visions that distress her.'

Katherine nodded and was silent. These past two days her kind hostess had been very withdrawn. For a while Katherine had wondered if she had done something to anger her, but then she realised that Alayne had something on her mind. She had not guessed that both Alain and Stefan were with the King, but now that she did she was anxious for them. Supposing one of them had been hurt or killed?

'Now you are allowing your imagination to distress you,'

Elona said as she saw her expression. 'Perhaps I should not have told you the truth.'

'No, I am glad that you did,' Katherine said and gave her a rueful smile. 'At least I understand now why Alain has not written again. I dare say he could not.'

Elona touched her hand in understanding. 'He will have been too busy. I have had but one letter from Stefan, and I believe that was written before he left, though it was delivered a few days later. I refuse to let myself worry. He came close to death when he was wounded by the wild boar. Since then I have lived every day as it comes and shall do while we both live. Happiness is too precious to let our fears cloud it, Katherine.'

''Tis true that life and death go hand in hand. Marguerite has lost her husband, and she is younger than you, I believe?'

'Orlando was quite a bit older than her,' Elona said. 'She loved him truly, but I do not think it was a great passion on her part. She was very young and innocent, and had seen nothing of the world when she married. I have hope that she will marry again one day—this time to a man she loves as I love Stefan. And as you love Alain.' Elona gave her a look full of mischief. 'I am not wrong, am I? You seemed so anxious for his sake that I thought it must be for love of him?'

'I would not have him know it,' Katherine confessed, smiling at her companion. 'But I fell in love with him when he first opened his eyes and looked at me.'

'You mean when your dragon felled him with her money-bag?'

Katherine laughed ruefully. 'I know that is what he calls my poor Maria—but she thought he meant to kill me.'

Elona laughed huskily; she was clearly amused by the confession. 'He told Stefan about it when they met briefly in London. You knew he came there on the King's business?' Katherine nodded. 'I think that was when he warned Stefan to expect a message from him—when they arranged that they would both fight for King Richard if need be.'

'I pray that it will not be necessary,' Katherine said in a voice that throbbed with passion. 'If He hath mercy, He will send them both back to us unharmed. I know that it is foolish of me to hope that Alain loves me as I love him, but I would see him safely home.'

'You wrong yourself, Katherine. Alain will be fortunate if he secures you for his bride.'

Katherine flushed and bent over her needlework. How could Alain love her when there were so many lovely women from whom he might take his pick? Elona saw her with affectionate eyes, but Katherine knew she could never lay claim to beauty.

'As to that, we must wait and see. For the moment I care only for the safety of those we love.'

'Amen to that,' Elona said and laid down her needlework. 'But I know that Stefan will come back. You see, although we have two sons, I do not yet have my daughter—and it was foretold that we should have two sons and a daughter.'

'And you believe in the prophecy?'

Katherine looked at her in surprise. She knew that it was some years since Elona had given birth to her twin sons—could she really believe that she would bear a daughter one day?

'I have always believed it,' Elona said and she smiled contentedly. 'And you must not worry too much for Alain. I am sure that he will come back to you when Richard is rightfully acknowledged as king once more.'

'I pray that you are right,' Katherine said. 'And now if you will excuse me, there is something I must do.'

Leaving her embroidery frame, she got up and walked from the room, making her way to her own bedchamber. There, she closed the door and locked it, before taking out the scrap of parchment bearing the verse that Alain had sent to her. Her first reaction had been to hide it, but now she realised that it might be all she ever had of him and she pressed it to her lips.

'May God keep you safe,' she said passionately and tucked the letter inside her bodice close to her heart. 'Come back to us, my love—come back to me, for I do not know how I shall bear it if you do not.'

'This arm pains me like the devil,' Alain muttered. 'It was but the merest scratch, but I think it must have taken harm.'

'You should not have ignored it,' Stefan told him with a frown. 'Infection may fell the strongest man. Sit still while I look at it, my brother—if there is poison we must cleanse it.'

'With a hot iron?' Alain pulled a face. In the Holy Land he had received a wound to his shoulder, which the Hospitallers had cauterised, and the cure had hurt far worse than his arm hurt now. 'Nay, it will heal soon enough.'

'Cowardly talk,' Stefan said and laughed, for he was no stranger to pain and had been to hell and back himself after the wild boar had gored him some years earlier. 'Let me look at your arm, for I have made it my interest to know something of these things…' Ignoring his brother's frowns, he opened up the bandages and looked at the wound, probing the open flesh ruthlessly. 'It is deeper than you told me, but I see no sign of infection. You have been lucky, and this salve Elona made for me should help the pain.'

Alain pulled a face, but the salve was cooling and he could

not but admire the way his brother administered it and rebound the wound with clean dressings.

'You seem to have a gift for healing, Stefan.'

'Nay, I merely follow what I have been taught by your mother, Alain. She has the true gift and we have all been glad of it, I think.'

'You speak more truly than you know. Had it not been so, I believe Katherine would have died at that inn, for despite Maria's devotion she did not know how to help her mistress.'

'And Katherine means a great deal to you, does she not?'

'Enough that I would have felt her loss had she died,' Alain replied, looking serious. He was still uncertain in his mind concerning both his feelings and Katherine's. 'I promised to write to her and she will think me faithless, for I have sent her but one poor poem. It has been too difficult to write since we encountered those brigands on the road.'

'We were unfortunate to be attacked by such rogues,' Stefan replied with a frown. 'Richard has regained his throne with no more than a few skirmishes—and for you to be injured in such a way when we were returning home is ill luck. They might have set upon any common traveller and to shoot at you from the safety of the forest was a scurvy trick. That arrow might have killed you had it struck its target, which was your back. If you had not turned the moment you did…'

'It was your timely warning that saved me.'

Stefan's brow creased, his expression angry. 'I should have been more watchful, but I believed all danger past. My one thought was to return home as quickly as possible so that we might bring the ladies to London for Richard's coronation. It makes me angry to know that you were injured by common thieves. I had no reason to suspect such an attack.'

'If they were brigands,' Alain replied, looking thoughtful. 'I believe it more likely that they had lain in wait for us, Stefan—and for no other. I was their intended victim and the arrow was meant for my back, not my arm.'

'You think the attempt on your life was simply that—they wanted you dead? Then they were not common outlaws, but assassins sent by your enemy.'

'Yes, I believe it is so,' Alain replied. 'If I were dead, Katherine would be more vulnerable. If Ravenshurst is behind this, as I suspect, he hoped to take us by surprise and be rid of the main obstacle in his path.'

'I know a little of the man,' Stefan said and his mouth curled in a sneer of dislike. 'The family is near to ruin, for the father was a foolish man who squabbled with his neighbours. Shortly before his death some years back, he fell foul of Prince John's men and was fined a huge sum. I think it near beggared him to pay it and Ravenshurst will have little or no inheritance on his return.'

'That may explain why he is so desperate to get his hands on Katherine's treasure.' Alain shook his head as Stefan's brows rose. 'It is a precious relic, I can say no more—except that men might pay a king's ransom for it.'

A wry grimace touched Stefan's mouth. 'King Richard hath pledged a vast sum for his freedom, and more besides. There are some who believe that he has tossed away his birthright, though he denies his oath was binding for it was taken under duress. 'Tis certain he will fight rather than surrender his kingdom.'

'It was a sorry business,' Alain agreed, for Richard had been forced to do homage to the Emperor for Burgundy and some whispered that his promise also gave Henry of Germany suzerainty over England. 'We must thank God that he is safely returned home and pray that we shall have peace at last in England.'

'With Richard on the throne?' Stefan smiled wryly. 'He is not called lionhearted for nothing, Alain. Much as I honour him, I know his temper too well. I dare swear that we shall be at war again within a year, perhaps less.'

'You will not answer the call?'

'Not I—nor will I fight on foreign soil again,' Stefan said. 'I was obliged to rally to Richard's aid this time, for his cause was right—but I have no love of war. I want to live peacefully with my wife and sons.'

'You are wise,' Alain said and looked thoughtful. 'Had I a wife, I think I might feel as you do—but I am not sure even then that I shall settle for a peaceful life.'

'Does ambition burn as brightly in you as ever?'

'Ambition—nay, I would not name it so. It is merely the desire to prove my worth, brother.'

'As a young, untried youth there was something to prove,' Stefan agreed. 'But you have fought in many battles. What can you have to prove now, Alain?'

Alain smiled, but shook his head. It would be impossible to explain his feeling that it was his sword that had won the battles—the sword his brother had given him, and that he truly believed had magical powers. He was afraid that without his sword he might be found lacking, a mere man, and not the mighty warrior the bards had named him in their tales. As a young man he had longed to do great deeds and win glory in battle, but he had discovered that war meant only death and suffering and brought no ease or satisfaction to his soul.

'In truth I do not know,' he said at last, for Stefan was eyeing him curiously. 'Perhaps nothing…'

'You search for something,' Stefan said thoughtfully. 'I see it in your eyes. I have felt as you do, brother, but I found what I lacked in love. Elona filled the emptiness inside me and I need nothing more than my wife and children, and to live in peace and comfort with them.'

'Mayhap I could find that same content with Katherine,' Alain said. 'Yet there is a need inside me that I cannot explain—perhaps it will never be met. I hoped that I would be a part of restoring Jerusalem to Christian rule, but it was not to be.'

'You feel that you failed?'

'Perhaps…how can we know what history will make of what we did there?'

Stefan saw that there was an aching need in his brother, but he could only hope that his feelings for Katherine would show him how to find happiness.

'Come, if you are rested, we should continue our journey. The Lady Alayne will not want to miss the King's coronation…'

'We shall go to see Richard crowned for the second time,' Alayne said decisively as soon as the messenger had delivered his welcome news. 'It will give us all the chance to visit the silk merchants and indulge ourselves.' She saw that Katherine looked uncertain and held out her hand to her. 'I speak of you as well as my daughters. You have made no complaint about wearing Marguerite's old clothes, but now you shall have new ones.'

'But…I have no money to pay for them,' Katherine said and blushed. 'Alain gave me my cloak and you have already given me so much. I cannot take more from you, my lady.'

'My son sent me some bales of material to use as I would, and that will provide some of the clothes we all need for winter. But I think a richer colour would suit your colouring and we shall buy something special. You must and shall have a new gown for the King's coronation,' Alayne said. 'It will be my pleasure to pay for it and I shall be offended if you refuse my gift.'

'Indeed, you must have a new gown for the occasion,' Marguerite said as Katherine looked uneasy. 'We shall all have them. It is a time for celebration and pleasure.'

Katherine was silenced. To argue further would seem churlish, but she was conscious of being beholden to her hostess, and it made her determined to do something about her situation as soon as she was able.

'I can only thank you,' she said shyly. 'I wish that I might do something to repay you…'

'Nonsense! Your company is recompense enough. I have enjoyed having you with us.' Alayne smiled. The news that had reached them only that morning was all that she could hope. Her instincts had been right. Alain had received a slight wound, but his arm was recovering. Both he and Stefan had arranged to meet them on the road and would swell their escort. 'God has been good to me, Katherine. Let me give what I can in return for all that I have.'

'But you give so much to others,' Katherine said and smiled at her. 'You saved me when I was close to death.'

'I nursed you,' Alayne replied. 'It was God who saved you, Katherine. You must never forget that all healing comes from Him. If I have a gift that helps me to help others, it comes from our Lord. If I did not believe that most truly, I could not continue to minister to the sick as I do.'

'Yes, of course,' Katherine said, for she knew that the Lady Alayne would never accept the praise for herself. 'But you were there when I needed you and I shall always thank God that you were sent to me.'

'Indeed, it was fortunate that I was already on my way to London—and it might not have been so, for we had almost decided to wait another three days…' She smiled at Katherine. 'You see, it was our Lord's intervention that brought me to you.'

'Yes, I see that you are right,' Katherine agreed. 'But you said that Sir Alain had been wounded in the arm…'

'Stefan's letter says that it is merely a flesh wound and he has applied a salve to it. Once we meet them on the road I shall be able to discover if there is more that needs to be done.'

'I believed there was hardly any fighting,' Katherine said. 'Sir Alain was unfortunate to be wounded.'

'It was not in the skirmish with Prince John's men,' Alayne replied with a frown. 'Stefan says that someone fired an arrow at him from the forest as they were returning home—' She broke off as she saw Katherine turn pale. 'What is wrong? You are not feeling ill?'

Katherine shook her head. Had Alain been attacked because he had rescued her from brigands in Italy and brought her here? Was it because of what she carried that an attempt to murder him had been made?

'No, I am not ill,' she replied, controlling her emotions with difficulty. 'It is nothing. I shall be perfectly able to accompany you to the King's coronation, my lady.'

Nothing would keep her here when Alain was hurt! She knew that she would not rest until she had seen him for herself.

Katherine was there with the de Banewulf family to see Richard wearing his crown in Winchester's great cathedral, and joined in the celebrations afterwards. All of them were wearing new gowns, but Katherine believed that hers was the most splendid. Fashioned of a rich, dark green with a surcote of silver, it suited her colouring, and the sparkle in her eyes had made her almost beautiful.

Her spirits had risen the moment she saw Alain and realised that, although still suffering from pain, he was not seriously wounded.

'It is merely a flesh wound,' he had told his anxious mother when she insisted on looking at his arm immediately, 'and Stefan's salve hath already eased the pain.'

Having inspected it for herself, Alayne announced that she was pleased with what she saw and gave her son a small measure of the medicine she always carried with her to aid his recovery.

Katherine was able to smile at him without betraying the anxiety she had felt, though she asked anxiously if he thought the attack on him had been because of her father's treasure.

'Nay, I do not think it,' Alain lied to comfort her. 'I dare say it was merely common thieves thinking to rob unwary travellers.'

She had pretended to believe him, though she suspected that he was trying to shield her from the truth. If her father's discovery had almost cost Alain his life, then it was time she was rid of her burden. It had been pleasant to dally at Banewulf, but she would tell Alain that she must leave for France as soon as the celebrations were over.

The church bells rang out joyfully all over the city. King Richard had once more asserted his right to the English throne and his people were glad to have him back, for few had prospered under John's rule.

Maypoles had been erected in the streets and people danced for the pleasure, for many of Richard's wealthy nobles had distributed gifts of food and ale to the poor of the city.

Katherine stood with Alain, Stefan and Elona to watch some mummers performing a play in the market square, laughing at the antics of the fool with his pig's bladder. They had been to a horse fair that morning, buying and eating hot pies as they wandered round the side shows and marvelled at the wares the pedlars offered. Katherine had spent some minutes looking at the stall selling holy relics, a frown creasing her smooth forehead.

'I do not know why people buy them,' she said to Alain as she turned away from the stall. 'If every fragment of the Cross offered for sale was genuine, it would have taken thirty men to carry it—and the saints can surely never have had so many fingers.'

Alain was amused by her observation, but then he saw that the thoughts underlying it were serious. 'You are thinking of your father's discovery?'

'Yes, it has been much on my mind of late,' she said and looked up at him, her anxiety plain. 'How can I hope to prove it is genuine without my father's notes?'

Alain hesitated, then, 'Perhaps I should speak to Ravenshurst?'

'Would it not be dangerous? I do not wish you to risk your life, Alain. I think it might be best if I return to France. I might then ask my uncle his advice.'

'It is strange that Baron Grunwald hath not replied to my father's letter,' Alain said, looking thoughtful. 'I wonder—' He broke off as a young squire wearing colours of dark green and gold approached them, his hand resting on the hilt of his sword. The youth came up to them and bowed respectfully to Katherine. Alain glared at him. 'Yes, what do you want, sirrah?'

'May I have permission to address the Lady Katherine of Grunwald, sir?'

'Who sent you?' Alain's eyes narrowed in suspicion.

'My master is Philip of Rotherham, sir. He is the lady's uncle through her late mother.'

'Yes, I know of him,' Alain replied, and laid a warning hand on Katherine's arm. 'I sent word that I wished to see him and received no reply. How can I be sure that you are who you claim to be?'

'I have a locket that the lady may have seen before—there was another just like it. If I may present it?'

'Give it to me.' Alain held out his hand to receive the locket, which was beautiful and intricately worked in silver. He showed it to Katherine, who gasped and turned pale. She looked so stricken that he reached out his hand to steady her lest she swoon. 'You have seen this locket before?'

'I have seen its twin,' Katherine said, picking it up to look at it more closely. She opened the clasp with trembling fingers and looked inside. 'When my mother died my father placed a piece of her hair inside her locket and kept it with him always. It was in his baggage and lost…but his had a tiny dent and this has not.'

'You may address the lady,' Alain said to the squire. 'What is your master's message for his niece?'

'Sir Philip begs that she will visit him at his lodgings, which are but two streets away. He journeyed here for the coronation, but he is sick nigh unto death and would see the Lady Katherine before he dies.'

'Do you wish to see him?' Alain's eyes dwelt on her face. She looked pale and anxious, the becoming colour from the morning air quite fled from her cheeks. 'You may refuse if you had rather not—for you owe him nothing.'

'My master begs that the lady will look kindly upon his request, for he wishes to make reparation for the wrong that he hath done her,' said the youth almost pleadingly.

'I shall see him,' Katherine decided. 'Not for the reparation that ought to have been my father's—but for my mother's sake. I know that she loved her brother dearly and it broke her heart when they quarrelled. Yes, I shall see him for her sake.'

'Very well, I shall come with you,' Alain said and called to Stefan that they would meet them later at their lodgings in the city. 'Lead the way, lad, for we are but strangers here.'

Katherine looked up at him, and he saw the anxious, slightly apprehensive expression in her eyes.

'You are afraid of what you may find?'

'A little nervous,' she admitted. 'I have never seen my uncle and know only what my mother told me of him. I think they were very alike, and he loved her—perhaps too much.'

'Then it is right that you see him,' Alain agreed. 'If he has suffered for his unkindness to your mother, this is his chance to reconcile his mind and relieve the burden on his soul.'

Katherine was holding the locket tightly in her hand, her heart pounding. Philip of Rotherham had been but a distant figure all her life, someone who seemed to exist only as a dream, but seeing the locket, which was the twin to the one he had given her mother, had suddenly made him very real. What would he be like? Would he still be angry that his sister had disobeyed him and married the man she loved? What would he feel towards his sister's daughter?

They had stopped outside a house. Katherine shivered in the chill wind that seemed to have sprung up of a sudden. The squire stepped up and rapped on the door, which was opened by an older man who might have been a steward by his robes. He nodded his head, his eyes moving over Katherine.

'I am Sigmund of Rotherham, lady.'

'And my uncle's steward?'

He inclined his head, his eyes intent on her face, searching it intently. 'You are not like your mother, lady.'

'No, I am told I favour my father in looks.'

'Aye, I remember him. Please follow me.' He glanced at Alain. 'Sir Alain—forgive us that we did not answer your letter more fairly, but my master is ill. He should not have made this journey, but he wanted to see Richard crowned once more. And when he was told that you were here, my Lady Katherine, he hoped to make his peace with you.'

'I have no quarrel with your master, sir.'

'Then perhaps you will consent to see him in his chamber, for his illness hath laid him on his bed and he cannot rise to meet you. The surgeon bled him an hour ago and he is very weak, though less feverish than before.'

'Yes, I am most willing to go to him.' She laid a hand on Alain's arm, as he would have accompanied her. 'Nay, it may be best if you stay here. I do not fear that I shall come to harm in this house.'

'I shall wait for you—but call out if all is not as it appears.'

'I thank you for your patience, sir.'

Alain nodded, watching as she followed the elderly steward up the stairs to the gallery above. It was a good solid house

of the kind owned by wealthy merchants and rented out to
men of rank at times like this, when the city was full of visitors. He had heard that Philip of Rotherham was a wealthy
man, though he knew little of him or his fortune, but perhaps
some good could come to Katherine through this visit.

Katherine walked the length of the upstairs gallery. The
wooden floors were covered with rushes to soften the sound
of their feet, and the walls were of a deep golden stone, which
was here and there hung with tapestry to keep out the cold.

The steward paused outside a door and turned to look at
Katherine.

'You may find the room airless and unpleasant, for the
doctors have ordered that a fire is kept going at all times, and
the windows are on no account to be opened.' He shook his
head sadly. 'I do not believe that my master has long to live.
I am glad that he has this chance to unburden his soul before
he dies.'

'I do not think my mother ever stopped loving him.' She
smiled at the steward, lifted the heavy iron latch and went in,
catching her breath at the heat and stench inside the room. It
was dark as well as stuffy and she had difficulty in seeing the
man lying in the large bed, approaching it with some apprehension. 'Sir…Uncle Philip…'

Now she was close enough to see his face. His skin was a
sickly yellow colour, the flesh stretched tight over his cheek-
bones, his eyes sunken. He had opened his eyes now and was
staring at her. She went closer so that he might see her. He
stared at her as if hoping to see another face, and a sigh left
his lips as he realised his hopes were unfounded. Katherine
was not his sister born again, but a very different person.

'I am Katherine,' she said. 'You asked to see me?'

'Katherine…' His lips moved awkwardly as if he found it difficult to form the words. 'My sister's child…'

'Yes, Uncle. I am here.'

'Give me your hand, let me touch you?'

Katherine obeyed and his fingers curled loosely about her wrist. They felt warm and damp, the flesh wasted almost to the bone. She felt a sharp pang of pity for his plight. How terrible it was to see any man reduced to this.

'Are you in pain, sir? May I do anything to help you? You might be more comfortable if the room were less warm…'

'No, no, leave it, child,' he told her. 'It pleases the physician to torture me for my sins, and I must bear it. I shall die soon and they cannot prevent it. If their treatment hastens my death, then so much the better. I have not been a good man, Katherine, and this sickness that eats away at me is a punishment from God—that is what they tell me and perhaps they are right.'

'I am sorry for your suffering,' she said. 'I know someone who might make you more comfortable even if it is not possible to make you better.'

'Nay, for if I suffer now, mayhap I shall not go to hell but win a chance for forgiveness.' He raised himself slightly from the pillows. 'I would ask your forgiveness for what I did to *her,* Katherine. I have wronged my sister and her child. Your rightful inheritance is already yours, the lawyers will see to that when I am dead. I have no wife or son—all that I have is yours. I ask only your forgiveness for the wrong I did your mother.'

'I cannot speak for my mother,' Katherine said. 'But she always spoke kindly to me of you, Uncle. I cannot think she hated you. I believe she sorrowed for the breach between you.'

He sank back against his pillows with a sigh, as if the effort had been too much for him, and she saw a tear squeeze from the corner of his eye and roll down his cheek. For a moment he lay in silence, gathering his strength, and then he looked at her once more.

'I loved her too well,' he said. 'The love I bore Helen was too passionate, too intense. It was not the kind of love a brother should have for a sister—do you understand me, Katherine?'

'I believe that I do, Uncle.' Her mother had given no hint of it, but Katherine's father had once said something that seemed to hint at some mystery in the past. Looking down at the sick man, she saw that he was tortured by his memories. 'Do not grieve, for I know that she forgave you.'

His hands worked on the coverlet, clearly still unable to release his tortured past. 'I begged her to love me, as I loved her. I wanted to lie with her. My body burned for her, but it was a terrible sin, and she refused me when I told her that she was the only woman I should ever love. I kissed her on the mouth and tried to force myself on her, but she fought me with all her strength and in the end I let her go. I spent the night in prayer for my sins, and in the morning she had gone. She went to your father, who had offered for her and been refused by me. She married him without my consent and so I held back what was rightfully hers. Now you shall have that and all that was mine. You will be wealthy beyond your dreams, Katherine. Men are evil, greedy creatures. Take care that you marry a man who will be kind to you.'

He was fretful, a little flushed as his fever seemed to return. She guessed that his mind was wandering in the past so that he hardly knew whom he spoke to.

'Yes, I promise that I shall marry only a good man, Uncle.'

For a moment he was silent and then, when he looked at her again, she saw that his mind was a little calmer.

'I have heard that you are under the protection of Sir Alain de Banewulf. The family is respected and I believe Sir Alain to be a good man. Will he marry you, Katherine?'

'I—I do not know,' she said. 'We are friends and he has been good to me. Were it not for Sir Alain, I might be dead.'

'Then I hope that you will find happiness with him. I have suffered for my sins, Katherine, and you see before you a miserable wretch who never knew a moment's peace after he drove his sister away.'

'Rest in peace, Uncle.' Katherine bent to kiss his cheek. His skin was papery thin and dry to the touch, and the stench of neglect was on him. She thought of Lady Alayne's sweet-smelling sheets, and the way she had been cared for when she was ill. 'Will you let me send someone to nurse you, Uncle? It might be that we could ease your suffering.'

'Nay, child. I shall not see you again. I have made my peace with you and may die now. Do not come again. Tomorrow my servants will take me home. I may live until we get there or I may die on the road. I care not either way. Go now, Katherine. You will hear soon of my death and the inheritance that is yours.'

Katherine's eyes stung with tears. She looked down at him sadly, feeling the waste of years, the pain and suffering he had endured because of a misplaced love.

'She understood, Uncle,' she whispered softly close to his ear and kissed him. 'And she never ceased to love you.'

She heard his sharply drawn breath, but turned and walked from the room without a backward look. The hurt went too deep, the regret too bitter to be washed away by the salt of tears. Perhaps if her uncle had sought forgiveness when she was still a child things might have been different. Had her father received what was owed him, he could have restored Grunwald and might never have set out on his travels. He might even have made friends with his wife's brother.

But it was too late for such regrets. She knew that her uncle spoke truly when he said that he would live only a short time. He would be fortunate if he died in his own bed.

Alain was waiting for her in the hall downstairs, standing gazing out at the street where the revellers were still dancing and celebrating the King's return, but he turned as she entered, his eyes searching her pale face.

'It was hard for you. I should have been with you.'

'Nay, for he spoke freely and he might not have done had you been there to witness his confession,' she said and held back a sigh of regret. 'I am merely sad at the wasted years and the unhappiness a foolish quarrel caused so long ago.' She spoke of it as a mere quarrel, for she did not want to reveal her uncle's shame at the moment, and because he had so sincerely repented, was truly ashamed of his wickedness, she was prepared to forgive him. Indeed, it was a terrible thing he had done, though driven by a love that went beyond what it ought.

'Shall I take you home now, Katherine—to Banewulf?'

'We shall talk as we return to our lodgings,' she said and turned to thank her uncle's steward before they left.

'You will hear from me soon, my lady,' he told her. 'For I know my master's wishes.'

'Yes, thank you. I am not sure where I shall be in the near future—but a letter to Banewulf will reach me.' He bowed respectfully to her and she took Alain's arm as they went out.

Alain looked down at her strained face as they gained the

street and began to walk slowly back towards the market place. 'Your inheritance has been restored to you?'

'And much more, I believe. It seems that my uncle has been pleased to leave all that he owns to me as reparation for the wrong that he did my mother.'

'You will be a wealthy woman,' Alain said. 'You must think carefully about the future, Katherine.'

'Yes, indeed, my uncle begged me to marry only if the man I chose was kind.' She felt heat in her cheeks and could not look at Alain, for she would not tell him what more her uncle had said concerning her marriage. 'But that is for the future and not something that need concern us for the moment. I wished to speak to you concerning my father's discovery. What do you think I should do with it? In truth, I think it a dangerous thing to own and would be rid of it if I can—but I owe it to my father to do what I am able to place it in the right hands.' If only she knew where that was! She had thought long and hard and still had no clear decision.

'For the moment it is safe enough in my father's strong-room,' Alain said and looked thoughtful. 'I believe I shall speak to Ravenshurst and ask him if he has the notes and if he will accept payment for them. It can do no harm and may help us to come to a settlement of this affair.'

'Do you think he would give them up?' Katherine looked at him earnestly.

'He must surely know by now that he is unlikely to get his hands on the cup,' Alain said. 'And I know that his estate is deeply in debt. It may be that he will bargain for the notes and documents—if he has them. Of course they could have been lost or destroyed.'

'Yes, I understand that, but if he has them…I could pay him

now,' Katherine said. Her eyes were anxious as she gazed at him. 'But I do not want you to put yourself in danger, Alain. I would rather throw the cup into a deep river than see harm come to you.'

'I beg you not to think of it,' Alain said swiftly. 'If your father's documents prove that it is indeed the cup our Lord used…it is too precious to be wantonly destroyed. Anyone who did that would be cursed forever. And rightly so. We may not lay this burden down, Katherine. It is our duty and our privilege to see this to the end.' There was a fervent note in his voice and she guessed that this meant more to him than an idle gesture. Perhaps because of the loss of Jerusalem, which she knew had pricked him sorely.

Katherine looked at him unhappily. 'It is a heavy burden to bear. I have wished that my father had never discovered it.'

'Where was it?' Alain asked. 'You have never explained that to me.'

'No, for I do not know exactly. I know that it was buried in a plain casket of bronze, and that it was wrapped in layers of cloth, together with a faded parchment that told how one of Christ's disciples had taken the cup. He had given it to a trusted friend for safekeeping, but it was stolen and then lost, lying undiscovered for years. Whoever wrote the words on that scrap of parchment did so many years later, according to my father. It was near Jerusalem that it was discovered, but only my father knew exactly where, though I believe it was some kind of tomb or catacomb.'

'Did he write down all the details of his search?'

'I believe he must have done so. He spent hours making notes, and, as you have seen from the fragment you have, they are very detailed.'

'Then Ravenshurst has the key to this,' Alain said. 'Unless the notes have been lost…'

'The casket was lost with my father's baggage. He believed the cup would be safer with me, and I carried it in a small cloth bag beneath my tunic until my room was searched in Italy, and then I gave it to Maria. She kept it with her always until she returned it to me at Banewulf and I placed it in Sir Ralph's strongroom.'

Alain nodded his understanding. 'Ravenshurst may have destroyed the papers in his frustration, but I think he has them still. He must understand the significance of what they describe. Why else would he have followed you thus far?'

'I dare say that you are right,' Katherine said and looked at him anxiously. 'So you think we should try to buy them from him before we do anything else?'

'Buy or steal them,' Alain said and gave her a wicked grin that would have made her laugh had the matter not been so serious. 'I have already sent men to following him, Katherine. He will know that his ruse of using men dressed to appear as brigands has not fooled us, and he will be waiting for our next move. I shall ask for a meeting on common ground and then we shall see…' He hesitated, then met her steady gaze. 'I had kept it from you but perhaps you should know that I suspect Ravenshurst's men of trying to kill me.'

She nodded as she accepted what she had always known in her heart. 'I thank you for telling me, for I had suspected it before this.'

'I think it best that you know the truth so that you may be wary in the future.'

Katherine knew he was right. 'And my uncle of Grunwald? What of him? Should I go to him for advice?'

'I think we should wait a little longer for his reply to my father's letter,' Alain said. 'To make the journey to France for no good reason would be foolish until we have settled with Ravenshurst. You must certainly see your uncle, but there can be no hurry.'

'No, I suppose not,' Katherine agreed. 'After all, I do not know if my uncle still lives…' The memory of Philip of Rotherham's wasted body was fresh in her mind. It was possible that her father's brother was also dead. 'And if your father has written to him, he may have good reason for not replying. Perhaps I should wait until he agrees to see me.'

Alain's eyes dwelled for some moments on her face. In truth, he was growing less and less inclined to part from her. He hardly understood this feeling inside him, but knew that it was unlike any he had experienced for a woman before this. Sometimes, when she had that teasing smile in her eyes, his body burned for her and he longed to make love to her, but at others, when she seemed vulnerable, he knew an overwhelming desire to protect her from all harm. It was a new and strange sensation, one that he had not experienced before.

Was the feeling he had for Katherine the love of which the troubadours sung? He had thought it merely a myth, a poet's dream of Utopia. Lust was a fleeting need that burned to ashes all too soon, but romantic love was a far sweeter thing. If that truly existed, if he might find it with Katherine…ah, then he would be fortunate. Sometimes he believed that he did indeed feel something special for her, and that he needed nothing more of life than to live with her in content as Stefan did with his wife and family—but at other times the restlessness was still strong in him. Why could he not be content? Surely he had seen enough of wandering?

'We shall return to Banewulf with my mother and Marguerite,' he said. 'I should like the chance to spend a little time with you, Katherine. It seems that there has always been something to take me from you since we came to England. Now that Richard is secure there is little for me to do for the moment and I shall spend some time at Banewulf with you and my family.'

Katherine gave him a tremulous smile, her heart beating faster as she saw the expression in his eyes. When he looked at her that way she could almost believe that he loved her as she loved him.

Chapter Eight

'We go home tomorrow,' Elona said as she and Katherine sat together in the warm sunshine, watching her twin sons playing tag in the gardens. The sound of their voices as they shouted and laughed at some mischief was a joyous sound and made Katherine wistful. Would she ever know the joy of a family of her own? 'We have been away for longer than we intended and Stefan has business that needs his attention. I shall miss you, Katherine. I wish you will not go to live in France with your uncle, but stay here with our family.'

There was a naughty gleam in Elona's eyes, which made Katherine blush, for she knew what was in the other's mind, and indeed, these past ten days since their return, Alain had seemed to be paying court to her. His smiles for her had been warm and merry, his words teasing but delicately laced with innuendo that she could not mistake, especially since he had written her more love poems.

'I must visit my uncle of Grunwald soon,' Katherine told her. 'It is only right and proper that I should, but I have been very happy here.'

Sometimes she tried to remember her life at Grunwald, but it seemed distant and far away. Even her travels with her father had faded into memories that were softer and sweeter for time. In her heart she knew that she wanted to stay here at Banewulf until she was wed and then go with Alain to his own manor—but did he really mean to ask her to be his wife?

Something made her look up at that moment, and she saw that he was walking their way, clearly intending to join them. Her heart beat faster. How could she hope that he would love her? He was all that a knight should be: tall, strong, clever and handsome. He could surely take his pick of women for his wife, and there were many far more lovely than Katherine.

Since their return from Winchester he had left off his soldier's garb of short tunic and braes and was wearing a longer gown of rich material such as he had worn for the King's celebrations. She noticed that he was rubbing his arm, and guessed that it was sore after his exercise, for it had not quite recovered from the arrow wound. He had spent some hours training with his brother that morning, and she and Elona had watched for a while, amused by the contest. The two brothers were well matched and delighted in trying to best one another, though they were as true friends as you might find.

'So this is where you are hiding yourselves,' Alain said with a teasing look at them. 'What mischief are you plotting now?'

'I was telling Katherine that we go home tomorrow,' Elona said, and then, with a lift of her head, 'Also that she should not think of going to live with her uncle in France.' Her eyes gleamed with mischief.

'It was to bring Katherine news of her uncle that I sought you out,' Alain said and frowned as if he were not best pleased about something. 'I have news for you at last, Katherine.'

'Then I shall leave you alone to talk,' Elona said and rose to her feet. She called to her sons, bending to say something to them that set them laughing and running ahead of her towards the house.

Alain sat down on the bench beside Katherine. 'I thought you would wish to know that we have had three messages this morning—all of them concerning you.'

'Three messages concerning me? I did not realise I had become so important,' Katherine said and laughed softly.

'The first and saddest is that Philip of Rotherham passed away at his home the same day that he arrived there. His steward has written to say that he will keep all in order for you should you wish to visit the property that is now yours. And he will prepare an inventory of all your uncle's wealth so that the lawyers may sign it and be satisfied that everything is as it should be.'

'My poor uncle,' Katherine said and made the sign of the cross over her breast. 'I pray that he may rest in peace.'

'Amen to that,' Alain said, an odd look in his eyes. 'So you are wealthy in your own right now, Katherine. Your uncle has not appointed a guardian for you—but I dare say your uncle of Grunwald is your guardian under the law. And that brings me to our next communication.'

'You have heard from Uncle Robert?'

'His steward writes to say that your uncle is from home but will write to you when he returns.'

'Away from home so many months?' Katherine wrinkled her brow in thought. 'Does that not seem strange to you?'

'I have discussed it with my father and he agrees with me that it sounds as if something may not be as it ought. It may simply be that your uncle does not wish to be bothered with his brother's daughter or perhaps he has been on a long journey somewhere…' Alain rubbed his arm, then became aware of what he was doing and stopped. 'My arm has not quite recovered from the arrow wound, but it is merely a nuisance. I think we were wise to delay your journey, Katherine.'

'Yes, for if my uncle was not there…'

'We do not know what we should find,' Alain agreed. 'So that brings me to my last message, and this is perhaps the most significant. Ravenshurst has asked for a meeting in London. He pretends to be unsure what my letter meant, but says he has managed to rescue something that belongs to you.'

Katherine's eyes took fire. 'That must mean that he has my father's notes! And it sounds as if he may be prepared to bargain for them.'

'Yes, I am certain that it does,' Alain said and smiled as he saw her excitement. He did not know how it was, but she seemed to have become a woman in a matter of weeks, and a lovely one at that. When he looked at her now it was almost impossible to remember the small brown child she had been when he rescued her from Ravenshurst's men. Gazing into her face, he had a sudden and urgent desire to kiss her, and without really knowing what he did, he reached out to touch her cheek with his fingertips. She did not draw back, but continued to sit gazing up at him with those brilliant eyes. He reached out for her, drawing her into his arms, his lips seeking hers in a kiss that was soft and gentle and only gradually deepened to passion. Yet when he let her go he found that he was shaken. He spoke from the heart, his doubts fleeing in that moment. 'I believe I have fallen in love with you, Katherine…'

She pressed her fingers to her lips and he saw that her hand was trembling. Then she clasped her hands together and raised her head proudly. 'I think you merely tease me, sir,' she said. 'For how can you love me? I am not beautiful or clever…'

'Hush, Katherine.' He pressed a finger to her lips and smiled at her tenderly. 'You wrong yourself, sweet Kate. You have a quick, clever mind, and though you are not beautiful as the world defines beauty, you are certainly lovely to me.'

'Then perhaps you do love me,' she said and laughed. 'For do they not say that beauty is in the eye of the beholder?'

'My love hath grown on me slowly,' Alain admitted, believing honesty best. Katherine would not be wooed with sweet meaningless words. 'At first I thought you but a thin, plain child, but you have changed in these past weeks, and I have come to appreciate you for many things. I always felt warmth towards you, though I will admit that it was not love at first sight. Can you forgive me for my plain speaking?'

Katherine's dark eyes sparkled with humour. 'If you had been anything less honest I should have thought you false, sir—but now I am inclined to believe you.'

'I have wanted to speak these past several days, but your uncle's bequest made me hesitate. I would not have you believe I value you for your uncle's fortune, Katherine.'

'I do not think it. You have wealth enough for any man, and, besides, I know you do not care for it so very much.' Katherine gazed up at him. 'I have sensed a hunger in you, Alain. I know not what it is you seek, but I think you have not yet found it—even in our love.'

'Do not blame me for my restless spirit,' he pleaded as he took her hand and stroked it with his thumb, sending little tingles of pleasure coursing through her body. 'I do most sincerely love you, Kate—but I admit that it will not always keep me by your side. Until this void is filled within me, I will continue to strive to prove myself.'

'But do you not know what is said of you—that you are the truest knight in Christendom? Other men admire you for your bravery in battle, Alain, but you are known as widely for your wisdom and your honour.'

''Tis my sword that won honour on the field of battle, for it hath magic powers of its own—and as for the rest, I am a mere man of no particular merit.'

'You should not think so little of yourself,' Katherine said and felt a prick of sadness that she could not ease that strange ache inside him. 'I know that there is something within you that will not let you rest, my love—but I want only to be by your side when I am needed and to have you love me.'

'You shall always have my love,' he vowed and went down on his knee in front of her. Taking her hand he kissed it and then held it as he looked into her eyes. 'Will you be my wife, Lady Katherine of Grunwald? Will you promise to live with me and love me all our lives? No matter if my wandering feet take me from you and cause you grief?'

'You know that I will,' Katherine said and her heart leaped with joy. His kisses thrilled her and she knew that she would only truly know fulfilment in his arms. 'You took your time to love me, Alain—but I loved you from that first moment, when you opened your eyes and looked at me. Any other man would have been angry after what Maria did, but you laughed and forbade Sir Bryne to harm us. From that moment I loved you, though I fought against the knowledge, for I believed you loved another.'

'If you mean Celestine, she was but a passing fancy, a moment of madness. Such a woman could never hold my heart. Besides, I did not trust her and it is best always to keep an enemy close. Only you have I truly loved, my Katherine.'

'As I love you.'

'Then we shall be wed,' Alain said and, taking her hands, drew her to her feet and into his arms. This time his kiss was hungry and passionate, arousing sweet desire in her. She felt his arms tighten about her, the throb of his need burned her through the rich material of the clothes they wore and she knew a longing to lie with him, to know the true fulfilment of their love. 'I want to make you mine, sweet Kate. I want to feel your flesh close to mine, to join with you in the sweetest coupling of all.' His hand trailed her cheek, the white arch of her neck and came to lie against her breast, making her pulses race.

'Take me now!' Katherine cried, suddenly urgent. He had aroused a need in her so fierce and strong that she longed for its release. 'Let us go somewhere we may be alone…'

Alain gave her one of his wicked grins. 'Oh, how you tempt me, Kate. If I had less respect for you, I would sweep you up and run off with you this minute, but I shall not dishonour you, my love. No other woman hath ever meant as much to me, and we shall wait for our wedding night, though we both burn for it.'

'I am immodest,' Katherine said and blushed. 'But I fear my thoughts have of late all too often been those that do not become a maiden.'

Alain laughed merrily, his eyes dancing with pleasure at her words. By God! She was a woman and a passionate one at that—and he had thought her naught but a child! 'I delight in your immodesty, sweet Kate, and would have you no other way. But should something happen while I am in London…I would not leave you with the possibility that you carry my child, for that would shame you.'

Katherine felt the chill at the nape of her neck. Shivers were running down her spine and she was afraid for him. Ravenshurst's men had already tried to kill him once.

'But you must take me with you! I cannot be parted from you now. We should be married at once and I should accompany you.' She looked up at him, her eyes wide and dark with pleading. 'Please say that you will take me.'

'No! I will not expose you to danger,' Alain said. 'Bryne is to meet me in London, and I have my loyal men to protect me. I shall make this bargain with the Baron, pay him what he demands and return for our wedding.'

'I want to come with you!' She caught his robe, her body urgent against his as she begged. She did not know why, but she was caught by a terrible fear of what might happen if they parted now.

Alain hushed her with a kiss that made her cling to him weakly, tears stinging behind her eyes. 'I love you too much, Katherine. I told you that my love would not always keep me by your side. You must accept that I shall leave you sometimes. It may be that Richard will need me in the future. There are other men who would be content to stay at home if that is what you need for happiness—Bryne for one. I know that he cares for you, and though he has deliberately remained in London and left the field clear for me, he would wed you if you gave him a sign.'

'How can you say such things to me?' She drew away, looking at him with hurt eyes. 'You know that I love only you.'

'Forgive me,' Alain said ruefully. 'But I thought you understood, Kate. I love you with all my heart, but I am not like my father and Stefan—I have not yet fulfilled my destiny. I cannot stay safe at home even if it hurts us both to part.'

Katherine gazed at him, fighting the tears that would shame her. She knew that he had spoken fair to her and that she must not ask too much. There was in him something she could not reach. He was ready to give her a part of himself. She would be his wife, bear his children—but she could not hold him if he would go. Until he had found that thing for which he searched, he would never be at peace.

'Then I must be patient,' she said and smiled at him. 'If you are determined to meet the Baron Ravenshurst alone, then so be it. I shall wait here until you return.'

'You will want to prepare your bride clothes,' Alain said, stroking his thumb over her full bottom lip as it trembled. He kissed her softly. 'Trust me to return for you, sweet Kate. My mother and sister will be delighted to help you fill your bride chest. They would not be pleased with me if I took you away at this time, my love. I promise that I shall come back to you very soon.'

'I shall miss you,' Katherine said, hiding the fear that raged inside her. He was his own man, not to be bound by a woman's tears and pleading, and she must learn to let him go. 'Kiss me again, and tell me that you love me.'

Alain drew her to him. He smiled down at her, gently caressing her cheek before he kissed her. This time his kiss was sweet and tender without the hungry passion of his earlier embrace, and she knew he was controlling himself for her sake. He loved her, wanted her passionately, but still he must be free.

'And now we shall go and tell my mother of our decision—for Elona will have hinted that she knows something and they will be waiting.'

'How could Elona know when I did not?'

'My brother's wife is always ahead of us all,' he said and laughed. 'Believe me, Kate, you may not have known that I meant to ask you to be my wife—but the rest of my family have been certain of it for days.'

'I wish I were not leaving, but we must,' Elona said as she kissed Katherine's cheek. 'We shall come for your wedding. I would not miss it for the world, but Stefan must go home for a time. There is much to be done.'

'I shall miss you,' Katherine said. 'Though Lady Alayne and Marguerite insist that I shall be too busy to miss anyone. We are to send for silks for my bride clothes, but Alain will take the list with him to London. In the meantime we are to visit the summer fair. I am told it comes to Banewulf every year and I may find some materials there, though perhaps not as fine as may be found in London.'

'But you will not need fine clothes all the time. Wait until your husband takes you to his manor, Katherine. You will find there is much to be done. I am never still when we are at home, but here at Banewulf everything is always in order. I dare say it will not be so at Alain's own manor.'

'Lady Alayne is a wonderful chatelaine. She has been teaching me so many things, and she does so much for everyone, the poor of the village as well as her own people.'

Elona agreed, for she, too, was fond of Stefan's stepmother, and they parted on the best of terms. Katherine had already said her goodbyes to Alain the previous day, for he had set out at first light and did not want to wake her so early. She was trying not to be anxious for his sake, but it was not easy. Baron Ravenshurst was a ruthless man and she knew that Alain might well be in some danger.

'Katherine…' She heard Marguerite's voice calling to her and went to meet her. 'My mother has found some material she thinks you could make use of for your working gowns. Come and see if there is something to your liking.'

Katherine followed her to the Lady Alayne's solar where a coffer had been brought down from one of the tower rooms. The lid was open and it spilled over with good woollen cloths in a variety of colours from grey to a deep blue. She was welcomed warmly and told to choose whatever she liked.

'You will need several new tunics and gowns,' Alayne told her. 'We may as well work on something simple until the silk comes for your wedding gown.'

There was no doubting that Alain's family was pleased that she was to be his bride, and the warmth of her welcome into this family made her spirits lift. Alain was well protected by his men, and Sir Bryne would meet him in London. Surely nothing terrible could happen to him—and yet a feeling of unease nagged at her.

She must stop worrying! Alain's arm was almost healed and he was both brave and experienced in matters of conflict. It was unlikely that he would fall into any trap the Baron laid for him.

She must do as the others had told her, give herself up to the pleasure of preparing her bride clothes. Alain could take care of himself. He was a man and a bold, fearless warrior. To cling to him would only annoy him and spoil their understanding.

She must throw off this cloud of unease and enjoy this time before her marriage, for her new friends were determined to make a great fuss of her.

* * *

Was the fair always so crowded? Katherine wondered, looking about her in excitement. The pedlars had set out their wares in a meadow on Sir Ralph's lands as they had for many summers past, and there was much to see and buy. The smell of roasting pig and a spicy pottage that one woman was offering to passers-by was tempting, but Katherine was more interested in the wares of those who sold fine cloth. She had already purchased beads and braid to trim the hem of the tunic she was sewing and she was heading for a stall that sold various trinkets when she saw Lady Alayne beckon to her urgently. She responded immediately, for she realised that something had happened.

'Is anything wrong?'

'I have received a message from my husband. He says that we must go home at once. I am sorry to curtail your pleasure, Katherine, but I believe it to be important. Perhaps we may come again on the morrow. The fair will be here for three days.'

'We must return if Sir Ralph sends for us. What can be so urgent?' She could feel a horrid prickling sensation at the nape of her neck. 'You do not think that something has happened to Alain?'

'No, for I should feel it,' his mother said. 'I believe that this is something that affects you, Katherine.' Alayne looked at her oddly. 'Something in this makes me uneasy. I know not why it should, but I fear for you, my dear.'

'But what could happen to me while I have the protection of your family?' Katherine was surprised because she could see that her future mother-in-law was genuinely concerned for her.

Alayne shook her head. She could not explain, but she sensed that something terrible was about to happen…

* * *

'Katherine…Alayne.' Sir Ralph came towards them as they entered the Great Hall. He looked anxious and ill at ease. 'I sent for you because Katherine's uncle of Grunwald has come to see her.' There was something in his look that warned them to be silent. 'Katherine—this is Baron Grunwald. He hath shown me letters of introduction and I can scarcely doubt them.' His words seemed to hint that he would refute the documents if he could and a chill started at the nape of Katherine's neck.

'Uncle Robert?' Katherine looked beyond Sir Ralph to the tall, thin man standing by the fireplace. She searched her memory, but found she could not recall him. Her uncle had been younger than her father by some years, and a stern, dour man. She had met him only once and the memory was dim, obscured by the years. 'I am pleased to meet you at last, sir.'

'Indeed? You surprise me, niece. Had you done your duty, you would have come to Grunwald long since and saved me the trouble of fetching you.'

'Saved you the trouble…' Katherine's breath caught in her throat. She felt cold all over, her mouth running dry with fear. He seemed to be saying that he had come to fetch her! Surely he could not mean it? 'But I am to be married, Uncle. Sir Alain intended to bring me to visit Grunwald once we are wed, but I do not wish to live there. My husband has lands of his own.'

'You are not married yet, niece, and your wishes in the matter are irrelevant,' her uncle replied in a cold, clipped tone. 'I am your guardian in my brother's stead. You may not marry without my permission and I do not give it.'

'But I love Alain!' Katherine cried, feeling desperate. She did not know this man and yet it seemed that he had power over her. He had the power to take her from the people who cared for her. That was the reason that Sir Ralph looked so ill at ease! Under the law he could not prevent her uncle taking her from Banewulf. 'You cannot take me from him. My father would have been pleased to see me happy. Why should you wish to deny me?'

His eyes were icy, his expression unmoved as he looked at her. 'My reasons are my own and I do not choose to share them. You are my ward. I have the King's own seal to the deed that makes me your guardian until I give you in marriage to a man of my choosing.'

'May I see it?' Sir Ralph asked. 'I do not doubt your word, sir, but I believe King Richard would not have set his hand to such a document if he knew that Katherine was to marry my son—and what the King hath given he can take back if it was gained unfairly.'

'King Philip of France—my sovereign lord—signed it. Katherine is of French birth. Her mother was an Englishwoman, but my brother was French. Therefore French law stands here.' Baron Grunwald handed Sir Ralph a document, which he examined with a frown and then returned. 'It is legal, as you see. Katherine has no other relative but me, for her mother's brother is dead. No one can dispute my right to take her with me.'

'No!' Katherine backed away from him. Something in his cold eyes filled her with terror. He did not care for her. He was imposing his will on her for reasons of his own. Her stomach was tying itself in knots and she felt sick. 'I shall not go with you. I want to stay here and marry the man I love.'

'You will prepare to leave here in two hours,' the Baron told her. 'Any attempt to hold you here will reap severe consequences. I shall use the law to wrest my property from any that would withhold it.'

His property! That was all she meant to him—something he owned to do with as he would.

Katherine turned to Alayne, her eyes wide with fear. 'Can he do this? Surely there must be some way to prevent him?'

'I do not know,' Alayne said, clearly desperate at this situation. 'I fear there is little we can do to stop him, if what he claims is true.' She threw a look of appeal at her husband. 'Husband—what must we do?'

'I could deny him,' Sir Ralph said. 'Our men outnumber his and we could overpower them. Would either of you have me do this? If you ask it of me, it shall be done.' He looked first at his wife and then at Katherine.

Alayne was silent, her face pale and stricken. Katherine saw her indecision and knew that she feared the consequences of such action. It would bring bloodshed and perhaps more. Sir Ralph might be arraigned before the King for dishonourable conduct and the penalty would be heavy. At the very least he would be forced to pay her uncle a huge sum for the loss of his rightful property—for she was his, to do with as he chose. There was no denying the law.

'No,' she said quietly and lifted her head, the pride shining from her eyes. 'I would not have you do that, sir. If my uncle demands that I go with him, then I must do as he says. I have no choice.'

'Katherine…' Alayne's voice was thick with emotion. 'Forgive me.'

'There is naught to forgive.' She smiled at the woman she had learned to love. 'Come with me while I prepare, Mother.' She held both her hands out to Alayne, who took them and then embraced her.

'Do not think to spirit her away and cheat me,' Baron Grun-

wald called after them as they went out. 'You will rue the day
if you deceive me, Katherine.'

She stopped and looked back at him, head high, eyes proud
and as cold as his own. 'You order me to leave all that I love
and I shall do it for the sake of those I care for—but do not
think to bend me to your will, Uncle. The law makes me your
property, but not your serf.'

She walked out, leaving him to glare after her.

Alayne put an arm about her waist as they walked up the
stairs to her chamber together. 'You must not abandon hope,
dearest. Alain will not let you go so easily. He will petition
the King. You are the heiress to a great fortune in England. If
Richard made you his ward, your uncle would be forced to
give you up.'

Katherine smiled wanly. She knew that Alayne was trying
to comfort her, but she believed that it was her fortune that
had brought Baron Grunwald hurrying to claim his rights
over her.

Katherine was his ward, which meant that he had control
of her fortune. He could refuse her the right to marry anyone
and keep her inheritance for herself. And if she died, it would
be his…

Katherine prepared herself to say goodbye to the family she
loved. She saw the anger and rebellion in Marguerite's eyes
as they embraced.

'We should kill them all!' she said fiercely. 'Father should
not let them take you like this.'

'To kill them would be murder. My uncle was clever when
he came with only a handful of men. Sir Ralph could not slay
them in cold blood, nor would I ask it of him.'

Katherine kissed her cheek. She went to Alayne, saw the tears in her eyes—but they had said their goodbyes earlier and merely embraced. Sir Ralph stood in angry frustration as she made her curtsy to him.

'Forgive me, daughter. I feel that I have failed you.'

'You could not do otherwise, sir. Tell Alain that I shall always love him. Whatever happens to me—my heart will remain with him.'

'You are brave and true, Katherine. Keep faith. This does not end here. I swear on all that I hold sacred that we shall meet again in better circumstances.' Sir Ralph's hands curled at his sides in frustration and she knew that he resented his powerlessness to stop her uncle taking her away from Banewulf.

'Come, Katherine. I shall brook no more delay.'

Katherine turned as her uncle's harsh command summoned her. She gave her hand to a young squire who came rushing to help her mount her palfrey.

'Say the word and I will kill him, my lady!'

'No, Edward,' she said recognising him as one of Alain's retainers. 'There shall be no bloodshed this day.' She looked for Maria, who was riding pillion behind one of the Baron's servants. At least Katherine had not been forbidden to take her faithful friend with her. She smiled at Maria, but said nothing as she rode out of the courtyard in the small cavalcade.

It was some hours before Katherine realised that they were not heading towards the coast, but further inland.

She spurred her horse forward, turning her head to glance at her uncle. His face still wore the same cold expression it had earlier and his eyes showed no emotion as she spoke to him.

'Are we not going to France?'

'We shall go to Grunwald when I am ready.'

'Where are we going?'

For a moment she thought he would refuse to answer, but then he inclined his head. 'Very well, I shall tell you. We are going to inspect the property Philip of Rotherham left to you, niece. As your guardian it is my duty to make sure that the lawyers do not cheat us.'

'Why should they cheat me, Uncle? Sigmund, who was my uncle of Rotherham's steward, wrote me a good honest letter. He is drawing up an inventory for the lawyers to sign. All is as it should be.'

'You may leave me to be the judge of these things, Katherine. You can know nothing of the matter. Property is a man's business.'

Katherine was silent. Angry words tumbled in her head, but she was wise enough not to let them flow out of her mouth. She had suspected that it was her fortune that had brought Baron Grunwald to England. He had ignored Sir Ralph's letter when he thought her merely a troublesome burden, but now he was here to claim her inheritance, not for his niece but for himself. When he spoke of property being a man's business, he meant that it was his! He would use it as he saw fit.

And she was powerless to stop him! Had she been a man she would have fought for her rights, but a woman had few rights and must rely on her guardians to keep her and her lands safe. She did not believe that she was safe with Baron Grunwald, for he had shown no warmth or feeling towards her. She was merely a pawn in the game he played. Alive she might prove of some use to him, but he would gain much more if she were dead.

Katherine realised she must be very careful. If she appeared to accept him at face value she might find a way out of this dangerous situation, but if he became angry…

But, no, she would not allow herself to think like that. Sir Ralph was no longer a young man and he had been forced to give her up to the Baron, who had the law on his side—but Alain would not let this go. She knew that he had done much to help Richard, both in the Holy Land and in his attempts to regain his throne. Surely the King would do something to help him now? If Katherine and her lands were made a ward of Richard's court, the Baron harmed her at his peril.

She dropped back in the cavalcade, watching her uncle riding ahead, and suddenly a picture came into her mind—a picture of her father and uncle riding together away from the castle of Grunwald. Katherine had been watching from the battlements, looking down on them. A tingling sensation started at the nape of her neck—something was not right.

The memory was so vague that she found it impossible to be sure—but she thought she recalled her uncle riding slightly lopsided. Now why had that been? Katherine tried to remember, but it eluded her at first. It was such a long time ago and so many things had happened to her since, but now it was beginning to come back to her. It had been a warm sunny day and she had climbed to the battlements to look out at her father's land, which she knew they would soon be leaving. She had noticed particularly that her father's back was straight and tall in the saddle while her uncle…her uncle Robert of Grunwald had a hunched shoulder and leaned sideways.

She remembered now! Her father's brother had a deformity of his back! He was not quite a hunchback, but there was something wrong with his right shoulder.

Why had she not remembered that when she was at Banewulf? She had only seen her uncle a couple of times, but she remembered him speaking to her father…something about wishing he had a straight body so that he might journey to the Holy Land.

'But I need you to be here, Robert,' her father had said. 'You must stay and look after the manor.'

'In truth, it is all I am fit for—but I shall do the best I can.'

This man was an impostor! Katherine was almost certain of it. His back was as straight as a board and, now she thought of it, he was probably older than her uncle of Grunwald, who had been several years younger than her father.

Katherine felt chilled. How could he have fooled Sir Ralph so completely? He had papers proving his identity, a document from the King of France—but how could they know the papers were genuine?

Yet Sir Ralph was not a fool. The papers might be genuine enough in themselves…and that might mean something had happened to the true Baron Grunwald.

Katherine went cold all over. Whoever was behind this elaborate ruse had gone to great lengths to get Katherine away from de Banewulf. He had chosen his moment well, after both Stefan and Alain had left their father's manor, and he had not risked using force, but stolen her by cunning.

How could an impostor hope to get away with stealing the fortune Philip of Rotherham had left to her? There must be people who knew the real Baron Grunwald, who would confirm Katherine's belief that her uncle had had a deformity of his upper back.

If she had only recalled this at Banewulf, then Sir Ralph would never have given her up. For the moment she was alone, Katherine realised. She could rely on her own wits to keep her alive and nothing else.

Chapter Nine

'This waiting irks me,' Alain confessed to Bryne as they drank wine together. 'Ravenshurst keeps me kicking my heels at his pleasure, but I must do my best to settle this business for Katherine's sake.'

'He hopes to drive the price up,' Bryne said. 'For my part I would consign him to the devil and rid myself of that cup. It hath brought nothing but trouble to you and her.'

'Katherine has spoken in much the same tone,' Alain admitted. 'But I believe it belongs to Christendom, Bryne. I do not think we have the right to forget it ever existed.'

'You are a man of high ideals,' Bryne said and looked grim. 'Few could live up to them—take care that Katherine does not suffer for your pride.'

'You think I would allow harm to come to her from this?' Alain looked at him hard, for the accusation was a harsh one. 'If she means so much to you, why did you not claim her as your own? I would have stepped back at the start if you had made your feelings plain.'

'I love Katherine more than she will ever know,' Bryne replied. 'But she loves you. I would not seek to press my claims when she hoped for a word from you.'

'You are a good man,' Alain said sincerely. 'Can you forgive me for taking her from you?'

'She was always yours,' Bryne said and smiled ruefully. 'Besides, I have it in my mind to return to Venice. I find England too cold and wet after the sunshine of Italy and shall make my life there. I wait only to see you wed to Katherine.'

'If this damned business was settled, that might be sooner rather than later,' Alain said. 'What do you imagine is behind his plan to keep me waiting here?'

'I wish that I knew,' Bryne said. 'I would swear he is up to some mischief, but we have no option other than to wait until he makes his move. At least we know that Katherine is safe at Banewulf.'

'I thank God for it,' Alain said. 'Were she not, I would suspect that Ravenshurst hoped to lure me here to spring some trap of his own. However, it would take an army to wrest her from my father's house...'

Had there been an opportunity on the journey, which took two days, Katherine would have tried to escape, but the man who called himself Baron Grunwald guarded her well.

They stayed at an inn for one night, and two men stood guard outside the door of her chamber the whole time. Maria brought food to her, for the Baron would not allow her to eat downstairs in the common parlour, and she told Katherine that the guards had been changed twice so that they remained alert.

'I offered to bring one of them wine,' Maria told her. 'For I could have drugged it and helped you to escape, my lady.

But he raised his hand to me and told me not to try my tricks on him.'

'Did he hurt you?' Katherine looked at her in concern. 'Be careful, Maria—this man is ruthless, whoever he may be.'

'So you have noticed it, too,' Maria said and nodded her head. 'I did not know what was going on until we were leaving Banewulf, but it did not take me long to realise that this man is not your uncle of Grunwald, Katherine. He is a base impostor and has stolen you from those who love you by treachery.'

'Be careful,' Katherine warned her, a finger to her lips. 'We are unprotected, Maria, and might be disposed of for less reason than a hint of suspicion. We must tread warily until we discover what he wants from me.'

'He means to rob you of your inheritance and then…' Maria's eyes were dark as she looked at her mistress. 'I shall kill him rather than let harm come to you, Katherine.'

'I would discover just what their plan is,' Katherine replied and looked thoughtful. 'I do not believe that my inheritance is the whole. I think this was a clever plot to steal my father's discovery.'

'You think that they want…?' Maria stared at her in horror. 'What will they do when they discover it is left behind in the strongroom at Banewulf?'

'It is perhaps fortunate for me that it is,' Katherine replied. 'Alayne asked me what they should do with it, and I told them Alain would decide its fate, for I could not. Once I saw how my supposed uncle behaved towards me, I was determined that he should not have it. And if in truth he is not my uncle…' She felt a thrill of fear. 'I think he must be in league with the Lord Hubert of Ravenshurst. The Baron has tried to abduct me, to steal the treasure from me—and to murder Alain. But this time he has succeeded by cunning where he previously failed.'

Maria's face was ashen with fear for her mistress. 'They will make you send for the treasure. They will threaten your life if you do not.'

'But they cannot kill me, for they must know that they would never get their hands on what they seek if I died—and Alain will not let this matter rest. He had already sent to Grunwald to find out what was happening there. I believe he will discover the truth—and then he will come to find me. I must believe it, Maria, for if I do not I am lost.'

'But he went to London to talk with the Lord Hubert…' She stopped and shook her head, afraid to go on because it would bring her mistress pain.

'Yes, I know what you cannot bring yourself to say,' Katherine told her. 'It was clearly a trap—but Alain will not fall into it. He will survive and he will rescue me.' He must come for her! She could not give up hope or she would die of her grief.

Maria looked at her dubiously, for she did not have as much faith in men as Katherine. There was not a knight in Christendom worthy of her darling in Maria's opinion, for her love blinded her, making her overprotective. She had begun to think that Sir Alain might just be worthy and he had sworn eternal love, but he should never have gone away and left Katherine to his family's care—and they should not have given her up so easily! Maria was angry, as she would always be angry whenever someone gave some hurt or neglect to her chick. However, she said nothing, for she knew that Katherine was in danger. They both needed to be on their guard and to keep their wits about them if they were to escape with their lives.

Maria would watch and listen, and if she suspected they meant to harm her darling she would kill them—the impostor and the Lord Hubert of Ravenshurst, if he should give her the chance. Her own life was nothing. She would give it gladly for the girl she loved.

'It was a trap,' Alain said to Bryne after reading the urgent letter from his home. 'Ravenshurst drew me here and then sent his creature to my father. His papers were good enough to fool anyone who did not know the truth, but I have received a disturbing report from Grunwald. Katherine's uncle disappeared some weeks ago, and his body has recently been discovered. He had been murdered, robbed of his jewels—including the ring with the seal of Grunwald, which is the proof of his rank. This man who claims to be Katherine's uncle is an impostor. And he may be a murderer…'

Bryne saw the way his mouth hardened and understood what he was feeling, for his own rage was hard to bear. 'They will not kill her, Alain,' he said gruffly. 'For to do so would expose them as rogues. You have proof that Grunwald is dead. You can stop them from stealing what is rightfully hers.'

'I care little for her inheritance,' Alain said. 'It is not that they want, though they will take it if they can—but if she is harmed…'

His eyes were dark with fear for her. Bryne smiled oddly. His own feelings for Katherine were strong and deep, and when he'd asked her to be his wife he would have been happy to be accepted…but things had changed. She was promised to Alain, and he would do all he could to see her restored to him.

'We shall find her and take her back,' he promised.

'I have kicked my heels here long enough,' Alain said and

smote the wall with his fist as his anger raged inside him. What a fool he had been. He should have married Katherine and made her safe before he left her. 'We must leave for France as soon as the tide is favourable.'

'That is probably what they expect you to do,' Bryne told him. 'They want you to waste your time looking for her while they force her to give them what they want.'

'My father says the cup is still in his strongroom. Katherine is so stubborn. She may refuse to give it up and then…'

Bryne gripped his shoulder. 'Courage, my friend. I think we must use our wits here. It is possible that they are elsewhere.'

'At Ravenshurst?' Alain frowned. 'I believe it could withstand a siege of several weeks—it is a stout castle, I am told.'

'Perhaps—and yet this man who claims to be Baron Grunwald…might he not want to try to claim her inheritance also?'

'You think he might take her there?'

'It is possible. Ravenshurst does not know that her uncle of Grunwald's body has been discovered. No doubt he imagines himself safe from discovery.'

'That is true, for it was hidden in a cave, and it was only chance that took a huntsman there in pursuit of a wounded beast. I believe you are right, Bryne. If he took her to Grunwald he would run the risk of being exposed for what he is, an impostor—no one will know that he is not who he claims to be at Rotherham. If my father was fooled, then so will others be.'

Bryne nodded. 'Rotherham is neutral ground. This man might not trust Ravenshurst enough to meet at the Baron's keep—and in that lies your hope, Alain.'

'You mean…' A wry smile touched Alain's mouth. 'We must pray that you are right, Bryne. Thieves often fall out over how to divide the spoils—and if the cup is still at Banewulf, Ravenshurst will be furious. He has Katherine, but not that he most desires.'

'Send word to your father and brother,' Bryne advised. 'I shall take my men and go to France to make certain how the land lies there. But first I shall seek an audience with the King, for you must be prepared for any tricks these ruthless men may practise, Alain. If one of them should force her to a marriage, you must have Richard's signed warrant to make that marriage illegal. If she becomes the wife of one of them she is lost to you forever.'

'If…' Alain's eyes burned with anger. The thought of Katherine wed to another, being forced to submit to him, was such agony that he could scarce bear it. 'She would rather die. I know her, Bryne. She would never consent. I think she would resist them to the end.'

'Then you must find her before it is too late.'

'Yes, you are right as always.' Alain smiled at him. 'I feared you would hate me for stealing her from you…'

'How could I hate a man I love as my brother? Besides, she was always yours. You could not steal her from me, for she loves you, Alain. You should have stayed at Banewulf and married her. They could not have stolen her away then.'

'You do right to upbraid me for my neglect,' Alain replied and the accusation smote him to the heart, for he knew it to be true. He should have placed Katherine's safety above all else. 'I believed there was no hurry—that it would be best to settle this business first—but you speak truly. Had she been my wife, they would have needed to storm Banewulf to take her from us.'

'Then you must lose no time in finding her. She will

never be safe until she is your wife, Alain. You owe it to her to make her safe—and you owe it to me to make her happy.'

'I know it.'

Alain needed no reminder from Bryne. He had cursed himself the moment he received his father's letter. Katherine was in danger and he loved her. He had not realised quite how precious she was until this moment.

'I swear I shall not leave her alone again…'

'You must settle this business for once and all, Alain.'

'I swear it shall be done.' He smiled grimly. 'So we part— you to the King and then France, and me to find Katherine, wherever she may be…'

Her uncle of Rotherham's property was a fortified manor house. Katherine was relieved to discover that it did not have a keep or massive fortifications, but merely a drawbridge, stout walls and a moat. It would not be easy to escape from such a place, but at least she would not be shut up in some grim dungeon here.

She had exchanged no more than a few words with the supposed Baron Grunwald since he had told her where they were going, merely inclining her head meekly every time she was told to do something. The impostor believed that she was truly deceived and it was better that way, for if he realised that she knew the truth he might decide to dispose of her. Dead, she could tell no tales.

Her guards never left her alone for long, and she was conscious of being a prisoner. They were taking no chances!

The small cavalcade clattered over the drawbridge and into the cobbled courtyard. One of her supposed uncle's men came to help her down. She accepted his help, suppressing the shiver of disgust that ran through her at the touch of his hand.

As she stood indecisively, someone else came hurrying up to her and bowed his head respectfully.

'Lady Katherine,' Sigmund said, beaming at her. 'It is a pleasure to see you here. We had no word until an hour ago that you were to be expected, but your chamber has been prepared.'

'Thank you, Sigmund,' Katherine said, feeling happier to know that she had at least one friend here. 'It is good to see you again.'

'You are Rotherham's steward?' The supposed Baron Grunwald's harsh voice cut through their greetings. 'I am the Lady Katherine's guardian. You will address yourself to me in future—and I shall want a full accounting of all that has been done here since your late master died.'

Sigmund looked startled, his eyes going from Katherine to the stern-faced man standing just to her right.

'You are Baron Grunwald?'

'It is not for you to question, merely to obey. Have one of the women take my niece to her chamber and then attend me. I am in control here now and I will be obeyed.'

Katherine nodded slightly as she saw the inquiry in Sigmund's eyes, but said nothing. What could she say? To denounce the man as an impostor could endanger all their lives. It would be most unwise to speak of her suspicions and she must at least pretend to think him the Baron for the time being. For the moment he must be addressed and treated as if he were indeed her uncle.

Sigmund needed no telling that something was wrong—her strained face was evidence enough. 'Of course, my lord,' he said, bowing low. He raised his hand and beckoned to a woman just behind him. 'Ethel will take you to your apartments, my lady.'

His look promised more—much more—but the next moment he was escorting the villain into the house, his manner subservient and as unlike his usual self as could be. Fortunately the alleged Baron did not know that and took it as his due.

'Have you travelled far, my lady?' An old woman came up to Katherine, giving a toothless smile. 'All is prepared for you and we are happy to see you here.'

'I thank you.' Katherine accepted her welcome with relief. At least the people here were prepared to be friendly. Her *uncle* might soon change all that, for his manner would make them fear to help Katherine lest he have them punished. But she believed that for the moment she was with friends.

It was a relief to get away from the watchful eyes of her *uncle*'s guards. Katherine was happy to be taken to her chambers, which were in the right corner tower and consisted of three rooms.

To gain access, she went through a sheltered courtyard and into the tower through a heavy oak door, which was studded with iron. Just inside was a spiral stone staircase, and there were three rooms in the tower at her disposal. The first was spacious and designed to be her solar, where she might sit with her women and do her needlework while the light prevailed. The second was her own bedchamber, which seemed smaller, because the privy had been sectioned off with a heavy curtain. The third room, above hers, was where some of her clothes would be stored, and where her women would sleep on straw pallets that would be packed away during the day.

The chambers for her own use were generously appointed with stools, rich hangings and articles that she might use for her comfort, including a beautiful lyre that she suspected had once been her mother's. Helen of Grunwald had loved to play her lyre and to sing sweet songs. There was a large oak coffer beneath the narrow window that looked out at the courtyard, also a tapestry frame, a trestle table and board covered by a heavy damask cloth, various religious articles, including a heavy bible and a wooden cross on the wall, and some silver trinkets.

'Shall you be comfortable here?' Ethel asked. 'You may have the late master's chambers if you find them more comfortable—but these were once occupied by your mother and we thought you would like to have them.'

'You could not have chosen better,' Katherine told her with a smile. 'I am very grateful to you for being so thoughtful.'

'It was Master Sigmund who gave the orders,' the woman told her. 'But we all wish to serve you, my lady—not just for your late uncle, but for your sainted mother.'

'Do you remember my mother?'

'I nursed her from a babe,' Ethel replied, her eyes filled with tears. 'I begged her to take me with her when she left, but she could not take us all—and she said it would be best if I stayed here to take care of her brother. She loved him despite…' Ethel closed her lips firmly. 'Is the man who came with you your uncle—the brother of the man *she* married?'

'Yes…' Katherine decided to say nothing of her suspicions for the moment. Ethel was clearly well disposed towards her, but she was not sure that she could be trusted to keep silent. 'Thank you for looking after me, but Maria will help me now. You may bring us food, if you will, for it is some hours since we last ate.'

'Yes, my lady. We are all happy to serve you.'

She went out and closed the door behind her. Katherine beckoned to Maria, speaking to her in a low voice.

'We must be careful for a while. Everyone seems friendly, but we cannot yet be sure they will keep silent. Do not let your suspicions show, Maria. We must bide our time and see what happens…'

'I shall discover what I can,' Maria promised. 'The impostor has hardly glanced at me, for he thinks me merely a servant, and it would be best that you show me no more favour than any other here. That way I may get close enough to hear what is being said…'

'If Hubert of Ravenshurst is to meet the fraudulent Baron here, he will not be long in coming,' Katherine said. 'As yet I have not been harmed, merely treated as if I were of no importance. We must discover what they mean to do with me. And then we shall make our plans…'

Maria nodded and looked thoughtful. 'Your steward is a good man, my lady. I believe you may trust him. It may be that he could help…'

Katherine placed a finger against her lips as they heard footsteps approaching. And then, quite suddenly, the door was flung open and someone appeared in the doorway. Katherine gave a little gasp of recognition as she saw the woman she had thought never to see again.

'Ah, so you are here,' Celestine said and smiled in a satisfied way as her eyes lit on Katherine. 'I could hardly believe that you had been such a fool, but it seems that Ravenshurst was right. He said that Sir Ralph would let you go without a fight.'

'Sir Ralph could not murder my uncle in cold blood,' Katherine said, raising her head proudly. Celestine was gloating, hoping to provoke her, but she would not lose her dignity. 'How came you here to my house? I do not recall inviting you.'

'I did not need your invitation,' Celestine said and smirked at her. 'Your *uncle* invited me himself.'

'But why should he do that?'

'I am to be his wife,' Celestine replied. 'How do you feel about me becoming your new aunt, Kate?' She laughed triumphantly as Katherine stared at her in shock. 'I see you are too shocked to take it in—well, I shall enlighten you. It was Ravenshurst's idea, of course—but I told Edgar that we did not need him. Why should we share with Ravenshurst when we could have it all?' Her mouth was sly, her manner bragging as if she had been very clever.

'I am sorry, but I do not understand you,' Katherine said, pretending to be bewildered. 'What are you saying? What was Baron Ravenshurst's idea?'

Celestine's gaze narrowed suspiciously. 'Are you so naïve? No, I do not believe it. Surely Edgar's story did not deceive you for long? You must have remembered that your father's brother was a hunchback?'

'You speak in riddles. My uncle's back is as straight as any man's.' Katherine knew she must keep up her pretence of innocence for if he guessed that she suspected him of being an impostor it might go ill for all her people.

'Edgar's back is straight, but your uncle of Grunwald was hunched in his shoulder. Can you not remember him?'

'I left France when I was but a child. I do not remember much about that time at all.'

Celestine frowned. 'Edgar said that you were convinced, but I believed you must have guessed by now. But you must know the truth soon.'

'What would you have me know, Celestine?'

'You will be released when you sign papers giving your inheritance to Edgar—and when we have the cup. You did bring it with you, didn't you? I know you carried it on your body all the time. I searched for it when you went on deck when we were at sea and I was sick, but could never find it—so you must have it on your person. Give it to me now and you could leave here this very night.'

'Does this man who calls himself my uncle know that you are here, making me this offer?'

'He is a fool,' Celestine said. 'He does not know about the cup. I warned Ravenshurst not to tell him. But *he* was a fool and missed his chances. Besides, why should I share the cup with either of them? I was the one who told Ravenshurst of its existence.'

'So you would betray them both? Is that wise, Celestine?'

'Edgar knows nothing of the cup. Give it to me now and I will persuade him that you should be allowed to leave here—once you have signed your property over into his keeping.'

'Have you no loyalty?' Katherine asked. 'Would you be faithless to all you deal with, Celestine?'

'Men have used me,' Celestine replied, a sour twist to her mouth. 'I was given in marriage when I was but fifteen to a man I hardly knew. My father bartered me for a stretch of land he desired, not caring that my husband was more than twice my age. I found a way to make my husband give at least as much as he took—but other men have taken advantage. Ravenshurst promised marriage and then changed his mind—but I have had my revenge on him, and now I shall be rich. I shall never need to smile at another man unless I choose.'

'You are so bitter,' Katherine said. 'I pity you, Celestine—but I cannot give you the cup, for I do not have it.'

Celestine's face darkened with anger. 'Do not lie to me—I can have you searched. You have no gallant knights to protect you now, Kate. Do not make me harm you, for I like you. I would have been your friend had you shared your treasure with me.'

'The cup belongs to the whole of Christendom,' Katherine said. 'I cannot give it to you, because I do not own it—nor is it in my possession. I left it…somewhere safe.'

Celestine's eyes flashed with temper. 'You are lying to me. Give it to me or I shall make you sorry you defied me.' She sprang at Katherine and began to tear at her clothes in a frantic attempt to discover where the cup was hidden.

Maria rushed at her and tried to pull her off amidst much screaming and shouting. So loud was the noise that none of them were aware of the door opening.

'What happens here?'

Celestine broke away as they heard the man's voice. She looked at him, then ran to his side, the spiteful cat becoming all at once a playful kitten.

'Thank goodness you came, Edgar. She knows you are not her uncle and she attacked me. She begged me to help her escape, and, when I refused, she attacked me.'

He looked at her, then at Katherine, his face sour with dislike.

'So, you have realised that you have been kidnapped, have you? Well, so much the worse for you. It was only a matter of time, for I have changed my mind about forcing you to sign your property over to me as your uncle. That might not serve once the deceit was discovered. I have decided that I shall marry you and then it will belong to me by right.'

'But you cannot!' Celestine cried. 'You are pledged to me. You swore you loved me…'

'Be quiet, woman,' Edgar of Achrington ordered. His face was cold, his eyes without warmth. 'Did you really imagine that I would welcome Ravenshurst's leavings as my wife? You came to me with your schemes and I agreed to them, but I made my own plans.' He smiled in a tight, cruel fashion as he saw her blanch. 'I dare say you had a scheme of your own to cheat me—but you are too late, Celestine. You told me that Katherine of Grunwald was a plain, dull creature, but you lied. I would have wed her for her fortune had she been as ugly as you described her—but she is fair enough and obedient, and we shall deal well together.'

Katherine stared at him. He could not mean it! She had been prepared to accept his anger, to sign what she owned to him had it been necessary—but to marry him! She would rather die.

'I shall never marry you, sir,' Katherine said quietly. 'Had you truly been my uncle I must have obeyed you—but you are an impostor. Tell me, sir—where is my uncle of Grunwald? Have you murdered him?'

'That was Ravenshurst's part of the affair,' he replied, eyes narrowed. 'I told him I had no stomach for murder and he called me a fool—but he was the fool. He went to London to lure your betrothed there and I did not wait for him to return. I have you now. Before he can return to claim his share of the spoils you will be my wife.'

'No!' Celestine launched herself at him. 'I shall not be cheated of everything. It was I who planned this, for neither of you had the wit—and I shall not be cheated of what belongs to me!'

Katherine saw that she had a knife in her hand and screamed. But he was aware of it and caught Celestine's wrist, twisting it so that the knife fell from her hand to the floor and was kicked away in the struggle. Maria hurried to pick it up, but at a shake of the head from Katherine made no attempt to attack him.

Celestine was screaming, biting and scratching at his face. Katherine thought for a moment that she would drive him off, but then she saw a change in his manner. His hands reached for Celestine's throat, and the look on his face was terrifying.

'You planned to betray me all along,' he said in a muffled tone. His eyes were glittering as his fingers tightened about her throat and Celestine began to gasp. She struggled for a little longer and then suddenly went limp. He let go of her and she fell to the floor, her eyes closed. 'No, let her lie,' he warned as Katherine would have gone to her. 'She deserved it. She is of no importance. Tomorrow will be our wedding day. Be ready, for I shall deal with you no less harshly if you defy me.'

His eyes glittered so strangely that Katherine was silent, watching as he turned and walked from the room. As soon as he had gone, she dropped to her knees beside Celestine, but Maria was before her. She laid her head against the other woman's chest, and then she sat back on her heels and looked at Katherine.

'She is dead. He strangled her.'

'Oh, no,' Katherine said and her eyes filled with tears. She and Celestine might not have been true friends, but she was shocked beyond measure at what had happened. It was too cruel, too cruel. 'How could he…how could he have been so wicked?'

'Such men are evil,' Ethel said from the doorway. She was carrying food and a jug of wine. 'I hid when he came out, for I heard everything, my lady. He is a wicked, evil man. I shall tell Sigmund and he will drive him out of your house.'

'No, stay your hand for a moment,' Katherine said. 'To fight this man would cause much bloodshed and I do not wish for anyone else to die. We must think of some other way to outwit him.'

'My lady…' Now Sigmund was at the open door. He stared at the woman's body lying on the floor, Celestine's beautiful face purple and ugly in death as it had never been in life. 'What mischief has happened here?'

'The villain, he who called himself my uncle, has killed her,' Katherine said. 'I do not know his true name, for she called him Edgar—and I have no knowledge of him beyond that, sir.'

'I knew at once that he was not what he claimed,' Sigmund said. 'How came he to abduct you, my lady?'

'By trickery,' Katherine said. 'I think he meant to force me into signing my inheritance to him, but has discovered a surer way to gain my lands. He means to marry me tomorrow.'

'I shall not allow that to happen,' Sigmund told her. 'There are fifteen men here loyal to you, my lady, and he brought no more than ten. We shall take them by surprise and kill them all.'

'But some of you will be killed,' Katherine said and the thought of more deaths sickened her. 'Is there no way that I could escape? Perhaps when he sleeps?'

'His men will not all sleep at the same time.' Sigmund said and frowned. 'But there is a way out, my lady. If that is your wish…'

'A secret way to leave this place?'

'Yes. Your uncle told me of it a few days before he died. It has been used in times of trouble in the past, when we were besieged. I speak of many years ago, before my time. In your great-grandfather's day there was often trouble, for King Stephen could not control the unruly nobles of this land and there was always fighting amongst them.'

'Then I shall leave this night,' Katherine said decisively. 'I shall need a man I can trust to guide me back to Banewulf—and my good Maria must stay here, for I will not have her risk her life.'

Maria protested at this, but was quietened when the steward told her that she would slow down her lady's escape. She embraced Katherine with tears in her eyes, telling her that she would pray for her safety.

'I shall send for you as soon as I am safe at Banewulf,' Katherine promised, and Maria nodded, though her eyes were moist with tears and it was clear that she disliked being left behind.

'I shall give you two men I would trust with my life,' Sigmund said. 'One is my only son, the other my sister's boy. Horses will be waiting for you in the woods yonder. Jacob and Fernor will come for you once it is safe and lead you to safety, my lady.'

'You are good to risk so much for me. The fraud will be very angry when he discovers I have gone. He may seek to punish you.'

'Do not fear for us, my lady. We shall find some way to mislead him.'

'Will you not come with me, Sigmund?'

'My duty to you compels me to stay here. My son and his cousin will lead you to safety.' He glanced down at the body of the murdered woman. 'She arrived alone only an hour or so ago and said that she was expected, poor lady. You should go up to your bedchamber, my lady—until all is made right here.'

'You will give her Christian burial, Sigmund. She was not my friend, but I would never have wished her to die so terribly.'

Sigmund made the sign of the cross over his breast. 'Had I come sooner I might have prevented it, but I fear I had other tasks. Forgive me, my lady. I would not have had you exposed to such a terrible thing as has happened here.'

'I shall go and pray for her soul,' Katherine replied, her throat tight with emotion. 'Treat her kindly, Sigmund, for my sake.'

He bowed his head to her and Katherine went to the spiral steps and walked slowly up to her bedchamber. She had begun to feel shivery and her body was trembling. She sank to her knees in front of the wooden cross set high on the wall, bending her head in prayer.

'God have mercy,' she said. 'Forgive her, for she sinned without knowing what she did, and forgive me that I have not yet fulfilled the trust that was put in me.'

She stayed for several minutes on her knees, and then rose. Maria was waiting for her and, as she saw Katherine's face, she came to put her arms about her as the tears burst out.

'Weep not for her, my sweeting,' Maria crooned. 'She would not have wept for you.'

Katherine drew away, wiping her eyes. Tears would not help. She must prepare to leave this place when the time was right.

'I shall take only what I need,' she told Maria. 'I did not order all my clothes packed before we left Banewulf. I shall take only those things that may be necessary to aid me in this escape.'

'You have no money,' Maria replied. 'But you may sell

something if you need it, though perhaps your steward will supply you with silver for the journey.'

'I believe you may rest easy in your mind,' Katherine said with a faint smile at Maria's anxious words. 'Sigmund's son and nephew are to help me, and he will see that we have all we need.'

'He is sleeping,' Sigmund said when he came to her chambers later that night, bearing a purse of gold, which he gave into Katherine's hands. 'I was able to get this for you, my lady—though he hath taken the keys into his own keeping. I had it in my rooms, for I was to have paid certain accounts, which shall now be left for the moment.'

'Thank you,' Katherine said and handed the moneybag to Maria. 'You have helped me to escape a fate I consider worse than death this night, and shall be rewarded for it one day— if I live to recover my inheritance.'

'I was charged to take care of you, my lady. My late master would have demanded more of me—and I would give it if necessary.'

'I would have no bloodshed,' Katherine said. 'You do not know how I came to escape, Sigmund. Remember, you know nothing of this.' She reached out to press his hand. 'Please, I do not want to hear of your death.'

'You shall not if I can prevent it,' he replied with a smile. 'Come now, quickly, my lady. He sleeps, but I know not for how long. I tried to give him drugged wine, but he drank only ale and water. I think he guessed the wine might be drugged and forced us all to drink the same ale as he all night.'

'I shall never forget you…'

Katherine and Maria followed quickly behind him as he led

them down the spiral steps and out into the courtyard. They hurried across the shadowed cobbles and into the chapel. After dipping to the altar respectfully, he led Katherine round it, and there behind a heavy drape was a small alcove where two young men stood waiting. One of them pulled a lever in the wall, causing it to slide back with a heavy grating noise.

Maria stepped forward to embrace her, then retreated, her face a mask of resignation as one of the men came forward, beckoning to Katherine.

'This way, my lady. I am Fernor and have pledged my life here at this altar to keep you safe this night.'

'And I, my lady.'

Katherine thanked them. They drew her into the darkness of a narrow passage, and she turned to see Sigmund watching her anxiously before he closed the door after them.

Jacob had taken a torch from a sconce in the wall. It smelled of burning pitch and the smoke made Katherine catch her breath. She controlled the urge to cry out in fear as she was urged deeper into the passage, which led down some steps and had become cold and damp.

'This takes us below the drawbridge and the moat,' Fernor told her. 'We must be as quiet as we can, because our men have been replaced on watch by the Baron's men. If they hear anything, they may alert him too soon. We shall not be safe until we reach the horses and my servant, who watches them for us.'

Katherine nodded, but made no reply. Indeed, she was not sure that she could reply. He hurried her on, then placed his finger to his lips, pointing upwards.

'The drawbridge is above us.'

Katherine heard a loud clanking sound and guessed that the

bridge was being let down. The clatter of horses' hooves across the bridge seemed to echo loudly in her ears and the noise was deafening.

Fernor looked up in alarm. 'Someone new comes,' he said. 'We must hurry, for if they discover that you have escaped they will scour the woods.'

Katherine followed as he set off at a run, her heart pounding wildly. She could not bear it if she were discovered and taken back to marry that impostor against her will.

It was so cold and damp and dark, and it seemed like a terrible nightmare that would never end. The hem of her under tunic was wet from water that had seeped into the underground tunnel by the time they finally emerged into the sweet night air.

It was said that demons and devils were abroad at night, but Katherine did not care. She had never been so glad to be out and was trembling from head to foot as Fernor threw her up into the saddle and mounted before her.

'It is best this way, my lady,' he told her. 'For we may be pursued and I know this forest better than you.'

She put her arms about his waist, a silent prayer in her heart.

'May God keep all my people safe this night,' she whispered. 'And deliver me safely to those who love me.'

Chapter Ten

'You have come. Thank God for it!' Alain said as he met his brother on the road to Banewulf. 'I would have gone on alone, but together we are so much stronger.'

'Our father set spies to watch where they took her,' Stefan told him. 'He was uneasy in himself after they had taken Katherine and is distressed by what has happened, Alain. He sent word that she has been taken to Rotherham, to the house of her uncle. Our father has asked me to beg for your forgiveness.'

'I find it hard to forgive, for he should never have given her up,' Alain said and his mouth was set harsh, all trace of his merry smile gone. 'I pray that nothing has happened to her. If Katherine is harmed—I do not believe that I could bring myself to set foot at Banewulf again.'

'You blame Father,' Stefan said. 'I would have felt as you do once, but I know he did only what he thought right, Alain. This man's claims to be her uncle appeared genuine and he had the law on his side. You must try to find it in your heart to forgive Father.'

'At this moment I can think only of Katherine and what

may be happening to her,' Alain said. 'I blame my father for
letting her go, Stefan, but above all I blame myself. Had she
been my wife it could never have happened.'

His eyes were bleak as he stared into the darkness of the
night sky.

'I can only pray that we are not too late…' He spurred his
horse forward, knowing that time was of the essence. While
Katherine was at the mercy of those unscrupulous men anything might happen.

'Wake up, damn you!' Baron Ravenshurst was furious as
he gazed down at the sleeping form of his erstwhile friend.
'Thought you would cheat me of my share, did you? You shall
shortly discover your mistake, Achrington.'

The other man opened his eyes as a *flacon* of water was
dashed into his face. He swore and jerked away, staring up at
the Baron in bewilderment for a moment.

'What was that for?' He blinked as he recognised the man,
his skin going a sickly yellow colour. 'Don't blame me, Hubert—it was all that scheming bitch. Well, she won't trouble
either of us again. She's dead.'

'Katherine of Grunwald is dead?' Ravenshurst growled,
misunderstanding him. 'You fool! You stupid fool.' He took
the other man by the shoulders and began to shake him as a
dog with a rat. 'If you have ruined it all by your stupid blun-
dering, I'll kill you.'

'No…' Edgar of Achrington coughed and fought him off.
'Not her—the other one. Celestine.'

'Oh, her…' Ravenshurst released him and he fell back
against the cushions of his couch. 'She doesn't matter. We're
well rid of her. I thought you meant Katherine. Where is she?'

'In her chamber.' Achrington turned pale as he realised his fate once Ravenshurst found out what he had planned to do. 'I thought to wed her—to make sure of her inheritance. They are sure to discover I am an impostor one day, and if she is my wife…'

'I care not what you do with her once I have what I want,' Ravenshurst said, causing the other man to sigh with relief. 'The Manor of Rotherham was always your part of it—but I want something else. Once I have that I shall leave you to your fun.' His mouth curled in a sneer. 'Methinks I shall pay the lady a little visit—she will be sleeping and may be more amenable now that she has had time to think on her fate.'

He went to the door of Achrington's chamber and yelled for the steward, glaring when Sigmund arrived clutching his bedgown about him.

'Ah, there you are, you lazy fellow. Where were you when I arrived? You should be whipped for your neglect. Take me to the Lady Katherine of Grunwald at once.'

'Yes, my lord,' Sigmund said. 'If you would care to follow me, sir. I believe the lady retired to her bed soon after she arrived, for she would not see me. She dismissed her women and said…'

Ravenshurst was not so easily deceived as his fellow conspirator and smelled a rat. Something was wrong here. He would swear it. The steward was lying and not as subservient as he pretended. He grabbed Sigmund by his gown and shook him until he gasped for breath.

'You had better not be lying. If she is not in her bed, you will be sorry, sirrah.'

Sigmund said nothing. He had known that he might pay the ultimate price for his lady's freedom, but his loyalty was such that he was prepared to pay it if need be.

'I am sure you will find she is sleeping, my lord.'

He led the way to Katherine's solar and wakened Ethel, who was lying there on a straw pallet.

'Go and fetch your mistress down, woman,' he said, giving her a warning look.

'I dare not wake her, master.'

'Do as you are told,' Ravenshurst said. 'Or you will feel my hand across your head.' He raised a fist at her. Ethel gave a cry and shuffled off as slowly as she could manage. Giving a shout of anger, Ravenshurst followed, pushing her aside so that she tumbled back, down the stairs. He burst into the bedchamber, and, seeing that someone was sleeping in the bed, pulled back the covers with a cry of triumph—only to discover that it was but a roll of straw. 'What trickery is this?' he cried and turned about just as Sigmund came up the steps behind him. 'Where have you hidden her? Speak up or you will not live to see the dawn.'

'Is she not sleeping, sir?' Sigmund asked. 'The Baron told me I was not to disturb her and I believed she was sleeping. I came to tell you that the Baron has called for his horse. I think he is trying to run away.'

'Damn him! He hath her hidden somewhere else—or has the cup more like.' Thrusting Sigmund to one side, he ran down the stairs and through the hall into the courtyard, where he discovered Achrington about to mount his horse. Grabbing hold of him, he pulled him back and threw him to the ground. 'What have you done with her?'

Edgar of Achrington had made a sudden dash for freedom. He had remembered that Ravenshurst was an unforgiving devil and his nerve had broken. Better to escape with his life—especially as he had no idea what it was that his erstwhile friend wanted so badly. It would do him little good to plead his innocence if Ravenshurst decided that he was hiding something.

'I know nothing,' he said as he lay quaking on the floor. 'She told me nothing of a cup...'

'Damn you, you lie!' Ravenshurst cried, pulling him to his feet and smashing his fist into his face so that he sagged and would have fallen again had he not been held in a tight grip. 'Tell me where she is or I'll kill you!'

'I told you I don't—' Achrington got no further for the other's fist smashed into his face once more, sending him reeling back and into the murky waters of the moat. He splashed helplessly around in the darkness, crying out for help until, receiving no reply, he went under the black, stinking water for the last time.

'Good riddance,' Ravenshurst muttered. 'So perish all cheats.'

He glared and shook his fist at the moat as if he would have liked to strike Achrington again, but then he turned towards the house. Katherine might have escaped. He would question those likely to know and then, if his suspicions were correct, he would set out after her.

God pity those who had helped her to escape, for he would show no mercy. With Celestine dead, that fool Achrington drowned and Katherine gone he was back at the beginning, his temper raging and ready to boil over.

Someone in this house knew where she had gone, and they would talk by the time he had finished with them!

'I am exhausted,' Katherine said. It was morning now, the sun beginning to shed its warming rays over them, trickling through the canopy of the forest. They had been riding throughout the night, not daring to stop lest they were pursued, and now she was weary, her limbs aching. 'We must stop for a while and find somewhere to rest and refresh ourselves.'

Fernor glanced at her, his gaze narrowed and anxious. He did not wish to alarm her, but he had heard dogs baying some minutes earlier and believed that someone might be following them. It could not be long once her escape became known.

'I know a place where you may rest,' he told her. 'It is but a few leagues from here, my lady. A house run by the good nuns and hidden away from the common view. It may be best if I leave you there and continue alone to Banewulf. Sir Alain's men may return with me to fetch you.'

Katherine hesitated, then shook her head. 'I thank you for the thought, good sir, but I would rather go on to Banewulf. If we may just stop for some wine and food…'

Fernor looked at her doubtfully, but made no attempt to dissuade her from her purpose. Yet the tiredness in her face made him anxious. He whispered to Jacob, who nodded and rode back the way they had come, towards the sounds of the dogs, which were coming ever closer.

'I heard dogs baying a few minutes ago. Jacob has gone to draw off their scent,' he told Katherine when she gave him an inquiring look. 'If it is us they are pursuing, he will lead them a merry dance and give us a chance to get away.'

'Then we must not waste time, but continue,' Katherine said, raising her head, a determined expression on her face. 'I can manage without rest for a while longer.'

'Forgive me, my lady. I know you must be very weary— but I would not have you taken prisoner again.'

Katherine nodded, but said nothing. She felt as if she might faint from weariness but refused to give in. She would rather die than let that impostor take her back again.

They continued to ride at a swift canter for some minutes. Fernor listened for the sound of the dogs, but it had stopped. Either they were after some other quarry or Jacob had managed to confuse them. He considered whether he dared risk stopping for refreshments at the Abbey. The sisters were of an order that gave succour to travellers and they were sure of a welcome at the visitors' house. Turning to glance at Katherine's white face, he decided that perhaps it was worth the risk, for she looked as if she could go no further.

It was when they reached the fork in the road that it happened, so suddenly that he had no warning and no chance to prevent it. A startled hart came dashing out of the forest, its path taking it across theirs and causing his horse to rear up. He fought valiantly to control it, but it was bucking and kicking and he heard Katherine give a little moan as she was thrown to the ground behind him. For a moment or two he wrestled with his frightened horse, gradually bringing it under control, and then he dismounted and hurried to where Katherine lay.

She was so still! She had not moved and he feared that she was dead. Her face was as white as death. He bent his head to listen for her breathing. There was a faint murmur so she lived.

What ought he to do now? He had sent Jacob to destroy the scent the dogs had been following, and he knew he must get Katherine to safety. He must take her to the Abbey and leave her with the nuns while he went on to Banewulf to alert her family.

Securing his horse so that the creature would not stray, he looked down at Katherine once more. She had not moved. It was clear that she needed to be cared for. Bending down, Fernor gathered her into his arms. The Abbey was not far. He would carry her there.

Alain reined in before the house of Philip of Rotherham, staring at the sight that met his eyes with a frown. The drawbridge was up and there was little sign of life. It seemed that he had come in vain. Yet now he looked again, he could see that something was dangling from above the portcullis—the body of a man, and a man that had been hanged.

'Something is amiss here,' he said to his brother, who was also staring at the fearsome sight. 'I suspect the worst, Stefan.'

'Have the herald blow up a demand for entry,' his brother replied. 'We must see what hath been happening here.'

The herald gave a blast and men appeared on the battlements above them as the sound died away. There was much shouting and gesturing, and then a man called out to ask who they were.

'I am Sir Alain de Banewulf and I demand entry in the name of my right as the Lady Katherine's promised husband.'

Some consultation took place and then the drawbridge was let down and Alain's horse was the first to clatter over it. He dismounted as several men clustered around him, three or four trying to talk at once.

'Where is the steward Sigmund?'

'On his sickbed,' an old woman said and shuffled towards him. 'They beat him, and then they took his son Jacob, whom they had captured, and hung him from the battlements as you see, my lord. Sigmund is confounded by his grief and swears he will die of it.'

'Who has done these things?'

'It was the Baron Ravenshurst,' one of the men said. 'He came looking for the Lady Katherine and was angry when he discovered that she had escaped with Jacob and Fernor.'

'Katherine was here?' Alain turned to him eagerly. 'You say she escaped—but that Jacob was captured. What of her? Did they take her, too?'

'No, my lord,' the man said. 'The Baron was furious when they came back with Jacob as their only captive. He set out in pursuit of her himself, and we raised the bridge. We do not know what to do, my lord. Who is our master now that Sigmund is like to die of his grief?'

'I shall see Sigmund and then make my decision,' Alain said. 'Take me to him—and in the meantime have someone cut down Jacob's body. He must be given Christian burial. Where are your wits to leave him there?'

'The Baron said he would return and punish us if we dared to cut Jacob down.'

'He will find a different reception if he dares to return,' Stefan said, coming to stand by his brother. 'Some of my men will remain here to help guard you until we find Ravenshurst and make him pay reparation for the evil he has done here.'

Alain was already striding away as Stefan began to organise the removal of Jacob's body and the strengthening of their defences. It seemed that they had come too late to prevent the mischief here.

Where was Katherine? How had she come to be separated from one of the men appointed to take care of her? Or had she been killed? Were Ravenshurst's men too frightened of their master to tell him the truth? Alain's mind suffered agonies as he reviewed all the possibilities.

His body was tense with fear as he followed the servant to

Sigmund's bedchamber. First he must see the steward and do what he could to restore order to this stricken community, and then he would set out after Katherine. If she was still alive, he must find her before Ravenshurst did!

Katherine stirred at last, her eyes opening. A woman was bending over her with a candle in her hand. She cried out because the light hurt her eyes and she was frightened. Everything seemed strange and she knew she was in a bed that was not hers.

'Are you feeling better, my lady?' a soft voice asked and a gentle hand stroked her brow. 'You have lain in a strange sleep this past day and we had begun to fear for you.'

'My head hurts,' Katherine said. 'And my mouth is dry. I would have water please.' She struggled to sit up as water was brought in a cup but fell back as her head swam. 'Where am I—and what happened to me?'

'Your servant brought you here. He said that a hart startled your horse and you were thrown. He asked us to take you in while he went for help. It seems that you were being pursued by a man who means you harm, Lady Katherine.'

Katherine nodded. Her head ached a great deal and the events of the last desperate flight from Rotherham were hazy, but she knew that she was escaping from a man who had tried to harm her. He had said he was her uncle, but then he had decided he would wed her... It was too difficult to remember anything more, because her head was very painful, and all she wanted to do was sleep.

'Sip a little more of this water,' the nun said. 'I am Sister Sarah and I have been appointed as your nurse. Do not worry, lady. Everything will be better soon and your servant will return with help.'

'You are so kind,' Katherine said and closed her eyes on a sigh. 'And I am so tired…'

She closed her eyes, a picture of Alain coming to her mind. There was comfort in the memory of the man she loved. Oh, how she needed him! Where was he and did he know what had happened to her? Was he even now on his way to look for her? She longed for him so desperately, for the touch of his hand and the sweetness of his lips on hers. Would she ever know such content again?

A tear trickled from the corner of her eye but she did not know it; sleep had claimed her, helping to heal the injury she had received in the fall. Sometimes she murmured in her sleep, but kind hands soothed her and then she began to dream and the dream brought a smile to her lips.

Alain was there beside her, taking her into his arms…

Fernor knew that he had been followed for some time now. He had ridden without ceasing throughout the night, but Banewulf was still some hours distant and he knew that the hounds were almost upon him. He could hear the sound of their baying; it chilled his blood and sent fear racing through his veins as he wondered what best to do. His horse needed to rest and he was not sure he could go much further himself.

Even as he wondered what he should do next, his horse stumbled and he knew it was lamed. He could ride no further and must try to evade capture on foot. Dismounting, he stroked the horse for a moment before setting it free.

'Find a new master, brave friend,' he said. 'For I fear I can do nothing for you now.' Releasing the beast from its harness and saddle, he moved away and began to run. He was running for his life, for he sensed that if the hounds caught him he was dead.

He had gone but a short distance when he saw the beast before him. A huge, great black creature with red eyes and sharp fangs, which it bared at him as it growled low in its throat.

Fernor stared at it as if mesmerised. He stood frozen to the spot, not daring to move for he knew that if he did it would attack, and, unless called off by its master, it would tear his throat out.

He could hear the thud of hooves approaching, and then the riders came into view. It was the end of the chase. He was cornered by the dog and could not escape. Yet he would rather die than reveal where his lady had taken sanctuary. Gathering his courage, he walked towards the dog, ignoring its growls as it prepared to spring.

'Hold, Brandon!' a voice cried, but it was too late. The dog had scented Fernor's fear despite his brave act, and its powerful hind legs pushed it forward as with one great leap it brought its quarry down and sank its yellowed teeth deep into the man's flesh. 'Damn it! Call that beast off at once before he kills the fellow. I want him alive and able to talk. If she lives, he is the only one who may know where she is…'

Katherine had begun to feel better. Her head still ached at times and she felt a little strange, for some of the events of the past few days seemed to elude her still. She knew that her false uncle had vowed he would have both her and her fortune—and, to her horror, she had seen him murder Celestine in cold blood.

Was it he who had been hunting them? Fernor had sent his cousin back to try to lead the hounds astray—but he had not come back to them afterwards. Had he been caught? And what had happened to Fernor? Had he been able to reach Banewulf and tell Sir Ralph what had happened to her?

She had been at the convent for more than a week now. The weather was fine and warm and she was able to walk in the peaceful gardens. She had made friends with some of the sisters and found it soothing to watch them at their work. They were always busy, tending their herb garden, making the cures and salves that they used to help others.

'It is so peaceful here,' Katherine said to the Abbess when she met her while walking in the herb garden and admiring all the plants. 'I almost envy your life here, Mother.'

'Yet I do not think you would want to stay with us forever,' the Abbess replied with a twinkle in her eye. 'I believe that you dream of a very different life, my daughter.'

'It is true that I hope to marry one day.'

'You must be patient, Katherine,' the kind woman said. 'Your servant may have met some difficulty on his journey, but if you do not hear from your friends within a few days we shall send word to Banewulf that you are here. Lady Alayne has stayed with us here on her way to London more than once, and she hath been generous with her endowments. I am sure that as soon as she knows you are with us, she will send someone to escort you home.'

'Thank you,' Katherine said and smiled ruefully. 'I do not mean to be impatient—indeed, there is no need, for this is a happy place to be. I have been at peace here.'

'I am glad that you feel it,' the Abbess replied. They were approaching a shrine of the Virgin Mary and she stopped to pick a rose in bud and lay it at the feet of the figure. 'We believe that our Lady cares for us and brings us the peace we crave.'

'It reminds me of a shrine I saw in Rome,' Katherine replied. 'It was so peaceful there—though it had been the shrine of a pagan goddess in the time of the ancient Romans. Yet I felt only goodness there.'

'Symbols of religion are a comfort,' the Abbess told her. 'Who are we to deny those who lived before us the comfort they drew from their own gods? For in the end there is only one God and yet we may all worship him in our own way.'

Katherine felt she was in the presence of a woman who had been touched by the Holy Ghost, for she knew that the Abbess's views were not shared by all. There were many that would excommunicate her for what they would call blasphemy, and yet there was something so right and good about the simple way she saw life and God.

Suddenly, she found herself telling the Abbess about the discovery her father had made, explaining her own doubts and the possibility that the full provenance could never be produced.

'It is a weighty matter,' the Abbess agreed when she had finished speaking. 'And a heavy burden for one so young. You must think very carefully, my daughter. In the wrong hands such a relic might be exploited—especially if it is truly the cup our Lord used at the Last Supper.'

'You think it may be true?'

Katherine had half-expected the Abbess to deny her, to say that it was an impossible tale and that the Holy Grail could not be the simple cup she had described.

'If your father was the wise and clever man you say, I do not doubt that he would make no claims he did not believe he could substantiate. If you truly believe the cup to be genuine, you must place it in the keeping of someone you trust beyond all others.'

'Yes, I see that I must,' Katherine said and smiled at her. 'Thank you for you advice, Mother. I shall think carefully before I do anything.'

'And now we must return to the house, for I see that Sister Sarah is beckoning. It seems that she has something to tell us.'

'Perhaps she has news.' Katherine's heart raced and she suddenly felt light-headed with excitement. It must be that Fernor had reached Banewulf and someone had come for her.

'Your lord has arrived, Katherine,' Sister Sarah called out to her. 'He is waiting in the visitors' room for you, for we may not allow a man into our house. Go through the gate and down the path and you will find him there.'

Katherine thanked her and turned towards the gate she had indicated. Her heart was racing as she ran down the path to the small building at the end. It was there that she had been brought on the night of her arrival, though she had not known it. The nuns had taken her into their infirmary where they nursed the sick, and afterwards they had allowed her to eat with them and worship in their chapel, most importantly to walk in their beautiful garden. However, no man was ever allowed beyond the gate.

She hurried up the path to the door and opened it, going inside to the large, dark room that lay beyond. It was cool after the warmth of the sun and for a moment she could not see— and then as her eyes became accustomed to the gloom she saw a man standing by the small window. The sound of the door closing behind her told her that there was another—and neither of them was the man she had come so willingly to see.

'So we meet at last, Lady Katherine.' Baron Ravenshurst made her a mocking bow. 'You have led me a merry dance. It was by chance that I stumbled on this place and came to inquire if they had seen you. Your kind friends were only too glad to tell me all I needed to know.'

'You tricked them into believing you my betrothed,' Katherine said in a choked voice. 'What do you want of me, sir?'

'You know full well what I want, Katherine,' Ravenshurst said, his eyes narrowed to greedy slits.

'I do not have it.'

'No, I dare say you have hidden it somewhere by now,' he said, a gleam in his eyes. 'But I believe that you could be persuaded to give it up—in time.'

'Is…*he* with you?' Katherine asked. 'The impostor who pretended to be my uncle of Grunwald?' Her mouth felt dry and she curled her nails into the palms of her hands. He must not see that she was afraid of him.

'You mean Edgar of Achrington, I imagine?' Ravenshurst smiled, his teeth bared like a wolf about to spring on its prey. 'I hope you held no love for him, lady—for he hath met with an unfortunate end in the moat at Rotherham's house.'

Katherine closed her eyes as the sickness rose in her throat. Yet she felt that the man who had pretended to be her uncle had received justice. 'I cannot pity him. He murdered Celestine. He has received no less than he deserved.'

'So you believe as I do in the law of natural justice?' He laughed, struck by her courage and her pride. 'I discover that I admire you, lady. You have spirit. It is a pity that you have defied me so long. Had your father accepted my offer, it would not have been necessary to do the things that have brought you grief.'

'Who else have you murdered?' Katherine demanded. 'If Sir Alain is dead, I shall never give you what you seek. You may take my life if you choose.'

'But you would not so easily give the life of others, I think?'

'What do you mean?' Katherine turned pale as he moved towards her. He was ruthless and she sensed that he would stop at nothing to gain what he desired.

'I do not believe you would see this place burned to the ground and the sisters raped and killed for my men's pleasure,' he said and laughed as she gasped and fell back. 'No, I did not think it. You are very brave with your own life, but you could not live with that on your conscience.'

'You could not do such a thing! You would burn in hell for all eternity.'

'Perhaps.' Ravenshurst moved a step closer. 'Yet I have seen worse done in the name of Christ. Our beloved King Richard murdered innocent Moslems at Acre and still thought himself the champion of God's cause. All religion is but in the mind of men and they make of it what they will for their own gain.'

'But if you believe that—why do you want the cup?'

'Then it does exist!' He reached out and grabbed her wrist, his fingers digging into her flesh in his excitement. 'Where is it? Tell me or I will make you sorry you were ever born.'

'At Banewulf in Sir Ralph's strongroom,' Katherine said. 'You cannot hope to take Banewulf, for it is heavily defended.'

'Why should I waste my time in fighting when I have all I need right here?' He smiled cruelly. 'I think Sir Alain will trade the cup for your life, lady.'

'Then you are wrong to think so,' Katherine replied with a toss of her head. 'Our marriage was one of property matters and no love match. If you think he will give up the cup for me, you are mistaken.'

He twisted her wrist, making her wince with pain. 'I think you lie, but we shall see. Now that I have you as my hostage, we shall discover whether your betrothed truly cares for you or not.'

'No!' Katherine backed away from him. 'You cannot take me from here. I have claimed sanctuary.'

'In the nuns' house I might have hesitated, but this is not consecrated ground. Besides, my warning stands good, lady— you will come with me now or see this place burned to the ground before your eyes.'

How evil he was! Katherine knew that she had no choice but to go with him. It seemed to her that all was lost, for if he had found her here he must have captured Fernor and that meant that her friends could not come to her.

'Very well, I shall go with you,' she said, pride coming to her rescue. She would not show fear for it would give him an easy victory. 'You leave me no choice—but I must warn you that it will do you no good to force me to give up the cup. It will bring you nothing but ill luck. It bears a curse and any who desire it for personal gain will perish if they dare to touch it.'

'Your lies will gain you nothing, wench,' Ravenshurst growled. 'You will come with me and a message shall be sent to Banewulf. Your life for the cup—the bargain is simple: either I have it or you die…'

Chapter Eleven

Alain looked down at the sick man, his brow creased in a thoughtful frown. He had had Fernor carried to Banewulf after their dog had attacked him, where he had lain in his sick-bed, too ill to speak this past week. Now at last he had woken from his fever and was gazing up at Alain fearfully.

'You have nothing to fear,' Alain told him. 'You are at Banewulf and I am Sir Alain. I want to beg your pardon for the attack on you by my dog. I tried to call him off, but he could smell the fear on you and I was too late.'

'Water…' Fernor croaked. He put his hand to his throat and felt the bandage there. He was lucky that the dog had not torn out his throat. 'I believed you were the Lady Katherine's enemy come to find her.'

'You should have stood still,' Alain told him. 'The dog was guarding you and would have waited if you had not approached it.'

Fernor gulped some of the cool water. His throat eased and after a moment he was able to speak again.

'I would rather have died than betray her.'

'Then you know where she is?' Alain moved closer to the bed, his pulses racing. This past week he had feared that Katherine must be dead, and the agony had raged ceaselessly inside him. 'Tell me at once. Where is she?'

'She was injured in a fall from the horse we rode,' Fernor said. 'I swear I could not prevent it, my lord. A hart dashed across our path and the horse reared up. I fought it, but she was thrown and when I was able to tend her she had lost her senses. I carried her to the Abbey and left her with the nuns. She is at the Abbey with the Sisters of Mercy.'

'And had she recovered her senses?'

'Not when I left her,' Fernor said. 'I waited some hours, but the sisters told me it might be a long while before she came to. I knew that she would be cared for and I came as swiftly as I could to find help for her. Then my horse went lame and—the rest you know, my lord.'

'The horse was recovered and has been tended in my father's stables,' Alain told him. 'I am told it is recovering—as you will, for you shall be cared for until you wish to return to Rotherham. And then you shall be rewarded for your services to my lady.'

'I thank you, sir. I must return soon, for I would know how my cousin fared.'

'Your cousin Jacob?'

'Yes, my lord.'

'I fear the news was ill, Fernor. Baron Ravenshurst murdered your cousin, and had Jacob's body hung from the battlements. I had it taken down and given Christian burial—and your uncle was persuaded that he must return to his duty, for he had surrendered to his grief and was like to die of it, but I think you will find him recovering on your return.'

'Jacob was his only son,' Fernor said and his eyes were dark with grief. 'I must go to him as soon as I am able, for he will need me now—though if my lady should have need of my services I would come to your call.'

'I shall remember,' Alain said and smiled at him. 'But you have been very ill and my mother will be angry if I tire you further. I shall leave you to rest now—but you will hear from me again.'

Alain went from the room, his boots clattering on the stairs as he ran down them. His mind was working swiftly and there was a look of grim determination on his face. He knew where Katherine was now and could only pray that she had recovered her senses—but what if Ravenshurst had already found her?

Stefan came to greet him as he reached the hall. Their eyes met and Stefan nodded understanding without need for speech.

'Good, you know where she is. When do we leave?'

'As soon as the men can be ready,' Alain said. 'She is with the Sisters of Mercy. She was hurt in a fall and Fernor left her there while he came on for help.'

'And the dog almost killed him for his trouble,' Stefan said. 'If he had died, we might never have found her.'

'I pray that no one else has,' Alain said grimly. 'Ravenshurst is out there searching for her, Stefan. The cup her father discovered has become an obsession for him and he will stop at nothing to possess it.'

'Then give it to him,' Stefan said as Alain frowned. 'Why not? We do not even know if it is genuine. The notes you have prove nothing except that a cup was found in the Holy Land— a cup that may be the one men have sought since the crucifixion, but could just as easily be a false relic.'

'It has brought Katherine nothing but grief,' Alain said,

looking thoughtful. 'I know she wanted it to be given to some-one worthy, someone who would keep it safe—but it is not worth her life. Yes, my brother, what you say is right. I shall take it with us and, if need be, the cup shall be given in ex-change for Katherine.'

'It is what he wants. If you are ever to be free of this evil man, you must either kill him or give into his demands—the choice is yours, brother.'

'I would kill him if he has harmed her…' Alain looked rue-ful. 'Yet if the cup is a holy thing, it would be a sin to give it into the keeping of a man like that, Stefan.'

'As I said, the choice is yours.'

'I shall have it brought up from the strongroom,' Alain said. 'But I hope that we shall find Katherine before Rav-enshurst does.'

Stefan was right. Alain knew in his heart that, as long as the cup was in their possession, Ravenshurst would seek to take it from them—and others might follow him. The greed of men was such that they would never be free until the cup was given into safekeeping.

Something must be done about it—but first he had to find Katherine and make sure that she had come to no harm.

Katherine had been given no chance to say goodbye to the nuns who had been so kind to her. She feared that they would think her ill mannered, but there was nothing she could do. If she resisted, the nuns might suffer a fate that she dared not contemplate. She knew that the Baron was a ruthless man and she did not doubt that he would carry out his threat to kill any who tried to stop him taking her—and innocent bystanders as well if it pleased him.

Far better to go with him, Katherine thought. She might seize her chance to escape, though she expected she would be well guarded. Ravenshurst would not allow his prize to slip easily through his fingers. He would keep her captive until the cup was in his hands.

She knew that she must give her consent to the cup being given up to him, though it grieved her that such a man should even touch it. She knew that her father had believed that he had found something so important that it was of incalculable value to the whole of Christendom, and she knew him well enough to believe that he would not make such a claim without good reason.

It would be sacrilege to let a man like Ravenshurst possess the cup that had touched our Lord's lips on that last night— but unless she could find some way to escape him it might be the only way to end this terrible affair. Too many had already died: her father, her uncle of Grunwald, Celestine—and Alain had narrowly escaped from the arrow that was meant to rob him of life. Surely it was enough? It must end before there was more bloodshed.

She rode in silence behind the guard Ravenshurst had set over her. Where was he taking her? She did not dare to ask, for she was afraid of arousing his anger. Yet as their journey progressed, she began to suspect that they were returning to her own house at Rotherham. She had thought that he would take her to his own stronghold, but perhaps that was too far from Banewulf, being in the north of England. She had not been told, but she imagined that a ransom note might already be on its way to Banewulf.

How long would it before Alain came? She could only pray that he was still alive and had not been another of the Baron's victims. Her heart was heavy as she thought of the man she loved. Would she ever see him again? Would the Baron let her go even if the cup was given up to him?

Sometimes it seemed so long since she had seen Alain, been held in his arms so lovingly that she was near to swooning for love. Tears gathered in her eyes when she wondered whether she would ever be held that way again.

'But…the other one claimed to be Sir Alain…' Sister Sarah stared at the man standing before her. She had wondered when the first knight claimed Katherine, for he had seemed a harsh, cold man, but it had not occurred to her that someone would lie so basely. 'She went with him…and never said goodbye…'

'She would not have gone willingly,' Alain said, his voice harsh with emotion. 'He used some threat to bend her to his will. Surely you thought it strange that she did not thank you before she left?'

'Mother Abbess thought it strange,' Sarah admitted, her eyes clouded with distress. 'She was very worried, but I thought Lady Katherine was overjoyed to see her lover…forgive me, sir. I led her into a trap. I did not know that he was the man she had been trying to escape.'

'You are not to blame,' Alain said. 'Tell me, how long have they been gone?'

'It was yesterday morning when he came for her…' Sarah was truly dismayed at what had happened. 'Had I known…forgive me, my lord. I did not know that he was not you.'

'How should you?' Alain smiled briefly to reassure her. 'Forgive us, we must go—but we owe you thanks for your care of her. I was not sure that she even lived until now. At least I have hope…'

He went out into the heat of a brilliant summer day and met his brother who had waited outside the gatehouse.

'She has gone?' Stefan read the news in his eyes. 'How long?'

'Yesterday morning.'

'Then we are not too far behind. We may catch up with them before they get there if we lose no time.'

'You think they go to Rotherham?'

'Ravenshurst has no keep or lands of his own within two weeks' riding. If he wants to bargain for the cup, he will take her somewhere nearby. For all we know he has already sent to ransom her.'

'Yes, mayhap, for we left before it could arrive,' Alain said. His eyes were dark with anxiety. 'She has been twice abducted from beneath our noses, Stefan. I fear that she may have given up all hope of rescue. She will believe we have abandoned her.'

'Nay, you wrong her,' his brother told him. 'She and Elona have become fast friends, brother, and I know that my wife thinks her a brave, clever woman. If she hath her wits about her, she will even now be looking for a way to escape her captors.'

Alain smiled. 'Yes, perhaps you are right,' he said. 'I have always tended to underestimate her, thinking her young and innocent, and must do so no more. If Katherine saw a way to escape him, I know that she would try—but that makes me fear for her even more. I believe him capable of anything. Who knows what he might do to subdue her?'

'You must not give way to despair,' Stefan told him. 'Elona was taken from me once and I learned too late how much I loved her. She did not know whether I would come for her, for she did not know that I loved her. Katherine knows you love her, Alain. That thought will keep her strong when all else fails.'

Alain's face was ravaged with his fear for Katherine. 'I pray that you are right, brother, for I do not know how I could bear her loss.'

'Understand this…' Ravenshurst's eyes were as cold as ice as they moved over Katherine, taking in the proud line of her body and the defiant tilt of her head '…defy me and I shall take a swift revenge, but I want nothing of you personally. Once I have the cup, you are free to return to your friends or stay at Rotherham. I shall not seek to force you into an unwanted marriage as that fool Achrington did. Nor do I want your inheritance. Had your father taken my offer, none of this need have happened.'

Katherine was filled with hatred as she looked at him. He was a big bull of a man with a thick neck and bulging eyes and she wished that she had the strength of a man so that she might punish him or die in the attempt.

'You admit that you had my father murdered?'

His eyes held the hard glitter of anger. 'Be careful, lady, for I shall tolerate only so much. Remember that you are my prisoner and that I am not to be deceived.'

'I have no desire or reason to deceive you. You may have the cup if it means so much to you. I would have no more bloodshed. If you give me your word that you will honour your own promises, the cup is yours.'

His eyes gleamed with sudden greed, but then his expression changed, his gaze narrowing in suspicion.

'You sing sweetly now, my bird, but what goes on in that devious mind of yours? I would swear you plan something to thwart me. Let me warn you that should you try to escape or trick me, you will wish that you had not.'

'In truth I would give you the cup now if I had it,' Katherine replied. 'I am sick of the pain and hurt it hath caused and wish that my father had never discovered it.'

'Mayhap you speak the truth,' Ravenshurst said, but he was wary. The cup was beyond price, no one would give it up so easily. 'Yet I cannot see your betrothed giving up such a valuable thing so easily.'

'If you think to find it a thing of value, wrought of gold or silver and studded with precious jewels, you will be disappointed, sir. It is but a simple plain thing.'

Ravenshurst glared at her. Clearly he did not believe her for one moment. Katherine felt a quiver of fear, for she was afraid that even when he had the cup he would believe himself cheated. He had created an image in his mind and would find reality very different. Yet she could only give him what she had and trust in Alain to save her from this man's wrath.

'You should send to Banewulf,' she said, looking at him eagerly. Until Alain came to claim her, she was this man's prisoner. 'If you wish, I shall sign my name. The cup is yours. I ask only that there is no more bloodshed.'

'I have already sent word,' Ravenshurst said, a sneer on his mouth. 'Unless the cup is delivered to me, you will never see Alain de Banewulf again.'

'Please, I beg you, do not harm him.'

'So, you love the man.' Ravenshurst nodded, a pleased smile on his lips as he realised that his bargaining power was greater than he had hoped. 'But does he love you, I wonder— or does he wed you for what he believes you will bring him? You are already a wealthy woman. Mayhap Achrington was not such a fool after all. Your looks have improved since I last saw you, lady—and besides, all cats look alike in the dark.'

He threw back his head and laughed as he saw her look of horror. 'Nay, you are not to my taste, Katherine of Grunwald. I like a woman of Celestine's mould. 'Tis a pity that fool killed her, for she amused me with her frowns and her smiling lips that told so many lies. He hath met his Maker and we must hope he burns in hell for his sins.'

Katherine crossed herself, a shiver running down her spine. 'Did you kill him?'

'I but gave him a helping hand. He drowned in the moat— and good riddance to him. However, I was obliged to punish the serf who tried to put us off the scent. I wasted days be- cause of him—but he will waste no more of my time.'

Katherine saw the malicious humour in his eyes and shud- dered. He had killed Jacob—Sigmund's only son—and she felt a burst of hatred for him. She had promised him the cup if he kept his word and she must not renege on her promise— but she hoped that one day he would be punished for the evil he had done.

'I wonder that you dare show your face at Rotherham again,' she said, raising her head in dignified pride. 'It was a cruel and useless revenge you took, sir. I pray that God will remember it and that you will reap your own reward.'

Ravenshurst laughed mockingly. 'You are not the first to have wished me to hell, lady. Your uncle of Grunwald begged for mercy on his knees, but I gave him none.' The leer faded to be replaced by glittering menace. 'I let none stand in my way. My standard bears the words, *Take what you want now,* and this is the measure by which I live. My soul may burn for it one day, but I doubt it. If *God* had been on our side in the land which we call *Holy,* then Richard would have had more wit than to fall out with Philip of

France and we should have taken Jerusalem from the infidel Saladin.'

Katherine stared at him in horror. Was this the man destined to possess the cup, which her father believed our Lord had drunk from on that last night? He was an unbeliever, a cynical man who had no faith but in the power of gold. And such a man was to possess the cup!

Something within her cried out that it must not happen. And yet she had given her word, but she had not known then how evil he really was. Now that she did, she was horrified at what she had done.

She prayed silently, fighting her fear for herself and for the man she loved. Somehow she must escape and foil this wicked man's plans.

'Oh, God, forgive me if I have betrayed the trust that was placed in me and help me to see what I must do...'

'They are but an hour ahead of us on the road,' Stefan said. 'My messenger saw them as he returned from Rotherham. None can ride as swift as he and I knew that he would not fail us. It seems that we are now one step ahead of Ravenshurst, my brother. He believes himself secure, but he is about to ride into a trap.'

Alain smiled at him. 'It is a good plan of yours, Stefan, to allow them entry into the courtyard and then, when they have dismounted and relaxed their guard, to surround them with your men. If we ride hard, we should be there to cut off their escape should they manage to fight their way free.'

'Ravenshurst has no idea that we were there. He will see something hanging from the battlements and believe that all is as he commanded. Once Sigmund has Katherine safe away, my men will overpower Ravenshurst's—and then we shall see how brave they are.'

'Your men have orders not to kill Ravenshurst?'

'I have reserved that pleasure for you, Alain. It is your betrothed he has harmed and yours should be the revenge.'

'He must die,' Alain said and there was no sign of his merry smile, no sign of the gentle knight Katherine had fallen so desperately in love with. His mouth was hard, his eyes cold. 'For if he lives then we shall never be free of him.'

'He surely deserves to die as punishment for all the lives he has taken,' Stefan said. 'Yet if it turns your stomach to see him executed, challenge him to single combat and let natural justice take its course.'

'That was my intention,' Alain confirmed. 'I know that I shall win for I think him a knave and a rogue, a blustering coward who hides behind a woman's skirts.'

'Is your arm recovered? If not, I would challenge him in your name.'

'My arm is still a little stiff,' Alain confessed, 'but well enough for what I must do, though I thank you for the offer.'

'I but offer to repay what you once did for me.'

'You were hardly risen from your sickbed. My wound was naught by comparison.'

The brothers smiled at each other, for the bond between them grew stronger with the passing years.

'As I said before, the choice is yours, my brother—but you must show no mercy, for Ravenshurst would show none to you or Katherine.'

Katherine could see the house now, and the sight of a blackened corpse hanging from above the drawbridge made her shudder and look away. The Baron was a barbarous, evil man and she despised him. Surely he must be punished for his sins?

The drawbridge was raised as they approached, but when Ravenshurst's herald blew his horn a man appeared on the battlements, and then there was a shouted discussion. A few seconds passed as if those within debated what should be done, and then the bridge was let down very slowly.

Katherine remembered her first visit and the horror of seeing Celestine murdered before her eyes. It was something that would remain with her for some time, as was the sight of the corpse hanging from the battlements. So much death and pain! And it was all because of her father's discovery. The guilt of it lay heavy upon her.

She felt like weeping as she saw Sigmund coming to greet her. He had aged in the short time she had been away, and she knew it was grief for the son he had loved that had brought those harsh lines to his face.

Regret swamped her. She felt his pain as if it were her own, her heart wrung with pity for him. She allowed him to help her down, and then held out both hands to him.

'Forgive me for what happened,' she said, her eyes moist with tears. 'I would not have brought such sadness to you for the world.'

'My forgiveness is not needed, my lady. It is not you I blame.' His gentle smile twisted her heart, for she could do nothing to comfort him. 'Come, my lady. You must be tired. Let Ethel take you to your room.'

Katherine saw something in his face and knew that he was agitated. She glanced at Ravenshurst, but he seemed to be laughing with some of his men, clearly well satisfied with the way the people of Rotherham had given way so swiftly to his demands. He had given orders for their horses to be led away, and seemed to be demanding wine and food for his men.

What was going on here? There was an atmosphere, a tension in the air. Katherine sensed something, but perhaps it was merely apprehension after the Baron's last visit. They were afraid of his anger. Yet she had felt something more, something hidden.

She allowed herself to be hurried away from the courtyard and into the house by the old woman. It was only as they mounted the spiral stone steps to her rooms that she asked Ethel what was happening. The woman gave her an odd smile, put a finger to her lips and shook her head as if to warn her to keep silent.

They were at the top of the stairs when she heard the first shout of alarm and stopped, looking at the old woman anxiously.

'Someone is hurt,' she said. 'I must go back. I must stop them hurting my people. Enough harm has been done as it is. He gave me his word that he would not shed more blood.'

'It is *he* whose blood will be shed,' Ethel told her, a gleam of malicious pleasure in her eyes. 'We have tricked him, for it is not Sigmund's son who hangs over the gate, but a common criminal hanged for his crimes. Things have changed here and he can no longer murder and torture as he once did. Do not pity him or his men, my lady, for they deserve their punishment. They came here to kill and plunder—and they shall die for it.'

'No…' Katherine shuddered with revulsion. She did not want this! 'I agreed to give him what he wants in order to prevent bloodshed…' She turned and began to run back down the stairs. This was foolish! Her uncle's men could not hope to win against the Baron's, and they would be punished terribly. Too many would be killed. 'This must not happen…'

Reaching the hall, Katherine saw that some fierce fighting was going on inside the house. She recognised some of the men as Ravenshurst's, but there were others not known to her. It was a few moments before she recognised the colours they wore—the colours of Stefan de Banewulf!

Had Stefan's men broken in and taken the Baron's by surprise? Or had they already been here? Katherine realised that it must have been a trap. Ravenshurst's men had been allowed into the courtyard in order to deceive them into thinking themselves safe before they were attacked.

She saw that some of the Baron's men were unarmed and had offered to surrender, but others fought on—and were cut down by the superior numbers. From the screams and yelling echoing in the courtyard, Katherine guessed that most of the Baron's men had chosen to fight. She covered her face with her hands as she saw men fall dying—one of them a man she knew to be her uncle's servant. He was but a youth, his only weapon a wooden cudgel he had taken up—a poor weapon against the swords of Ravenshurst's men at arms. A pool of his blood was spreading over the flagstones, reminding her of other atrocities—the murder of those innocent hostages at Acre!

It was too terrible! Unbearable. Katherine had never wanted this. She had hoped that all might be settled without so much blood and pain. Ravenshurst himself deserved to be punished, but his men had but obeyed his orders—and they would not be the only ones to suffer from this night's work. She cried out as she saw another of her uncle's servants fall to the floor, bleeding from a wound to his side.

'Come away, my lady,' Ethel said, pulling at her sleeve. 'This is men's work, leave it to them.'

'We must fetch salves and linens,' Katherine told her. She was sick to her stomach, shocked at what had happened, distressed that she was inadvertently the cause of so much evil. 'These men will need treatment for their wounds. Call my women—Maria is still here?'

'Yes, my lady, for when you went without her you told her to remain until you sent word.'

'Then she will know what to do,' Katherine said. 'Ask her to help you, and bring the things to me here. We shall do what we can to help those who suffer.'

Ethel hesitated, for Sigmund had told her she must not let her mistress witness the slaughter that was planned, telling her to lock her in her chamber if need be, but Katherine was the mistress here and she could not defy her.

'Will you not come away?'

'Leave me be. Do what I tell you, Ethel. I am mistress here and you will obey me.'

'Yes, my lady.'

Ethel hastened to obey. Katherine was no longer a prisoner, but a woman who knew her own mind.

Katherine watched the slaughter continue. It sickened her, demeaned her, and yet she could not look away. Who had ordered this terrible revenge?

At last she could see that the Baron's men had their backs against the wall with no hope of escaping their fate. She walked forward and called out in a ringing tone.

'Stop! I command that this bloodshed cease at once. Lay down your swords, all of you. I will not have such evil done in my name.'

At her command the Baron's men threw down their swords, dropping to their knees, their eyes turned towards her as if they knew that their only hope of mercy lay in her.

'Have mercy on us, lady.'

'We but obeyed our orders.'

'These men have surrendered,' Katherine said. 'They must surrender their arms and give their promise to do no more harm here—and then they shall be allowed to leave.'

'I beg your pardon, Lady Katherine,' one of Sir Stefan's men said, inclining his head in a respectful manner towards her, yet clearly defiant. 'But Ravenshurst's men show no mercy to their victims and deserve none granted.'

Her head was up, her manner proud and commanding. 'Nevertheless, you will obey my orders. I am the mistress here—and I gave no permission for this bloodshed.'

The soldier looked at her, clearly at a loss to know how to answer her. He had been following his orders and served his lord, not the lady of this manor.

'I have my orders—'

'The lady speaks truly,' another voice said and then Stefan de Banewulf strode into the hall. 'The fighting is at an end, Zachary. Those who swear an oath to repent of their evil and sin no more may go in peace. Our quarrel is not with these men—but with their master.'

'Sir Stefan!' Katherine cried and ran towards him. 'I thank God that you have come. I did not want this bloodshed. Too many have died needlessly. I had promised Ravenshurst the cup if it would prevent more deaths.'

'It would not have served,' Stefan said and his manner gave no quarter. 'There are times when only force will do. Ravenshurst is an evil, ruthless man and would have reneged on his bargain given half a chance. We had no choice but to fight for you, Katherine—otherwise he might have taken the cup and still have kept you.'

Katherine shook her head. She was close to tears, moved by the pitiful cries and moans from the wounded. In her heart she knew that Stefan spoke truly, but the sight of so much blood had sickened her. It was like Acre all over again—and the slaughter of the hostages that had occurred afterwards when King Richard received no promises of exchange from Saladin and wreaked a bloody revenge. Something that would be a stain upon his name for evermore.

'You may be right,' she said and brushed the tears from her eyes. 'I shall not argue for I must be grateful to you for what you have done for me—but I wish it had not happened.' She looked about her. 'Is Alain here?'

'He is outside…' Stefan laid a hand on her arm. 'He intends to see Ravenshurst brought to account. If the Baron still lives, he must be punished.'

'Yes, he should be punished,' Katherine said. 'It is for the King to decide his fate—which shall probably be death.' Her face paled as she saw Stefan's look of denial. A thrill of horror ran through her. He could not mean that Alain meant to kill the Baron himself! 'No! There must be no more bloodshed! I forbid it…'

She broke from Stefan. He swore as she dashed towards the door that led to the courtyard, following her. But at the doorway she stopped and stepped back, for Alain had entered. She stared at him in horror as she saw the blood on his hands, a few spots spattered on his face and still dripping from the sword that he held.

'No…' Backing away from him, Katherine felt the gorge

rise in her throat. She had believed him a gentle knight, a good Christian, but he was no different from any other. His eyes were glittering with the lust of battle, a gleam of triumph writ plain upon his face for her to see. 'I did not want this…I would have given him what he wanted…God forgive me… forgive you…' She shuddered as the sickness turned inside her.

'Katherine?' Alain was bewildered by her reaction. It was no pleasure to him to kill, though he knew that there were times when it must be done. His triumph was in finding her apparently unharmed when he had feared she might be dead. 'Has that devil harmed you? Forgive us for letting that impostor who claimed kinship take you. My father will never forgive himself for being duped as he was…'

'No!' Katherine cried as he reached his hand to her. 'No, do not touch me…'

She turned and fled from him, running up the stairs to her chamber and closing the door. There, she flung herself down on her couch and let the tears flow.

'Katherine…'

Alain's voice called to her from the doorway, but she did not lift her head nor look at him. She could not bear to see him stained with blood. In her mind she could see women and children lying dead in the dust of Acre's streets. The suffering she had witnessed there became one with the bloody fighting she had witnessed below in the Great Hall, inextricably entwined with the death of her father.

'Leave me. Please leave me alone.'

'I am sorry that you had to see this, Katherine.'

'Please do not,' she begged. 'I would have given up the cup—even to that monster—rather than that it should come to this.' She felt the touch of his hand on her head and shuddered. His hands were stained with blood, and she felt herself defiled by it. 'I beg you, leave me. I cannot bear what you have done.'

'But Ravenshurst killed your father and your uncle—and Sigmund's son.'

'And should have been punished by the law.' She sat up at last and looked at him, her eyes drenched with tears and yet proud and angry. 'Do you think I can love a man who would murder in cold blood? Your hands are as stained as his. Please leave me now, for I am sickened to my stomach by what has happened here.'

'Katherine…' Alain stared at her in disbelief. To hold him as one with Ravenshurst was a cruel insult and it struck him to the heart. That she who he loved could think so ill of him! 'You cannot mean this. I had to take you back from him. I could not allow that man to hold you, perhaps to deflower you…you must understand. I had no choice but to fight.'

'I understand that you killed men that had no choice but to serve their lord,' Katherine said coldly. 'I understand that innocent men have been killed here this day, because of what you and your brother have done.'

'Katherine…no,' Alain said feeling the sting of rejection as he saw the disgust in her eyes. 'Katherine, I love you. I had to do it…'

'He would have taken the cup and let me go,' she said, knowing even as she spoke that Ravenshurst might still have kept her despite his promises. 'Leave me, I beg you.'

'Katherine, please…' Alain took her by the shoulders, raising her up to kiss her. It was a hungry, despairing, savage kiss that shook her yet left her cold. She was too shocked and she could smell the blood on him, taste it in her mouth. He felt her restraint and let her go, his eyes reflecting his hurt at her rejection. She felt a pain deep inside her heart, but could not reach out to him. He had the stench of death on him, the death of innocent men. 'Go away. I have work to do. The wounded must be tended.'

'It is already being seen to,' Alain told her. 'Join your women if you choose. I shall not hinder you. I have other work.' She stared at him, her eyes dark with the horror she had seen that day. 'Ravenshurst and some of his men escaped. I must go after him—and he shall be brought to account for his sins, though you hate me for it.'

Alain…don't go… The words were in her heart, but not on her lips. *Forgive me…*

Katherine remained silent as he turned and left her. She heard the clatter of his boots as he ran down the steps and felt the crashing despair as her world fell in on her. She had loved him so much—still loved him—but could she ever bring herself to forget what had happened here?

Chapter Twelve

Five days passed before Alain returned to report that he and his men had failed to find Ravenshurst. In that time Katherine and her women had worked day and night to tend the wounded. She had discovered to her relief that there were more left alive than she had imagined. Stefan's men had not killed ruthlessly, and many of the Baron's men had surrendered after seeing they were outnumbered. At least ten of them had elected to swear fealty to Stefan as their lord, and she heard them speak of him with admiration.

It was true that there were nine dead and six so badly injured that there was little chance of saving them. Others had superficial wounds that were easily treated. Katherine was relieved to discover that the man she had seen fall was the only one of her own servants who had been killed.

'Vester was Jacob's friend,' Sigmund told her. 'He begged to be allowed to fight and was proud to offer his life for you— and in revenge for my son's death.'

'I am truly sorry for Jacob's death,' Katherine told him. 'If it were possible, I would go back and change things—had I known what would happen here I would not have run away.'

'Jacob gave his life gladly for you, my lady,' Sigmund said, looking at her sadly. 'He but did his duty and I am proud of him. He would not want you to suffer for his sake.'

'What do you mean?'

'We all know of your tender heart, my lady—but Sir Alain merely did his duty.' Sigmund met her eyes steadily. 'And what he did here was right. Baron Ravenshurst was an evil man, my lady. It was right and proper that he should be stopped. You do not know what he was capable of—what might have happened here had Sir Stefan not caught him in his net.'

'Too much blood has been shed in my name,' Katherine said and looked sad. 'I know that you speak as you believe, my friend, and I would have had revenge for your loss—but of one man alone. The others did only as their lord bid them. I would not have had them die for my sake.'

'Many of them were shown mercy,' Sigmund replied. He hesitated, then, 'Think carefully, my lady. Sir Alain is a good man and you may regret it if you shut him out of your life.'

'I thank you for your advice,' Katherine said, lifting her head proudly. 'You may leave me now.'

Sigmund sighed. He had done his best, but what more could he say? If Ethel had but done his bidding and locked her in her chamber, Katherine might have been spared the horror that had wounded her tender soul.

He was sure that she had loved the man she was to marry, and it grieved him to see her suffering now. Sir Alain was suffering, too. It was there in his eyes, though he gave no outward sign. For such an honourable knight to be accused of evil by the woman he loved was indeed a heavy burden.

* * *

'Your lord bids me tell you to prepare to leave,' Ethel said when she came to Katherine's chamber later that day. 'Would you have your women begin to pack, my lady?'

'Sir Alain is not yet my lord,' Katherine said. 'You may tell him that I am not yet ready to leave. Perhaps tomorrow or in a week's time.'

Ethel hesitated, then sighed and went out. Her mistress was more stubborn than any had realised hitherto and it seemed that she was not to be persuaded into being sensible or forgiving.

'Was that wise?' Maria asked after the old woman had gone. 'I would have thought you would prefer to leave this place. It can give you little satisfaction to be here.'

'I wish I might never have to see it again,' Katherine said with a shudder. 'The memory of that night will always remain with me. It should not have happened, Maria—so many killed and injured…'

Maria looked at her sadly. 'It is the way of war. You were not thus at Acre.'

'Because I believed that a just cause,' Katherine told her. 'And it was only afterwards, when I saw…' She closed her eyes as she recalled the slaughter of the family she had cared for in that fierce bloodletting. But that was something she had promised herself she would forget. 'Our men fought for right and for God—though what happened after was something that will never be forgot.'

'There is a beast in all men,' Maria told her with a sigh. 'When it is roused things are done that are afterwards regretted. King Richard hath a temper and his treatment of the hostages was a shameful act. Sir Alain is not like him. He is a gentle knight, a true knight—what he did here was for your sake. For love of you, Katherine.'

'Do you think that makes me feel better—to know that slaughter was done in my name?'

'You think it was slaughter because Ravenshurst's men were taken by surprise?' Katherine nodded and Maria sighed. 'Do you not see that it was done to save lives—and to protect you? Had Sir Stefan and Sir Alain laid siege to this house, many more would have died. It could have gone on for weeks, causing terrible hardship for all here. At least this way, Ravenshurst's men were given the choice to surrender. Several of them did—they would not have had that opportunity if they had been besieged. Their master would have hung any who dared to disobey him—and your own people, too, I dare say. Sir Alain dare not take the risk, for you might have been ravished or killed in revenge.'

'You have changed your mind mightily,' Katherine said, stung by her friend's chiding. She knew that Maria was right and yet she could not think of Alain with blood on him without shuddering. 'You thought him a monster and vowed to kill him for me once.'

'And would have had he harmed you, but he hath done nothing but care for you and protect you,' Maria told her, for Alain's true love for Katherine had won her over at last. 'Had I been given half a chance, I would have killed that evil man who took you from the Abbey. I am not as forgiving as you, my lady.' She looked at Katherine strangely. 'Why can you forgive others and not your betrothed?'

Katherine turned from her, unable to answer such a telling question. Maria was right to chide her. How could she show forgiveness to men who had been involved in her father's murder, even tend their wounds and pray that their lives might be saved, when she could not forgive Alain?

It was stupid, ungenerous and unlike her. She knew that there was a part of her that wanted everything to be as it had been, that she wanted to confess her love and ask his pardon, but another part would not give way. Was it merely pride?

She was not given long to ponder the question for the door was flung open and Alain strode into the room. One glance at his face told her he was angry. Ethel must have given him her message and it had brought him to her straightway. She trembled inwardly, for she had never seen him look that way.

'We must leave here in three hours if we are to reach a safe haven by this night,' Alain told her, his face hard and cold. 'Your ladies must pack what you need for the journey. Anything left behind can be sent for later.'

'And if I do not care to leave?' He was bad as Achrington or Ravenshurst! She looked at him resentfully. Why must she always do as a man told her? She was tired of being treated as if her wishes counted for naught. 'Supposing I wish to stay here?'

'It is not safe,' Alain replied. 'We are returning to Bane-wulf until Ravenshurst is taken. He hath not the strength to take this place by force, for I shall leave some of my men here to guard it—but I do not trust him. I shall take you back to my parents' home and then go to London. With a royal decree against him, Ravenshurst will be outlawed and shall be brought to justice one way or another.'

'I shall go with you on one condition,' Katherine replied, lifting her head proudly. 'You will give me your word that he shall not die by your hand. I shed no tears for him, for he surely deserves to be punished by the law for his evildoing— but not by your hand.'

Alain looked at her in silence for some seconds. Katherine's heart beat fast and she held her breath. Would he refuse?

'Very well, you have my word,' Alain said at last. His expression was cold, unforgiving. 'You are my betrothed and I hope that you will come to accept me, Katherine. The promises we made to one another cannot be undone. You would be dishonoured if you broke yours—and I shall not break mine. We shall marry, though you will not be forced to suffer my presence. I dare say there is a foreign prince somewhere that will buy my sword.'

'You would fight for any who paid you?' Katherine was horrified. Was this the knight she had believed the truest in Christendom?

'Why not?' Alain's mouth curved in a derisive smile. 'I have blood on my hands, Katherine—the blood of innocent men, you said—why should I not fight for any who will pay me?'

His anger and his words shook Katherine. Maria had almost convinced her that she ought to forgive him, and she was trying to erase from her mind the memory of him coming towards her stained with the fresh blood of his enemies—but now she was sickened. She felt a pain in her heart as if a knife had pierced it, but she gave no sign of the wound he had dealt her as she raised her head and looked into his eyes.

'As you say, I cannot break my promise, and as you will not we shall marry—but after that I shall go to the Sisters of Mercy and ask to join them. Not as a nun, but as someone who will work with them to help the sick and poor.'

For a moment Alain's eyes blazed and she thought he would deny her, but he merely inclined his head.

'As you wish, Katherine—but first I shall claim you as my wife. For one night you shall be mine, and afterwards…' A harsh laugh escaped him. 'Then, my sweet Kate, you may go to God or the devil if it pleases you.'

Katherine stood as if turned to stone as he swivelled on his heels and walked out of her chamber without another word. He could not mean what he had just said? Surely he would not force himself on her if she would not yield?

Alain had never felt such anger. The look in Katherine's eyes—the disgust on her face when she had first seen him— had stabbed him to the heart. How could she think so ill of him?

Did she not understand the danger she had been in? Ravenshurst would never have given her up, no matter his promises. Once he had the cup he would have seen that her inheritance was a rich one, for she was more wealthy than she dreamed. He would have forced her to be his wife and then… Alain could not bear to think of her eventual fate.

Ravenshurst would have used and abused her until he decided it was safe to rid himself of her. To think of Katherine at that evil man's mercy was more than Alain could have borne. He would have killed twice as many men to set her free—but he had not killed in cold blood. Neither he nor Stefan had ordered senseless killing.

In battle there was always some unnecessary bloodletting. For some men the killing became a mindless slaughter that they could not control, though they might afterwards feel shame. Others killed cleanly, coldly, enjoying their sport.

Alain knew that when Richard had ordered the slaying of the hostages there had been others killed; innocent men, women and children were dragged from their homes and killed in the streets. It was a stain on the honour of those who had taken part, and Alain had done his best to control such evil where he could—but there were times when there was no choice but to take life.

Katherine must understand that this had been one of these times. If she could not, then the future was indeed bleak for them.

It seemed that he had killed her love. Having seen the horror in her eyes, he knew that she could not love him and it hurt him more than he had expected. Until this moment he had scarcely known how precious she was to him—and now it was too late.

She hated him, but he must marry her. She would not be safe from other unscrupulous men until she was his wife.

He would marry her, and he would know her as his wife— even if she went to her grave hating him for it!

Katherine held herself aloof on the return journey to Banewulf. A part of her wept bitter tears as she watched Alain riding just ahead of her, his back straight and stiff with a mixture of pride and anger. She wanted to make up their quarrel, to tell him that she still loved him, but she could not. Something inside her was still recoiling from the look in his eyes as he had come to her fresh from the lust of battle. It seemed that the knight she had loved so desperately had either vanished or had been merely a figment of her imagination.

For his part, Alain gave her no indication that he wished to make up their quarrel. When he looked at her his expression was cold, indifferent, and there was no sign of the merry smile that had enchanted her. He had become a stranger and one that she did not much like.

'You should beg his pardon for so misjudging him,' Maria told her as she undressed her mistress for bed on the last night they would spend upon the road. They were staying at a monastery, and the guestroom was cold and cheerless, the bed hard and monstrous uncomfortable. 'It is no wonder he is angry with you. How could you accuse him of murder when he came to rescue you and be avenged for your father's and your uncle's murder?'

'Be quiet,' Katherine said, her mouth set stubbornly. 'I will hear no more of your scolding, Maria.'

'I have been friend and comforter to you for most of your life,' Maria said, refusing to be silenced. 'And if I do not prick your conscience, who will?'

'I do not care to have it pricked.' Katherine glared at her. 'You did not see that slaughter happening as I did.'

'And whose fault was that? Had you listened to Ethel, you might have spared yourself the pain.'

Katherine ignored her, refusing to answer. Yet as she lay upon her hard pallet that night she found herself unable to sleep. Maria was right, she knew it in her heart. Alain had done what he had for love of her, to protect her. He had a right to be angry after the harsh accusations she had made.

Yet the memory of so much bloodshed was hard to bear and she could not shut it out of her mind no matter how much she tried. It was impossible to reconcile the picture she had built in her mind of Alain de Banewulf with the bloody avenger she had seen in the Great Hall at Rotherham. Were there two men in him, and, if so, which was the real one—or was the picture she had built for herself of him simply false? Katherine could no longer trust her instincts.

She wanted to love him, but could she ever forget that sight— could she find the merry, gentle man she had loved again? If he were lost to her forever, she believed that she would be best to retreat to the Abbey and spend the rest of her life in prayer.

* * *

After a restless night, Katherine was tired and heavy eyed as they continued their journey, her face strained and weary. Alain's gaze dwelled on her for a moment and she thought he might say something, hoped desperately that he would find words to bridge this gulf between them. When he turned away without speaking, she knew that it was over between them. She was a prisoner of her own despair, and he no longer cared whether she loved him or not.

Holding her tears inside, Katherine rode in silence. She was glad when Banewulf came into sight. At least when they reached it, Alain would leave her. He had said that he would go to London to petition the King, and she hoped that, before he returned, he would come to see that to go on with their marriage would be a mistake.

She was so weary that when a young squire came to help her down she almost fell. The tears were very close, and to her shame she felt them trickle down her cheeks when Alayne held out her arms to her.

'My poor Katherine!' Alayne cried. 'I have prayed for your return every night. Forgive us for letting that wicked man take you away from us. We believed he had the right, but we should still have made him fight for it in the courts. My son was so angry with his father for allowing you to leave that I believe they may never be on the same terms again.'

'He should not blame Sir Ralph,' Katherine said, her throat choked with emotion as she fought her desire to weep. 'It was neither his fault nor yours, my lady. I chose to go…'

'Knowing that it would cause trouble for us if you refused.'

'It was not only that,' Katherine replied. 'I did not want more bloodshed. I hoped to spare your people and his. There has been too much, too much....' She faltered as she saw Alain was standing close to her, his face a mask carved out of stone. 'While I believed that man my uncle, I hoped that he would relent and allow me to marry Alain, but I would have borne anything rather than see innocent men die.'

She heard Alain exclaim furiously. He walked away and she realised that he had misinterpreted what he had heard. Did he imagine it would have cost her nothing to give up her hope of being his wife? It would have cost her more than he knew, for she would never have been another man's wife in anything but name. She would have died rather than let any other man claim her.

'Well, you are safe with us now,' his mother told her, putting an arm about her waist. 'You have been through a terrible experience, my dear daughter, but we shall help you to forget. You will soon feel better and then you will learn to be happy again.'

'Perhaps...' Katherine checked her tears. She would not give way to her desire to weep like a weak woman. 'Yet it is not of myself I think—but all those who lost their lives because of something I had. It would have been better if I had cast it into the sea.'

'No,' Alain said and she turned to see he had come up to them again without her realising it. His expression was harsh and she was unable to read what was in his mind. 'The cup is too precious to destroy, Katherine. Your father's papers were recovered from the baggage Ravenshurst left behind at Rotherham in his haste to escape justice. I have read them and I believe they are proof positive that the cup he discovered is indeed the one that our Lord used at the Last Supper.'

'Yet still I would be rid of it,' Katherine said. Why could

he not understand her feelings? To her the cup had become
tainted by the evil that had surrounded it. 'It has caused nothing but evil and I believe it is cursed.'

'Have a care,' Alain warned. 'You speak of a holy relic and
one that belongs to Christendom. It should be in Jerusalem
and would be had that city not been lost to us—but failing that
it belongs in Rome. Now that we have provenance we could
take it there after our wedding and seek an audience with his
Holiness.'

'You may care to make the journey, sir,' she said, her face
cold. 'I do not. For my part, I would destroy it before it costs
more lives.'

'I shall not permit such sacrilege.'

'You will not permit?' Katherine could barely control her
anger. How dared he behave in such a high-handed manner? He
spoke as if he owned her—as he would in truth once she
was his wife.

She would not marry him. She would refuse him—run
away if need be. Wild thoughts of leaving Banewulf chased
through her head, but were soon dismissed. In truth, she would
not be safe wherever she went while she still had the cup.

Once they were wed Alain had promised to let her retire
to the Abbey. She hoped that he might keep his word, even
though it meant that she must pay a price before he granted
her her freedom.

She would have said more, but the puzzled look in Lady
Alayne's eyes held her silent. This quarrel between them was
private and must not be allowed to bring grief to others. Lifting her head, she forced a smile.

'Of course, sir,' she said. 'I must accept your decision in
all things, must I not?'

Turning proudly, she walked away from him, making her way inside the house and going up to her chamber. Once inside, she stood with her back against the door, gathering her wits. Alain was determined that they should marry and that she should be his wife in truth as well as name. How could she bear that? How could she give herself to him and then walk away from the marriage?

Katherine despised and hated him. Alain could not doubt that, for her manner to him was reserved and cold. She had smiles for his mother, and even his father—who he had still not quite forgiven for letting Katherine be taken from them—yet there were none for him.

He had hoped that once she was back at Banewulf she would begin to relent, to see that he had done only what was right, but she seemed determined to avoid him, to shut him out of her life.

There were moments when he felt like walking away, from Katherine, his home and all that he knew. Bryne had returned from France with the news that Grunwald was little more than a shell, its walls fast crumbling into dust, much of it carried away by the peasants to build their cottages and cow byres. Perhaps if he were gone Katherine would marry Bryne and be happy.

It might be better for them all if he just accepted that she hated him. And yet there was a part of him that would not, could not, give her up.

She was his and somehow he would make her love him again.

Katherine was disappointed if she imagined that Alain would leave at once. He lingered for two days and she was forced to bear the silent accusation in his eyes every time he looked at her.

'I thought you meant to go to London, sir?' she said when he came up to her when she was walking alone in the gardens.

'I have sent word ahead,' he told her. 'It is perhaps not as important as I thought. Ravenshurst has little money and no friends. We are safe enough here in my father's house, Katherine. I have decided that we should get to know each other a little better before our wedding. I have had little time to court you, which was unfortunate.' Had she known him better, she surely could not have thought him a man of Ravenshurst's ilk?

Katherine's eyes flashed with pride. 'It is too late to speak of courtship.'

'Do you say so?' Alain's eyes were intent on her face. He had never seen this woman. Where had his little brown bird gone? She was neither the shy maiden she had been before she was abducted nor the child he had first thought her, but a proud woman—and she enchanted him. Yet it seemed impossible to break down the barrier between them. 'Would you have me come to your bed as a stranger, Kate? It might be better for you if we could at least be easy with one another.'

Her eyes flashed with temper. Did he care nothing for her wishes?

'I wish you would not come to me at all. Since you say we must marry I have no choice, but I shall not be a loving bride. If you ever cared for me, sir, let me go to the Abbey.'

'Nay, I do not think you suited to the life,' Alain said and reached out to touch her cheek. The touch of his fingers made her jump as if she had been scalded, her breath coming faster. He moved towards her, his eyes transfixing her like a rabbit caught by a stoat. She could neither move nor resist as he drew her into his arms, kissing her with a fierce passion that left her shaken when he at last released her. He let his fingers trail down her throat, his hand lingering for a moment in the sweet valley between her breasts, his thumb moving over to caress the nipple beneath her gown. His touch in such a sensitive place made her shiver, though she hardly knew whether it was for pleasure or fear. 'I have longed to love you, Kate. You have haunted my sleep for many nights—many more than you might guess. You shall be my wife and I shall take my rights as your husband and then we shall see…'

She looked at him, her eyes blazing with a passion from deep within her, and in that moment she had a beauty she would never realise was hers, nor the effect it had upon her betrothed.

'You are mine, Katherine,' he said huskily and she saw that he had been as affected by that kiss as she. 'I do not intend to give you up, nor shall I leave you again before we are wed. I shall tell my father to bring the ceremony forward and the business with Ravenshurst may wait…'

'No! I do not want…' She knew that she lied even as the words left her lips. Despite all, she had felt a stirring of desire as he kissed her. She knew that if he wanted her she would never have the strength to leave him. 'This is not chivalrous, sir. I do not want to wed you.'

Turning, she fled away into the garden, leaving him to stare after her.

Alain was determined that the wedding should go ahead with no delay. His mother pleaded with him to give her more time to prepare, but he would not listen.

'Katherine is vulnerable until she is my wife.' He answered

his mother's pleading in a curt tone that brooked no defiance and she sighed over the loss of the sweet, gentle man that had been her son before he left for the Holy Land. 'We need only our family and close neighbours about us to witness our vows. We shall be wed in six days and that is my last word upon the matter.'

'I do not know what has come over him,' Lady Alayne said to Katherine. 'He was never like this—so angry and harsh. I swear I do not know him.'

'I fear he may be angry with me,' Katherine told her. 'It is not you who has angered him, Mother.'

'Why should he be angry with you—is it over that cup you placed in our strongroom?'

'In a way, yes,' Katherine said and decided that she ought to tell Alain's mother the whole story. She spared no details, telling of her love for Alain from the beginning, and the revulsion she had felt at seeing him with blood spattered all over his face, clothes and hands. 'My father's discovery had caused so much grief already. Alain thinks we should take it to Rome, and that was my wish also at the start. I thought it too precious to give into the hands of anyone but the Holy Father—but since then I have come to think that it may be cursed, that it is not a holy relic but something of the devil's forging.'

'Yes, I can understand that,' Alayne agreed. 'My son did what he had to do to rescue you, Katherine. I know how you feel, and I think you must try to forgive yourself for having brought suffering on others—but the matter of the cup is different. If it is cursed as you say, then perhaps we should destroy it ourselves. Alain is certainly changed. He took the cup with him when he came to rescue you, but it is back in Sir Ralph's strongroom now. I wonder…'

'It is but a fragile thing,' Katherine said. 'We might destroy it easily…'

'I shall fetch it,' Alayne said decisively. 'We will take it to the chapel and place it on the altar and pray for guidance. If it truly hath powers, either for good or for evil, they will surely manifest themselves in such a place.'

'Yes,' Katherine said, looking at her seriously. 'If, as you say, it is God's wish that the cup should go to Rome, we shall surely feel it.'

'Go to the chapel and wait for me there,' Alayne told her. 'I will fetch the cup and bring it to you.'

Katherine agreed and they parted.

The sun was warm as Katherine made her way through the courtyard, watching men hard at work in the small craftshops that made up a part of the manor; bakers and carpenters, stone masons and farriers were all hard at their daily tasks. And at the far end of the courtyard some of Sir Ralph's men were training with their swords and weapons.

Katherine turned her face from the sight, the sound of metal upon metal bringing back the horror of that night at Rotherham. Would she never be free of it? Sometimes she thought she could forget, but then it would return, her memories crowding in on her.

It was cool and dark inside the chapel, and she knelt before the huge silver cross on the altar, her head bent in prayer as she asked for guidance, quite unaware of the man who lingered in the shadows watching her.

When Alayne entered the chapel some minutes later, Katherine got to her feet and turned to greet her. She was feeling a little comforted by the peace all around her and, when Alayne handed her the small cloth bag in which the cup had been carried all the way from the Holy Land, she suddenly felt at peace.

'Place it upon the altar,' Alayne said. 'We must both pray for guidance, Katherine. What you do now is important, and we must be sure that whatever you choose is the right thing.'

Carefully unwrapping the cup, Katherine placed it on the altar cloth. It looked small and insignificant against the ornate silver goblets that were used during religious ceremonies. And yet Alayne drew a sharp breath as she saw it and sank to her knees.

'We ask Your forgiveness, Lord,' she said. 'And we pray that You may give us guidance and the strength to carry out Your wishes concerning the cup.'

Katherine joined her in silent prayer. After that terrible night of bloodshed at Rotherham, she had wanted to be rid of the cup, believing it evil—but now she understood that it was men who were evil. Evil men had sought the cup for its value in gold, for there were many that would pay to have such a precious thing for themselves.

'At last…' The triumphant cry startled both Katherine and Alayne and they opened their eyes, jumping to their feet as a man appeared out of the shadows and moved towards the altar, sword in hand. 'At last it is mine…'

'How have you come here?' Katherine whispered.

How could he have passed the guards? Yet looking at his dress, no one would take him for the Lord of Ravenshurst. He looked more like one of the beggars who often came to Bane-wulf for charity. He must have mingled with the village folk as they entered on their lawful business.

The two women rose to their feet in alarm, for it was obvious that the man was dangerous. His eyes glittered with a fanatical fervour, his hair and beard were wild and matted and he seemed as if he had lost all reason.

'No!' Katherine cried as he moved towards the altar. 'You may not take it! You are steeped in the blood of innocents and your touch would defile it. I forbid you to touch the cup. It must be given to the Holy Father and kept in Rome where all may see it.'

'Who are you to defy me?' Ravenshurst advanced on her menacingly, his sword at the ready. 'You are nothing—a beetle I shall crush beneath my feet. No one shall stop me taking what is rightfully mine.'

Katherine moved away from him, her eyes never leaving his face. He was surely insane? His desire to own the cup had driven him out of his mind. He was determined to have it at all costs, to kill or die for it, and she in her foolishness had brought it here to this place where he could see and touch it.

Suddenly, she knew that he must not have it. No matter what it cost she must keep him from taking something that was so precious it belonged in a safe haven where the greedy men of this world could not use it for their own ends.

'You shall not have it,' she said in a strong voice and stood in between Ravenshurst and the altar. 'No matter what you do, you shall not take it.'

'Let me by or it will be the worse for you, Katherine.'

'No.' She lifted her head proudly. 'You shall not pass…'

'Then I have no choice.' Ravenshurst lifted his arm, his sword glittering in the candlelight. 'Prepare to meet your death…'

Chapter Thirteen

'Stand back from her!'

Alain's voice rang out and suddenly he was there beside Katherine. She glanced at him and saw that he was unarmed, wearing only a short tunic and braes, his feet softly shod in leather slippers. Yet there was about him a determination that she had seldom seen. Fear gripped her—she knew that without his sword and armour he was at a disadvantage. Beneath his beggar's robes, Ravenshurst wore his chain-mail, and a tunic still splattered with the blood of that night at Rotherham.

'You must not fight him,' she said to Alain, for without his sword and suit of chain-mail he was vulnerable. 'Please, Alain, do not.'

'I do not forget my promise to you,' Alain said harshly, but his gaze never faltered as he looked at Ravenshurst, who was moving towards them, sword in hand. 'Stand away. Go back to the house with my mother and leave this to me.'

Katherine shook her head. She could not leave him, knowing that he must be killed if she did not find some way to help him, but she moved to one side, looking about her for some weapon.

'Come away,' Alayne urged, but she shook her head stubbornly.

'You go. I shall stay.'

'I'll fetch help.'

Katherine did not turn her head as Alayne went swiftly from the chapel. She was watching as the two men circled one another in what was clearly meant to be a dance of death. Ravenshurst yelled fiercely and struck at Alain with his sword, but he dodged back, nimbly avoiding the blow. Then he picked up a wooden stool and began to use it as a shield to defend himself from the furious onslaught as Ravenshurst charged at him, slashing wildly to left and right.

There was a long wooden pike standing at one side of the church where a display of armour had been set upon the wall as part of a thanksgiving for some long-ago victory. Surely Alain would snatch the weapon and drive his opponent back? But he had ignored it, his expression grim but unflinching. Her heart lurched as Ravenshurst made a series of wild lunges at Alain.

She watched as he used his stool, seeming to bait his opponent, making him lunge angrily and miss his target time and time again. Yet he made no attempt to strike back, merely defending himself from the Baron's attempts to wound him.

Why did he not strike back? Why did he not avail himself of the pike, which would have given him the advantage? She puzzled over it, but then suddenly the answer came to her as in a blinding flash. He was honouring his promise to her!

He would keep Ravenshurst from harming her or taking the cup—but he would not fight back. He would not kill the man who was trying so hard to kill him, because of his promise to her. If need be, he would die for his honour! And she had accused him of being no better than the man he fought. How cruel and wrong her accusations had been. So much did he value his honour that he would not do more than defend himself.

Oh, the foolish, foolish man! Katherine felt like screaming aloud in her frustration, but she dare not distract Alain, for one stumble would bring him down. He was trying to contain Ravenshurst until someone came to help him. Oh, let him not be killed before that help came!

She could barely hold back her scream as she saw the Baron's sword rip through the sleeve of his tunic. Fresh blood spurted and ran down Alain's arm.

'Arm yourself,' she murmured, but so softly that none could hear. 'Oh, my dearest love, do not die for my sake. I was such a fool to think so ill of you. God forgive me for hurting you as I did.'

She seized a heavy candlestick from a small side table, holding it at the ready as she saw that Alain's wound was hampering him. He was still keeping the Baron at bay, but only just. She moved closer, waiting for her chance, and then seeing that Ravenshurst had his back towards her, she brought her weapon crashing down across his shoulders. He gave a shout of anger and turned on her, thrusting at her with the blade of his sword. In that moment, Alain brought his stool down hard on Ravenshurst's sword arm; there was a cracking sound as a bone splintered and with a grunt of pain he let go of the sword, allowing it to fall unheeded to the ground.

The Baron snarled like a wounded beast and moved away from them, his eyes moving from side to side as if he thought Alain would close in for the kill. Backing away from them, he reached the altar, and picking up the cup, he held it aloft.

'I have it now and defy you to take it from me.' He laughed demonically, a sound that made Katherine shudder. He must surely be mad, for he had lost all reason. 'I call upon the power of this cup to strike you down, de Banewulf, and all your…arghhh…' His eyes bulged suddenly and sweat stood upon his brow as his body was gripped by terrible shudders that racked him from head to toe and the cup seemed to fly from his fingers to the stone flags of the chapel floor. It smashed into twelve pieces. Ravenshurst sagged to his knees before it, covering his face with his hands, his body shaking as he cried out in fear.

Neither Katherine nor Alain could move. It was as if they were rooted to the spot, able only to observe. The Baron stayed where he was for some minutes, and gradually the shudders subsided, and then at last he stood up and Katherine was struck by the look on his face. It was as if the madness had left him and a new calm had descended on the man who had been willing to kill ruthlessly only seconds earlier. Yet it was the calm of a man with the mind of a child.

'Forgive me,' he said, looking at Katherine but not seeing her as he stared into the darkness beyond her, 'if I have harmed you, lady. I shall go now and cause no more trouble to you or yours.'

Katherine turned her head to watch as he walked unsteadily from the chapel looking neither to left nor right, a man broken in spirit and body. Then, as she turned back, she saw that Alain had knelt by the broken pieces of the cup, but even as he reached out to gather them, they began to glow and shimmer with a warm yellow light.

'Do not touch them,' Katherine warned. She knelt by his side, watching as the light grew brighter and brighter until it almost blinded her and she had to cover her eyes. It was then that she seemed to hear the voice, and in the voice was love and peace, telling her all she needed to know.

When she was able to open her eyes again she saw that the light had gone and the cup was once more in one piece. Looking at Alain, she knew that he was as stunned by the miracle they had witnessed as she had been.

'It is a miracle…'

'It is whole again…' Alain breathed, a look of wonder in his eyes. 'It broke into twelve pieces—one for each of the disciples—and then it healed itself.'

'It cannot be destroyed,' Katherine said in an awed tone. 'It is the reason it was there for my father to find after more than a thousand years. It must truly be the Holy Grail, Alain.'

'Yes…' He turned to look at her, giving her his hand to help her rise. 'Do you realise the power this cup has—the source of good or evil it might be for those who possessed it?'

'But Ravenshurst could not touch it…you saw what it did to him. He was like a child…an innocent. He will never be a man again in the true sense of the word. He is helpless…'

'It was his punishment.' Alain looked solemn. 'Better that he should seek succour from the monks or live a life of penitence rather than bring harm to others.'

'It is a fearful thing to posses, Alain.'

'We must give it to someone who is able to care for and protect it, Katherine.'

'I think…' Katherine hesitated momentarily, then, 'When the light was so powerful and I closed my eyes, it was as if our Lord spoke to me. I believe he told me what I should do with the cup, Alain. To keep it safe and away from greedy men who would take it for their own gain.'

Alain picked up the cup and replaced it in the cloth bag Katherine held out. His eyes were intent on her face.

'Tell me what you want to do with it, Katherine,' he said and she did.

'I am glad to see that you are safe and well,' the Abbess told Katherine. 'We were worried for you, my child, and Sister Sarah blamed herself for allowing you to walk blindly into a trap. We should not easily have forgiven ourselves if harm had come to you.'

'She was not to blame. I went with Baron Ravenshurst because otherwise he would have set his men loose on the sisters—and your house would have been burned to the ground. I could not allow that to happen for my sake.'

The Abbess looked grave. She made the sign of the Cross over her breast. 'It would have been a severe loss to us all, Katherine, had our home been destroyed, and who knows what else may have happened. We thank you for risking your own safety to save us.'

'It would have grieved me to see such destruction, for I felt a sense of peace here in your gardens,' Katherine said. 'And that is why I have come here today, to ask a favour of you.'

The Abbess looked puzzled. 'You do not want to join us?'

'No. I have no vocation and I am to be married…' Katherine blushed as she recalled her harsh words to Alain when she had spoken of leaving him to live at the Abbey. 'I want to leave something in your safekeeping, Mother.'

'I am sorry. I do not quite understand you, Katherine.'

'It is a long story.' Katherine paused for a moment. 'I told you of the discovery my father made. But you do not know what has happened since I left here.'

'Ah, yes, my child. I understand. Please tell me what you would have me know.'

The Abbess inclined her head. She listened patiently as the tale unfolded, saying nothing even when Katherine described the miracle she and Alain had witnessed when the cup healed itself. The silence after her story was done was tense and hard for Katherine to bear. Did the Abbess believe her or suspect her of lying?

'Why do you want to give the cup to us?' The Abbess spoke at last, her gentle eyes dwelling steadily on Katherine's face. 'Do you not know what interest would be caused by the discovery of such a treasure? There are kings who would pay a fortune to possess the cup that touched our Lord's lips at the Last Supper. His Holiness would very likely reward you with honours and blessings. Have you not thought of these things, Katherine?'

'A thousand times, Mother. It has lain heavy on my conscience these many months. I had thought to give it to his Holiness. I want no reward yet I believe it must be placed somewhere worthy of its significance. Once I thought Rome was the proper place, but now I think...I believe that our Lord told me to bring it here to you. Men have died for the greed of others, those that sought the cup for their own gain. If it was widely known of, it might be that other men would try to take it for themselves. I believe it should be kept secret, hidden somewhere to keep it safe.'

'And yet it must have the power to do good,' the Abbess said, looking thoughtful. 'If the power of Christ can pass through this simple cup—and I must believe the things you have told me, for I believe you honest, Katherine—what more miracles might be brought to pass? What good it might bestow upon those who visited its shrine? Think of all those who suffer who might be healed.'

'Yes, I know this is true,' Katherine said. She looked into the eyes of the woman sitting opposite and saw the true goodness of her soul. 'But would it ever be safe? If its existence was proved so that all knew and believed, would it not provoke quarrels—even wars? Rome, France, Germany and England might all lay claim to it.'

'You are very wise for one so young,' the Abbess said and smiled at her. 'But you must allow me a few days to think and pray. If it is truly our Lord's wish that the cup remains with us, He will surely guide my thoughts to the right path.'

'Thank you for hearing me and for believing me,' Katherine said and rose to her feet, curtsying reverently to the Abbess. 'I shall return to Sir Alain, who waits outside the Abbey gate. We are to marry soon. If we return when we are wed you may have your answer ready.'

'I am sure that I shall. Go now and may God bless you and your union with Sir Alain.'

Katherine thanked her and left the cool peace of the ancient Abbey. Outside in the sunshine Alain was waiting for her, his back turned towards the Abbey gardens. Seeing the way he paced restlessly, she guessed that he was tense, perhaps wondering if she would return to him or choose to stay with the nuns.

'Alain…' He swung round immediately, his eyes dwelling on her for a moment, and then he smiled, holding out both hands to her. She went to take them, gazing into his eyes for some seconds. 'The Abbess asks for a few days to consider. I told her we would return after we were wed.'

'You told her that?' He looked deep into her face, his expression solemn. 'Are you ready to marry me, Katherine?

Can you forget the horror of that night—the sight that so shocked you? I said then that you had no choice but to wed me, but I was angry. Your accusations cut me to the heart and I was afraid of losing you—but I cannot force you to be my wife. If in your heart you wish to be free…'

'No.' Katherine smiled and placed a finger to his lips. 'I was horrified by what happened that night—seeing you with blood spattered over you and the glow of triumph in your eyes. For a while I thought that I should never forget, but in the chapel…when the voice spoke to me…I was healed. I saw that the cup was whole again and I, too, became whole. I have known in my heart that what you did was for my sake, but still I felt sullied by all the evil that had been done in my name. Now I know that neither you nor I was to blame. There is evil in some men, and there are other men who fight against that evil—and sometimes blood must be spilled in a righteous cause.'

'I, too, have felt sullied by injustice and the wasteful loss of life that occurs when men fight,' Alain told her. 'When I fought at Acre I believed that what we did was right, that it was God's work—but when those hostages were killed because Richard was angry that Saladin did not accept his terms of exchange…then I, too, was sickened. I wondered if that was the reason we failed to take back Jerusalem, because we were not worthy.'

'It was a shameful thing,' Katherine said. 'I saw innocent men and women die and my heart wept tears of blood for what had been done in the name of Christendom. My father said that he felt it a burden all devout Christians would carry on their souls.'

'And we were not strong enough to take Jerusalem back

from the infidel,' Alain went on, his face working with the
sense of failure this still held for him. 'I have longed to do
something for Christendom, something that would compen-
sate for our failure…'

'That is why you were angry when I said I would destroy
the cup,' Katherine said, understanding now why he had been
so harsh. 'You thought it would give something back to make
up for all that the Christian Empire has lost.'

'Yes, something of the sort,' Alain admitted. 'Perhaps in
a way I was as guilty as Ravenshurst of wanting something
for myself—even if it was not gold or fame. I wanted to feel
that I had been instrumental in giving something precious to
Christendom.'

'And you have been,' Katherine told him. 'But for you it
would have been stolen from me long ago.' She looked at him
anxiously. 'Are you disappointed that I have brought it here
to the Abbey?'

'No, for I, too, felt something when the cup restored itself,'
Alain told her. 'I did not hear our Lord's voice, for He chose
to speak to you—but it was as if I had found peace within myself.' He smiled oddly. 'Before I left for the crusade my
brother gave me a sword that was supposed to have magic
powers. And truly, when I held that sword in my hand I felt
invincible. I believed that none could touch me, that I had the
strength of ten men.'

'A magic sword?' Katherine smiled. 'I have seen you fight,
my lord, and I believe that the magic lies in your own courage—for in the chapel you had no weapon but a wooden
stool.'

'And my love for you,' Alain told her with a loving smile.
'I would have died rather than let him hurt you—but I had

given my word that I would not kill him. Even had my sword been to hand I must have kept that promise, Katherine.'

'And so you defeated him with nothing but a wooden stool. Surely that tells you that you need no magic sword?'

Alain's eyes danced with the merriment that had been missing for a while. 'I know not whether it was that or the miracle we witnessed, sweet Kate, but something has changed in me. That restless spirit, the need to prove myself to myself, hath gone.'

'Then you will not leave me to offer your sword to a foreign prince?'

'They were but idle words,' Alain told her softly. 'I have been a long time in understanding my heart, Katherine, but I know it now—and it belongs to you. When we are wed I shall never want to leave you.'

'I do not see why we should ever be parted,' she said and gazed up into his eyes. 'I want nothing more of life than to be your wife and to bear your children.'

'Then we shall be wed as soon as the priest may marry us,' Alain told her. 'Come, my love, let us return to Banewulf.' She sighed as he drew her into his arms and kissed her, her body responding to the hunger in him. 'For I cannot wait to make you my bride.'

'You look lovely,' Alayne said as she dressed Katherine's hair for her wedding. It hung upon her shoulders in luxuriant tresses, shining and soft. She wore a simple coronet of flowers on her brow, her dress of white silk caught with a silver girdle. 'My son may think himself a fortunate man to gain such a bride.'

Katherine glanced at herself in the mirror her future

mother-in-law had given her as a wedding gift, puzzling over the image she could see in the polished silver.

'I do not think I am beautiful, Mother,' she said. 'But if you see me through the eyes of love, then perhaps that is how Alain sees me, too—and I am content if he thinks me attractive.'

'I am sure my son thinks you beautiful,' Alayne said and laughed. 'When a man like Alain loves, he loves with all his heart—and you have worked a miracle, Katherine. I thought the gentle, sweet-natured youth I loved so much had gone forever, but it seems that you have brought him back to us. These past few days he has scarce stopped smiling and teasing us all.'

'He seems happy,' Katherine replied. 'But I am not sure it is I who have worked this miracle in him.'

They had decided not to tell anyone but the Abbess of the miracle they had witnessed in the chapel. Not because they did not trust Alain's family, but because it was something that was best known to only a few. If the Abbess decided to accept Katherine's gift, they would never tell the whereabouts of the cup to anyone.

'It is the miracle of love,' Alayne told her. 'I have seen it work in others and I know its power. Love can overcome pain and hardship, Katherine. It can sustain when all else fails, and it can bring great happiness. Guard it well for if lost it can never be recovered.'

'Yes, I know,' Katherine said. She had believed Alain's love lost after that night at Rotherham, and knew herself fortunate to have a second chance. 'I shall not let Alain's love slip through my fingers again.'

The two women smiled and kissed and went down the stairs, walking together to the chapel, where Alain was waiting with the rest of his family and the priest. As he turned to look at her, Katherine's heart beat faster as she saw the promise in his eyes.

She went forward to stand by his side and the priest began the service that would make them man and wife.

'You are so lovely,' Alain said as he looked at his wife. They were alone in their bridal chamber, the feasting done for them, though the sounds of laughter still floated to them through the open window. 'I do not know how I ever thought you a thin, plain child.'

Katherine laughed, for she loved it that he was honest with her concerning his feelings towards her at the start. She would never be a vain woman and she could not have believed it had he showered her with pretty compliments. All she needed was to know that she was loved.

'I am happy that you find me attractive, my husband,' she said and held her hands out to him in welcome. 'But I shall pray that our children take after you in looks—at least our daughters. Perhaps it is not fair that our sons should be too handsome.'

Alain shouted with amusement, for he had begun to appreciate the sense of humour that lurked beneath Katherine's serious looks. She was so much more than he could ever have guessed when he first rescued her from the rogues who would have abducted her.

He moved towards her, gazing down at her lovely face, touching her cheek with his fingertips, trailing them down to the white arch of her throat. He kissed the tiny pulse spot at the base of her throat, then slipped her tunic back so that his lips could seek out the sweet rose of her nipples that budded with desire.

She moaned with ecstasy as he initiated her into the secrets of pleasure known only to true lovers. Kneeling before her, he let his tongue trail slowly over the sweet curve of her navel, burying his face for a moment in the tight curls that covered her feminine mound. Then he swept her up in his arms, carrying her to their bed, where he lay her down on the fresh linen prepared for them.

The bed had been sprinkled with rose petals, and there amongst the fragrance of crushed petals, Alain took his bride slowly, gently, along the path to exquisite pleasure. His touch was sure and certain as he played her like a stringed instrument, bringing forth such delicate feelings that she gasped and arched beneath him. With lips and tongue and stroking, he brought her to such a pitch that when he entered her she felt little pain, and that soon swept away in the tide of desire that lapped over her like warm water.

Afterwards, she lay in his arms, her limbs melting in the languorous aftermath of desire, replete, content.

They talked for a while, loved again, finding themselves caught in the strength of their feelings that left them shaken and, afterwards, able only to sleep, entwined as one, limbs locked together in a lovers' knot.

'You must not be nervous,' Alain said as he saw the expression in her eyes. She looked anxious and uncertain, her hand trembling a little in his as he helped her to dismount. Three days had passed since they had married and now they had returned to the Abbey to hear what the Abbess had to say about Katherine's request before making their way to Alain's own manor. 'If she will not accept the responsibility, we shall take the cup to Rome.'

'Yes…' Katherine felt the warmth of the sun on her head. She could smell the fragrance of flowers from the walled garden, roses and lilies and jasmine. 'But I believe the cup belongs here.' She stopped for a moment to bow her head to a small stone statue of the Virgin Mary, which stood on a plinth before the garden gates. 'I believe it would be safe here.'

'Then I pray the Abbess thinks as you do,' Alain said. 'Go to her now, my love, and I shall wait here for you.'

Katherine smiled and went through the gate into the garden beyond. The peace of the old garden surrounded her and she smiled as she listened to the sound of birdsong and the humming of bees. She was surprised to see the Abbess coming towards her, almost as if she had been waiting for her to arrive.

'Katherine, my daughter,' the Abbess said and smiled at her. 'I knew you would come today, and I have my answer ready for you.'

Katherine did not need to ask, for she could see that the Abbess looked serene. She had decided that the cup should remain with them for safekeeping.

'I am glad that it will be here with you, Mother.'

'You know that I can never acknowledge it? The whereabouts of your father's discovery must remain a secret, known only to you, your husband and I.'

'I would not wish you to reveal it. Only if you keep it secret will it be safe from the greed of men.'

'We understand each other.' The Abbess smiled at her. 'Our Lord has spoken to me, and I have done as He asked. The cup lies in its final resting place and the secret will die with me.'

'That is as it should be,' Katherine said and a feeling of

great peace came over her. 'Thank you for what you have done, Mother. It has taken a great load from my shoulders.'

'And given me a blessing I had not expected,' the Abbess said. 'Our Lord has asked a service of me and I am truly fortunate. Go now, Katherine, and join your husband. My blessing goes with you and my hope for your happiness.'

'Thank you.'

Katherine turned away and went out to join Alain. He came towards her, taking her hands, gazing down at her. His eyes searched her face and found the answer he sought.

'All is well?'

'All is well. The Abbess keeps it secret and none shall ever know where it lies.'

'Then we have done our duty,' Alain said and drew her towards their waiting horses. 'Come, my lady. It is time that we went home…'

Afterword

The miracles began a year after the cup passed into the hands of the Abbess. A sick man and his wife came to pray to the shrine at the gates of the Abbey, begging the Virgin to give them some hope. The man was cured of his sickness and went away to tell of the miracle that had restored his wasted limbs.

From that time on until the Abbey was destroyed in the reign of King Henry VIII there was a total of two hundred and fifty miracles attributed to the Virgin's statue at the Abbey of the Sisters of Mercy. After the building was burned to the ground, the statue lay in the ashes of the Abbey gate, surrounded by briars that grew over it, remaining undiscovered for many years until…

But that is another story.

0805/04b

MILLS & BOON®

Live the emotion

Historical
romance™

THE ABDUCTED HEIRESS
by Claire Thornton

City of Flames

Lady Desire Godwin's gentle existence is shattered
when a handsome brigand crosses the parapet into
her rooftop garden. She watches, dismayed, as the
impudent stranger is carried off to gaol. But as fire
rages across London Jakob Balston uses the confusion
to escape. He expects that Desire will have fled town
– only she's still there, alone...

TEMPTING A TEXAN
by Carolyn Davidson

Fatherhood hits wealthy banker Nicholas Garvey
from completely out of the blue. He's the legal
guardian of a niece he never knew he had! And then
he's rewarded with an even bigger surprise – the
child's beguiling nanny, Carlinda Donnelly, a woman
who makes his blood race and his passions soar...

On sale 2nd September 2005